Deadliest Intuition

Deadliest Intuition

E. Raye Turonek

www.urbanbooks.net

Urban Books, LLC
300 Farmingdale Road, NY-Route 109
Farmingdale, NY 11735

ISBN 13: 978-1-64556-234-4
ISBN 10: 1-64556-234-4

First Trade Paperback Printing August 2021
Printed in the United States of America

10 9 8 7 6 5 4 3 2 1

Distributed by Kensington Publishing Corp.
Submit Orders to:
Customer Service
400 Hahn Road
Westminster, MD 21157-4627
Phone: 1-800-733-3000
Fax: 1-800-659-2436

Deadliest Intuition

by

E. Raye Turonek

Acknowledgments

Looking back at what I was facing four years ago, my challenges seemed insurmountable. But that being said, God puts blessings along your path. Me? I've had more than a few. My wonderful husband has been the best blessing of all. Our family could not function successfully without him home, tag teaming the day with me. He is my support system and lifelong partner. To the woman that took a chance on a new writer, I thank you, my mentor and friend. I appreciate you more than words could ever express, N'Tyse Williams of Boss Magnet Media.

Along with these godsends, I've had an exemplary support system, including Diane Rambert of Diamonds Literary World, Robert White of Robert's Reading Room and Reviews, Martha Weber, Martin, and Ebony Evans of Eye CU Reading & Social Network. Many more have had their hand in ushering me along on my journey to accomplish my legacy. I want to say thank you to all of you from the bottom of my heart. This is only the beginning. Aspirations, here I come.

—E. Raye Turonek

*The punishment which the wise suffer who
refuse to take part in the government,
is to live under the government
of worse men.*

—*Plato*

Chapter 1

Shield of Lies

Tearing out of the building into a torrential downpour of rain, Joe made a beeline for his pickup truck. A shimmering full moon obstructed by storm clouds neither helped nor hindered his way, thanks to the lights atop strategically placed posts landscaping the parking lot. He kept his head down low but flashed his badge at the security guard manning the booth at the gate's entrance. The uniformed man exited without pause as the liftgate whipped back upon the guard's approval. Now he was only fifty feet or so before making it to higher ground. His ten-hour shift at the youth correctional facility had ended. By the time Joe hopped inside his pickup truck, all he wanted to do was get home to a cold beer and a pair of dry pajamas.

"Gonna be one helluva storm," he remarked, wiping the fog from his windshield as he attempted to peer out into the nearly empty lot.

The once-over he had given the glass not doing the trick, Joe started his engine, then turned on the defroster and wipers.

"It's looking like a helluva storm out there. Hopefully, everyone is home, tucked safely inside and not out there on the road. Those of you who are out there navigating this monster of a storm, Godspeed," the radio disk jockey commented just as the radio had popped on.

Joe flipped through the AM stations, searching for some sports talk before beginning his journey home from work. The old melody "Take Me Out to the Ball Game" being played in the background of a commentator's rhetoric prompted him to settle on the current station. Patriotic rhetoric was one of Joe's favorite forms of entertainment.

A tall, lanky figure stood at the road's edge cloaked in a translucent rain poncho with hands resting on his hips as he surmised his dilemma. The conversion van he was driving just minutes earlier had slid off into a ditch, trapping the front tires in the mud. No matter how many times, or alternate angles he had tried to reverse it, the tires would merely spin in place. There was no way he was getting out of there without assistance. Lucky for him, there was a truck coming up the road right toward him.

From afar, Joe could barely see the man. What he could see was the vehicle seemingly stranded on the side of the road. He fought with himself about if he should lend a hand, but by the time the headlights of his vehicle illuminated the shimmering, chrome badge clipped on the man's waistbelt, there was no question of what he needed to do.

Joe pulled up to the ill-fortuned stranger, lowering his passenger window. "Looks like you've gotten yourself in a pickle."

"I'm stuck in the mud. I think I'm going to need a tow," the stranger responded over the sound of roaring thunder.

"I have a hitch and tow on the front of my pickup. I can hook it to your frame and try to pull you out."

"Thank you. I think that would do it," the stranger replied as he seemed to hold his trembling arm at his side.

"Anything for a fellow man of service. Let's get you out of this storm. You may want to go and get that arm checked out if you hurt it in the crash," Joe rambled on as he hopped out to attach his tow to the conversion van's underbelly. "I'm Joe, by the way. What can I call you?"

"Ronald. Ronald Doolally."

"Nice to meet you, Ronald Doolally. I wish it were under better circumstances, I must admit."

Before Ronald could respond, a loud click sounded off. "That's it. It's hooked. You can go ahead and hop inside. When I flash the lights at you, put it in reverse and start backing up."

Ronald climbed inside of his van as Joe climbed into the driver's seat of his pickup. Within a few seconds of tugging, the plan had proved fruitful. Ronald's conversion van was out of the mud and back on solid ground.

Joe hopped back out of his truck, ready to receive kudos for the brilliant idea and save, but once he made it to Ronald's driver's-side door, something else caught his eye. "Your front tire is nearly flat. That's probably why you couldn't get out of the mud on your own. You really shouldn't drive with your tire like that. It's way too slick out here," Joe warned.

Ronald climbed back out to assess the damage.

"I have a spare. I can change it," he calmly replied as he opened his side door to grab a tire iron and jack.

"I'd love to be of more assistance, but I just worked a ten-hour shift."

"No need to explain. You've done enough. Besides, I have a raincoat on. You should probably get home and out of those wet clothes. I appreciate your help."

"Like I said, it's a pleasure helping a fellow man of the shield. I hope your night gets better from here." Joe tipped the brim of his hat, then turned to head back to his vehicle.

"Much better than yours, I'd imagine." Ronald lifted the tire iron above his head, then came down with such force that the blow to the top of Joe's skull knocked him out cold, sending his limp body crashing to the ground.

When his lids opened, he found his legs had been bound at the ankles and arms at his wrists and tied to a metal beam supporting the ceiling. The duct tape covering his mouth kept his lips sealed. Screaming for help wasn't an option. His eyes studied the hollowed-out cement structure still in the early stages of being constructed. Steel beams lined the ceiling while drywall sat off to the side waiting to be installed. There were holes made for windows but no glass encasing them, which allowed rain from the storm that had yet to let up to pour inside. Joe had no idea where he was or how he had gotten there, for that matter. The last thing he remembered was pulling Ronald's conversion van out of the ditch.

What the hell is going on? Why would he do this to me? Joe thought as he struggled to break free from the bondage holding him captive.

That's when he heard the steel door open, then slam shut. Footsteps neared him second by second until they stopped alongside his head.

Ronald bent over, ripping the duct tape from Joe's face with one quick snatch.

"What the fuck is going on here, man? You need to let me go. I work for the county, ya know? You're making a big mistake. Hey, I *helped* you. Don't you remember? The guy who got you out of the ditch? Why would you do this to me? Is this how you repay a Good Samaritan?"

"You're no Good Samaritan. You're what we call a wolf in sheep's clothing."

"What the hell are you talking about, man? I'm no threat to anyone. Look, I've got a wife and kids. You've got the wrong guy," Joe pleaded.

"We'll see about that. You yell for help, you die," Ronald threatened before hooking the winch and cable to the rope around his ankles. He untied the rope keeping Joe attached to the beam before leaving the room, yet left his arms bound.

Joe sat up immediately, fueled with the motivation to get the hell out of there. First, he had to get his wrists and feet untied before his captor would return. He reached for his ankles, but before getting a grip on the rope, his body started to slide across the floor. It was slow, initially, giving him the impression that he had time to loosen his restraints. Then, suddenly, his body yanked back. Head slamming against the concrete floor, he was dragged out of an opening in the structure.

Joe hollered out in horror, fearing he would surely plummet to his death, the sound of his screams drowned out by sounds of crackling thunder. He dangled there in the air, upside down but eye to eye, with Ronald seated in the wrecking ball crane. It only took Joe a moment to realize his body had replaced the missing wrecking ball.

"How many?" Ronald asked, assuming Joe knew why he was hanging there.

"How many what, man? I don't know what you're talking about," Joe contested as the blood rushed to his head, leaving veins protruding and his face beet red.

"I know what you've been up to, Joe. This is your opportunity to confess and avoid being buried alive." Ronald maneuvered the controls, swinging Joe's body hard to the right.

"No! Please . . ." The fresh grave Joe had found himself hanging over did plenty to convince him that Ronald meant business. "Come on, man. I've got a family to take care of. You can't kill me."

"Then for your family's sake, you better get on with it."

Joe yelled in frustration, knowing there was no way he was weaseling out of the situation. "I don't know how many, man. I didn't keep count." He let out an exhaustive sigh.

Ronald scoffed, disgusted at the very sight of him. "People like you *always* keep count. How many?"

Joe hesitated before eventually muttering the answer under his breath, "Twelve."

"Louder, so that we can hear you," Ronald demanded.

"Twelve," Joe screamed. "Twelve. Got dammit. What else do you want to know? You want to know where? When? How? I bet you'd like that, wouldn't you, you fucking psychopath." Secrets having been laid bare, Joe released his fury in an onslaught of insults. "How dare you sit there and judge me? Look at what *you're* doing. You think you're better than me, you sick fuck? How many people have *you* hurt? Huh? How many, you fucking reject?"

Ronald allowed Joe to air his grievances over panicked breaths before launching his body further right, then abruptly left, driving him toward the building as if he were wrecking ball.

Joe protested, fearing it would be his end. "Stop. Nooo."

"Lights out," Ronald teased just as Joe's body collided with the cement structure. "The chickens have come home to roost, Joe."

Chapter 2

Coping

The next morning, Ronald lay atop the leather sofa, yet again recalling the day his life had changed for good. . . .

That fateful afternoon back in 1972, the pitter-patter of little feet echoed through the old wooden, two-family flat on Gable Street—wood creaking as infectious giggles bounced off the walls.

"Knock it off, you two. It sounds like you're going to go through the floor," Mrs. Doolally called out to her children as she rubbed the porcelain saucer dry to place it inside the cupboard. A soft smile wrinkled her cheeks near the edges of her mouth. Still, she shook her head, that not having been the first time she had to instruct her rambunctious twins to settle down. The sound of her children's laughter, although distracting, touched the warmest spaces of her heart. Mrs. Doolally loved her little family . . . herself, her husband, and 7-year-old twins, Ronald and Cecilia, both pale with freckled cheeks and thick, ginger coils.

Cecilia's pigtails bounced atop her shoulders as her brother gave chase through the kitchen, past the apron-draped woman who then stood swatting a hand towel in their direction. "If you two don't get out of here with that," she threatened, shooing them from the room.

The pair didn't skip a beat, Cecilia being the first to tackle the basement stairs. After dashing halfway down the staircase, she grabbed hold of the banister, swinging beneath it as a shortcut into the Michigan basement. The moment her red Chuck Taylors hit the cement, she darted off into the darkness.

"I'm gonna get you, Cecilia," Ronald vowed, having kept on her tail until then.

Cecilia was as smart as a whip with a keen intuition to boot. Once, a neighbor attempted to lure her into his home under the pretense he'd give her mounds of sugary sweets. Something about him, though, told Cecilia the man was bad news. So much so, her hand had begun trembling at her side. It was her way of determining when she could not trust the energy around her. She could sense it, the evil in him.

Her big, gray eyes widened, attempting to see beyond the blackness in front of her. "You'll never catch me, Ronald," the little girl teased, rounding the living space.

The basement, spanning the length of the home, was a circle with a furnace room at its center. Cecilia had landed in the laundry room but made her way around into the other rooms, ducking behind dampened bed linens hanging from cords lining the ceiling. If not for the clanking of the buckles affixed to the suspenders of her blue jean overall skirt, he would never have found her there hiding underneath the table in the dining area.

"Told ya I'd catch ya," he whispered at the base of her earlobe, having snuck up beside her.

His presence sent a shock wave through her tiny body, catapulting Cecilia off into another escape attempt. That time, she shot up a separate set of stairs, leading to a large, wooden door. A loud, dragging sound erupted as she pulled the door open, allowing beaming rays of sunlight to shine in. Ronald missed her by an inch, almost laying a hand atop her shoulder before she took off into the big backyard. Attempting to tire him out, Cecilia took a couple of laps around their aboveground pool. Ronald, most times, would succumb to exhaustion, leaving his twin sister the victor. But let's just say that day Ronald had eaten his Wheaties.

Being the reigning champion, Cecilia had a few more tricks up her sleeve. She took her chance tearing off toward the humongous, blooming apple tree, kicking fallen green apples from her path along the way. Her target was the garage alongside the rooted monster. Anyone could tell it was ancient. Other neighborhood children found it frightening. Torn bark depicted the image of a face howling in pain, a fact that didn't stop Ronald and Cecilia from finding solace between its branches. They often climbed its limbs to hop over onto the roof of their garage, the pair's star-gazing spot.

But alas, then was a time to play chase. She leaped with one hand in the air, her foot catching a groove in the tree at the same time her hand grabbed the branch above her head. From then, the little girl was off to the races. Once she reached her exit spot, Cecilia paused, testing her mode of transport. She gave it a tug or two, approving of the safety the branch would provide. One big swing and she safely planted her feet on the garage alongside them. Cecilia made her way across the roof, then looked down over the edge, eyeballing the basketball rim affixed above the big metal door. *Should I do it?* She turned to see what progress her brother had made just as he'd made his landing. As she had expected, he was closing in on her.

"I'm coming to get cha, Cecilia."

"Never," she proclaimed before climbing down onto the rim.

She used it to hang as low as she possibly could to get the leverage needed to get on the roof of her mother's old banana-colored Chevy Malibu. Cecilia sprinted across the hood, then windshield, the bottoms of her Chucks leaving dirt impressions on the glass. Her frame was small enough not to cave in the roof of the vehicle as she shot across, then down to the opposite end.

"Mom's gonna kill you," Ronald warned, feeling a bit sour due to the butt kicking he was receiving courtesy of his sister.

Currently under construction, the soon-to-be house across the street had become one of their spots of exploration. The two were fascinated by the rock piles, cement blocks, and heavy machinery outfitting the half-acre lot.

Cecilia took her chance darting across the street after glancing both ways to ensure the coast was clear. "Come and get me, brother," she challenged him, tackling the fifteen-foot gravel pile in front of her. It took her less than a minute to reach the top, then to stand there victorious.

"Dun dada dun dun dun dada dun," she stomped, singing the Rocky anthem with her fists held high in celebration of the accomplishment.

"Don't be a show-off," Ronald complained, finally reaching the summit's peak.

That's when the rocks shifted. Cecilia's foot came down on sliding gravel, taking her down into a hole that the workmen had dug for the basement.

"Ronald, help me," she squealed, a look of sheer terror in her eyes as she plummeted.

"Cecilia!" His brows wrinkled with worry over his sorrowful brown eyes as the boy stood in disbelief at what he was witnessing. He'd reached for his twin sister's hand but a moment too late.

Cecilia's little body had rolled down the slope, only worsening the pile's instability. When her frail structure hit the bottom of the pit, an avalanche of rocks began to topple down on her.

"Ronald, please, help me." For the last time, she called out to her brother for help as a white cloud of dust permeated the air.

One second, he could see her hand reaching up out of the rocks, then the next, her body had become completely covered with stones. Cecilia had been buried alive, and there was nothing Ronald could do to save his dear twin sister.

"Cecilia," Ronald called out in terror. Tears welled up in his ducts.

A soft, monotoned voice calling out to him pulled the now fully grown man back to the present.

"Ronald, can you hear me?" His psychiatrist snapped her fingers.

The scruffy-faced gentleman opened his eyes—one brown, the other gray. "I hear you," he replied, staring fixedly at the dimmed light fixture in the ceiling.

"How does it feel remembering that day?" Dr. Martyr pressed on, keeping her voice as passive as she could.

"It feels like torture." He turned to her. "I feel helpless. I feel like," Ronald paused, fighting the aching lump in his throat more than the truth he hesitated to admit. "I could have done more to save her."

"Ronald, as long as you harbor guilt over the death of your sister, the inner turmoil you're facing will never cease. You must release it. Ronald, you *have* to release her."

She peered into his sorrowful eyes with intent.

He knew she meant well and that her concern was genuine enough. But to be quite honest, she had no idea what she was dealing with. Neither did Ronald, for that matter.

"That's easier said than done, Doc. She's my twin. Sometimes, I feel like she'll never leave me."

"Are you ready to talk about what triggered your episode last week?" she inquired, intertwining her fingers before placing them atop the ledger on her lap.

Dr. Lisa Martyr, the youngest psychiatrist in her practice, had just earned her doctor of medicine. As a child, she was always attracted to the wounded. Even if they looked put together outwardly, it was as if she could sniff out the pain in a person. Healing that pain provided her fulfillment. Ronald happened to be her favorite patient. She fancied him yet would never reveal her true feelings, as it was against her code of conduct. Besides, he was nearly twelve years younger than she. Dr. Martyr would often describe him as a handsome young man, barely legal to drink.

"Do you need more time?" the doctor continued, sensing his hesitation.

Stuck in his head, Ronald flashed back to the episode in question.

Crouched on hands and knees, beads of sweat poured down Ronald's profile out of his long, curly, red coils as he frantically burrowed into the ground, bare-handed.

"Ronald?" Her voice yanked him from the memory, pulling his focus back to reality. "You've been very distracted lately. Have you gone yet to get that MRI I referred you for?"

"They put me on a list," he responded, huffing as he lifted from a lying position on the plush leather sofa.

"Ronald, do you want to be cured?" his psychiatrist asked in the softest voice she could mimic. She didn't want him to feel as if she were antagonizing him. Her inquiry was genuine.

"What kind of question is that? I wouldn't be here if I didn't want to fix what's happening to me. You think I want to live like this for the rest of my life? Coming in here to tell you about how I can't get over the deaths of my family isn't something I particularly enjoy, Doc."

"I believe you, Ronald. I believe you want to live a normal life. Maybe even have a family of your own someday. For you to do that, though, we have to work through these blocks. We need to find out what it is about your sister's death that you can't seem to let go of."

"I've heard that same line since my adolescence."

"I promise, I'm going to help you, Ronald. I know it has been a long, hard road for you, but you can get over this. Tell me, when was the last time you went out on a date?"

"I don't have time for a date." Ronald blew off the notion.

"How so?" she frowned. "Has school become too demanding?" his psychiatrist pressed forward.

"Between work and school, it's hard to find free time." Ronald had to tell Dr. Martyr something besides the truth. If she knew he was seeing his sister's apparition while he was awake, she'd have him committed. Coming to her gave Ronald someone to talk to. She was his last remaining outlet. Unfortunately, he had absolutely no confidence in the fact that she could help him.

"You should try it. Have you seen anyone you might be interested in?"

"I can't say I've been looking." Ronald stuck to his guns.

"Ronald, you attend a university full of beautiful, intelligent beings. You should try mingling."

He looked down at his wristwatch, not wanting to open that can of worms. "I think it's about time for me to go."

Dr. Martyr glanced down at hers realizing their session was due to end in several minutes. "Oh . . ." She pushed one side of her shoulder-length brown hair behind her ear. "Well, I guess you're right. No worries. We can pick back up where we left off on Wednesday." She stood, tugging at the helm of her black business skirt to assure its length was appropriate. "Don't forget, Wednesday at eleven o'clock," she reminded him, hoping he would show up.

"Thanks, Doc." Ronald headed for the exit.

"That's a very nice broach, if I must say so myself," a waiting patient schmoozed the secretary just outside Dr. Martyr's office.

"Why, thank you, sir. I appreciate you saying so, again," she remarked politely, a bit put off by his constant compliments each visit. Fraternizing with the patients was against company policy, but Rochelle would never in a million years date a patient even if it weren't. Besides, she didn't exactly see Mr. Arthur Columbus as handsome.

His third chin looked completely unnecessary, considering he was, at most, 150 pounds soaking wet, wearing full fireman's gear. He sought out Dr. Martyr's assistance after seeing a posting on campus alleging one month of free counseling. Arthur wanted desperately to be cured of his insecurities. Often, the mass of self-doubt that plagued him caused him erectile disfunction. That, atop of his high blood pressure medication, a condition that made him a looker most times as opposed to a completer of the act. *Oh, but when I do . . .* The thought sent him salivating.

A mildly exposed bosom under a fitted champagne-colored business suit introduced Rochelle's hourglass frame at which Arthur stood gawking, choosing to fade out the sound of her voice as she attempted to usher him inside.

"The doctor will see you now, Mr. Columbus," she remarked, having recognized Ronald emerge.

Dead air followed her instructions, lengthening the moment of anticipation that he'd take his creepy ass inside. She called out to him once more. "Hello . . . Earth to Mr. Columbus." Not even the snap of her fingers caused his leer to wane.

"Hey, man, don't be a creep," Ronald chimed in, tapping Arthur's shoulder.

The moment he turned, making eye contact with him, Ronald's hand began to tremble.

"What are you gonna do, hit me or something? I was simply complimenting the woman's broach."

"Liar. That wasn't all he was doing," Cecilia's voice rang true in his mind.

Ronald didn't believe a word he said. How could he? After Cecilia's burial, Ronald's nagging headaches manifested into much more, eventually revealing itself to be the voice of his dead sibling. For years, he tried his best to block her out, but ultimately, he accepted that it was his punishment for Cecilia's death, and so he gave in to the apparition. So much so that one of his eyes had gradually transitioned to gray. His mother always had suspicions it was because he'd lost his twin, the change came. The once-vibrant little boy became shy around strangers, preferring to stay to himself. It was because he could sense the evil in a person. All thanks to the twin sister who refused to leave him.

He focused on stopping his twitching hand before responding. "Of course not. Why would I hit you?"

Mr. Columbus sucked at his teeth, shooting Ronald a brief scowling stare to which the young man huffed in amusement.

"Are you finished here? I'd like to confirm my next appointment."

"I'm done here," Arthur reluctantly remarked, a bit embarrassed he'd overstayed his welcome.

Rochelle rolled her eyes, relieved he'd gone on his way. "Thanks. I appreciate the interference."

"It's no problem. Next Wednesday at 11:00 a.m., right?"

"I'll mark it down in Dr. Martyr's calendar."

Ronald mashed his stretched strawberry lips, avoiding a full smile. "I'll see ya then." He continued his way out of the office with his sister's apparition right alongside him, looking just as she had the day she was crushed by rocks. Ronald tried his best not to look at her.

Cecilia's dark, sunken eyes were foggy, her clothes tattered and dingy, down to her calf-length socks. Even her fingernails looked as if they had been dipped in soot. Ronald kept his eyes elsewhere as often as he could. Nevertheless, it didn't stop him from hearing what she had to say. Most times, her voice bored into his psyche, causing her will to be that of his. Even after twenty years of life, it remained Ronald and his sister alone.

A sinister whisper nagged at him as he exited the building. *What a bad, bad man. Bad men deserve to be punished.* Cecilia's voice drowned out everything else in the vicinity.

Even the sound of the woman's voice bidding him a good day as he hopped into his burgundy Chevy conversion van remained mute. Ronald smiled, guessing what she meant to convey, attempting to ignore his sister's demand.

"Listen to me, brother. Why are you ignoring me?" The apparition turned up the volume. Her thin, black, crusted lips stretched wide.

Bang! He slammed the door of his vehicle upon climbing inside. "I hear you, dammit. I hear you. You're all I can ever hear." A frustrated Ronald rapidly pounded his closed fist atop the steering wheel, hoping against his better judgment that the noise would stop.

"If you want me to stop, then do as I ask," she demanded once more.

Ronald breathed an exhaustive sigh, pulling his seat belt over his chest to buckle himself in. "As if that's ever worked before," he contested in a low lull.

"One's Karma has to be fulfilled. This is your Karma, dear brother. Your Karma for letting me die."

"I didn't kill you. You slipped," he snapped, staring into the rearview mirror to finally face her.

"You're the reason the rocks slipped. You're the reason I'm dead. Face it," she snarled.

Ronald lowered his head in shame, deep down believing Cecilia's accusations. "What do you want me to do, Cecilia?"

"The path to redemption is good works, dear brother. You can redeem yourself by punishing him."

"Fine," Ronald replied, resistance fleeting. "But I have to be sure he's evil. You can't just go around punishing people without proof they've done wrong."

"You felt it, didn't you, dear brother? His evil evoked my senses. You can't deny you felt it. It's only a matter of time before someone falls victim to his sins. But don't you fret, brother. I'll lead you to the truth of it all . . . I always do," Cecilia proclaimed.

Ronald started his van, headed off on a quest to seek the truth. Cruising down highway I-75, he recalled the first time his sister's apparition appeared to him, marking his initiation into his new life.

Chapter 3

Cecilia's Return

Cecilia had been deceased for over a year. Regardless of that fact, her side of their room remained decorated with his late sister's belongings. Scooby-Doo paraphernalia covered the walls. The analog clock above Cecilia's bed, the covers, even the drapes over the windows were that of Scooby-Doo and the gang. Drapes Mrs. Doolally had sewn herself, with ruffles added for a feminine touch. Sure, you'd think Scooby-Doo would be more of a boy's choice, but Cecilia had her reasons. Her favorite character Daphne was what attracted her to the show. She had long, red hair like hers. Only Cecilia's was full of beautiful, red coils, which often, her mother braided into two pigtails. The little girl always wondered what it would be like to straighten her hair. Yet, she wouldn't dare volunteer to be under the hot pressing comb her mother heated under the stove's flame. Unfortunately, her death came before she ever got up the courage to try it out.

Plagued by night terrors after his twin's death, Ronald regressed from a social atmosphere, preferring to stay home rather than play with friends. The night terrors were the precursor to his headaches. Then the latter foreshadowed the surfacing of Cecilia's apparition. A bad dream ripped him from his sleep in a cold sweat that had dampened the pits of his white T-shirt. The panicked *little boy had become accustomed to the nightmares but seeing her there in front of him once he'd regained focus upon rubbing his eyes free of sleep terrified him to his very core. He hollered at the top of his lungs, but alas, not the faintest squeak could be heard.*

The apparition crept up beside young Ronald, who sat frozen in terror—panicked breaths barely filling his lungs before being forced back out.

Seeing the fear in his eyes, she spoke. "It's me, dear brother. Why are you afraid?" Cecilia's apparition paused at the foot of the bed.

"Cecilia's dead," he faintly uttered as a tear fell from the liquid welled up in his eyes.

Feet never touching the ground, the apparition inched closer. "Only to the others, dear brother." Cecilia sat on the bed beside him. "I'll never leave you."

Ronald nearly jumped out of his skin when the apparition laid its filthy hand atop his, but not wanting to offend his twin sister, he sat as still as a scarecrow, allowing her to embrace him. "I don't understand what's happening. I'm scared, Cecilia," the little boy finally admitted.

"In time, you'll come to understand why it's you, just as I had to learn why it was me chosen to die, dear brother."

Ronald was barely a third-grader when his sister appeared to him for the first time, assuring him of the role he would play from then on. Currently, he was an adult in college and well into acting out his said role. Every day, he prayed silently that one day, his sister would transition into the light. It was a wish Ronald would never admit aloud. Deep down, he'd grown tired of not having a normal life, one where he could enjoy the company of another. His life had been so wrapped up in the demands of his sister that he barely got to live his own, a punishment he once thought to be fair. As time passed, though, with his psychiatrist's help and the counseling received, Ronald began to see things from a different perspective. He truly wanted to live. However, wanting something is much different than taking the steps necessary to implement the change desired. Was Ronald ready for that? It was a question he'd asked himself quite frequently over the past few years. The answer, unfortunately, was often an emphatic no. Thinking about his dilemma weighed heavily on his shoulders. By the time he'd made it to his exit, not a solution had surfaced. Ronald feared Cecilia's request for him to punish Arthur Columbus would be fulfilled sooner than later.

Chapter 4

Their First Encounter

Their neighborhood over the years had vastly transitioned. In the '70s, the Doolallys were the only mixed-race residents, adding a bit of color to Gable Street. Now, the neighborhood was a melting pot, housing people of many diverse cultures. Construction on the house across the street ceased after Cecilia's death. After hearing of the accident, the owners declined to build on the property. The Doolallys gladly purchased the land, leaving it as a shrine to their fallen daughter. "Cecilia's Lot" sat decorated with wildflowers surrounding her headstone. Although her body had been laid to rest at the cemetery, her greatest testimony could be seen right from Ronald's bedroom window, a fact his parents had no idea would go on to torture their son throughout his adolescence.

Ronald cruised past the memorial, pulling into his driveway. He remained in the house they grew up in even after his parents died. Unable to overcome her daughter's death, Mrs. Doolally took her own life only a few years after Cecilia had passed. Mr. Doolally eventually succumbed to alcoholism, dying of kidney failure just before Ronald's eighteenth birthday. All the couple owned was left to him. That, along with the memories, were all he had, memories that damaged Ronald much more than they could ever heal.

He pulled into his driveway, shutting the engine down when the memory surfaced.

Mr. Doolally flipped burgers and hot dogs on his barrel-style smoker offsides as young Ronald played basketball in the driveway.

"One hand, son. You dribble with one hand at a time, no matter what," he coached on as the little boy panted, trying to catch his breath.

"I'll tell you what. I've got an idea. You'll be an expert in no time." Mr. Doolally ducked inside the garage briefly before resurfacing with a small rope.

"Now, what do you plan to do with that, sweetheart?" Mrs. Doolally spoke up from the sidelines, slightly nervous about what her husband was about to do.

"I wouldn't harm a hair on his curly head, my love. Don't you worry." He turned to young Ronald, "You trust me?"

"I trust you, Daddy," Cecelia shouted from the blanket spread atop the lawn along the driveway.

Mrs. Doolally smiled, rolling the end of one of her daughter's pigtails around her index finger as she admired her little girl's beauty.

Meanwhile, her husband had tied the short rope around one of young Ronald's wrists, then attached it to the beltloop on his jeans. "Now, you have no other choice than to dribble with one hand."

The memory drifted as Ronald heard the screen door to the unit next to his close. He hopped out of the van to head inside.

"Mrs. May, how are you?" the young man politely inquired as he jetted up the porch stairs.

"I'm doing just fine, Ronald. How are you?" she replied, looking up at him, surprised he'd even furnished her more than a wave. May Constance had been his neighbor for years, and in that time, he'd barely spoken more than a few words to her.

"Pretty good. You have a good day," he quickly ended the conversation, unlocking his door, then shutting himself inside.

"What an odd young man," the old woman remarked as the door closed in her face.

The first thing Ronald gave his attention happened to be the personal computer that sat atop the desk in his living room. Most people would have thought it odd Ronald didn't have a television in the sitting room, but he never had company. When Mr. Doolally died, Ronald rented out the flat alongside him. Even though he and his neighbor were in separate units, it was the closest he had to a roommate, being they shared part of the basement. It was the only space with a washer and dryer connection.

His current position had helped him to choose a neighbor befitting his home. Under the guise of watchful eyes, they were all subject to Ronald and Cecilia's scrutiny. The security job he had obtained at Wayne State University before he'd decided to enroll officially as a journalism student made him all-knowing as to the comings and goings on campus. He hoped to one day become a writer. Releasing the many stories that had been trapped inside him for so long was tempting. Though they wanted out, if revealed, Ronald's freedom would be at serious risk. His descriptive writing class would surely allow him to create a fantasy around those sinful deeds threatening to boil to the surface. At least, Ronald surmised as much.

The mentally exhausted young man plopped down in his office chair, rolling across the wood floor toward the bookcase against the wall beside him. He pulled down a book, *Compelled to Murder,* by E. Raye Turonek. Of course, he had read the book more than a few times already, as it not only fueled him with ideas of inspiration as to his aspiring writing career, but it also housed the key to his knowledge. Ronald used an algorithm that frequently changed his password so that the chances of him being hacked or found out were slim to none. Had anyone stumbled upon the fact that he'd hacked into the college's security footage, he would be jailed—posthaste.

Ronald cracked open the book on page 133, which happened to be the same time his twin, Cecilia, was pronounced dead. Wedged in between the pages sat a small piece of paper with the current password printed. He rolled back over to his personal computer, then proceeded to log in.

That's when the doorbell rang, initially causing him to pause. *I don't have time for this.* He huffed, then sprang up from his chair to peer out of a small opening in the miniblinds he had created with a nudge of his finger. He could see her standing, arms folded across her abdomen, waiting for him to answer. Ronald tried surmising who she was along with what she wanted before answering. After drinking in her voluptuous frame, big, rounded beautiful eyes, and abundant long, black coils, he couldn't recall having ever laid eyes on the young woman.

Ronald twisted the brass knob, pulling open the front door but left the iron security gate closed to greet his unannounced guest. "Hello, is there something I can help you with?"

Damn . . . Auntie was right. He's packed full of gorgeousness. Her eyes jutted open wider. "Hello, my name is Gertrude, Gertrude Liberal. I wanted to introduce myself, being I'll be staying here now with my aunt."

"Excuse me?" Ronald unlocked the security gate, opening the screen door for clarification.

"My apologies . . . I didn't mean to interrupt you while you were getting ready."

"It's fine. I'm actually ready for the day."

"Oh . . . Then, I think you may have forgotten something." She blinked, attempting to clue him in before blurting it out. "You have one gray eye and one brown." She snickered at what she assumed was an innocent mistake.

"I don't wear contacts, but I promise they won't change any other colors," Ronald admitted.

For a moment, Gertrude stood staring in awe of him but eventually snapped out of it, noticing his look of anticipation. "I'm so sorry. How rude of me, standing here staring at you like some sort of lab experiment. My aunt May rents the connecting flat. She told me you were the landlord. I wanted you to know I'll be staying here awhile with her. Until I finish school at least."

"School?" His brows wrinkled.

"I'm officially enrolled to take classes at Wayne State University. It's downtown Detroit."

"I'm aware of it. I attend school there also, so I guess I'll be seeing you around."

Gertrude smiled, showcasing a row of straight, gleaming white teeth. "That's comforting. I don't know anyone in the area except for my aunt. Would you mind showing me around the campus? My student advisor seems a bit too busy helping out the—" she paused for a moment of contemplation, trying to find just the right words—"pretty girls."

Although Ronald found Gertrude quite beautiful, he understood precisely what it was she meant by the statement. "Seems he's misjudged."

She blushed at his kind words. "So, can I count on you to show me around?"

I guess it can't hurt to show her around, he quickly convinced himself before announcing the good news. "Sure. Why not? I know the campus pretty well. I'll show you around."

"Thank you so much. I truly appreciate it. And to show my appreciation, I'm going to liven this place up. You could use a good gardener. Maybe I can plant some gorgeous flowers like they have in that lot across the street."

"That won't be necessary," Ronald replied, the reminder of his sister's death having instantly soured his mood.

"Oh, it's no problem. I think my aunt could use the added scenery. She'd do it herself if she could. But then, what kind of niece would I be if I let my elderly aunt do gardening while I'm living here rent free? No way. I'm not that kind of person. I'm going to create you both a beautiful landscape, and I'm happy to do it."

"Sounds like you've made up your mind."

"I have," Gertrude grinned, hoping to see Ronald lighten up a bit.

To her dismay, the sour expression on his face had yet to wane.

"Well, I didn't mean to monopolize your time. Not today, anyway." She flashed an innocent smile. "I guess I'll see you tomorrow morning? My classes start at 8:00 a.m."

"I'll be up and ready at 6:00 a.m. If we get there by 7:00, that'll give us plenty of time to peruse the campus," he responded.

"Perfect. I guess I'll see you then. I mean, I *will* see you tomorrow morning. I don't want you to think by me saying 'guess' that I'm going to stand you up. Not that I would ever do that anyway. I'm not that kind of girl," she rambled on.

Ronald could sense Gertrude's nervousness yet failed to realize it was due, in most part, to her fondness of him. "I'll see you in the morning, Gertrude Liberal."

"Oh. Well, I guess that's my cue." She waved goodbye, then scurried off toward her end of the porch as Ronald shut the door to continue the task at hand.

Chapter 5

Duty Calls

Cecilia was there waiting as Ronald turned to head back to the living room, blocking his path. *"You like her, dear brother."*

"What are you going on about, Cecilia? She's just a neighbor and seems to be a genuinely nice person." He continued, passing right through the apparition as if she weren't even there.

"We'll see how nice she is."

"Cecilia, just stop," Ronald implored with a sigh as he plopped back down into his chair in front of the computer. "Don't you have bigger fish to fry?"

"Arthur Columbus," she hissed with a seething glare.

"Let's see if we can find Mr. Columbus on campus." Ronald clicked at the buttons on the keyboard, bringing up security footage at the college. "I do know that he works at one of the restaurants on campus," he continued, looking closely at the monitor until spotting his person of interest in the student center. "There he is, enjoying some tacos on his lunch break," Ronald uttered in a low lull, not taking his eyes off Arthur. "I don't know. Looks pretty standard to me, Cecilia."

"Look closely, dear brother. Under the table," the apparition suggested, leaning her face in toward the monitor.

Only then did Ronald see it—Arthur's hand under the table, snapping pictures of the woman sitting across from him at a separate table. A blue jean skirt barely reaching the halfway point of her extremities allowed sight of her most private places. His disposable camera was perfectly positioned.

Ronald sat back in his chair, allowing the realization to set in. "Guess he isn't as innocent as I thought."

Without looking away from the monitor, the arm of the apparition stretched behind her, gripping Ronald's forearm as it rested on the armrest of the chair.

"That's just the tip of the iceberg, dear brother," Cecilia rejoiced, forcing a flood of Arthur's past transgressions into his psyche. His head fell back, leaving his eyes and mouth wide open. Ronald could see everything through the eyes of his sister's apparition. All the filthy things Arthur had done to those unsuspecting young women came clear.

Upon Cecilia's release, Ronald's head shifted up right. "I should never have doubted you, dear sister."

"I would never steer you wrong."

"I guess you're right."

Ronald spun round in the direction of the kitchen just as the security alarm affixed to the wall chimed, alerting him of something awry. "Well, look at that. I think our guest must be awake." He slowly lifted from the seat to settle the issue, not too concerned with whatever happened to be setting off his alarm.

He moved through the living room into the kitchen, where nothing seemed out of sorts. Not that he'd expected it to be. Decorated with the same daisy-printed wallpaper his parents had themselves chosen, the rounded kitchen was spacious. It had more than a few exits leading to various rooms in the house, a bathroom, the basement, the back hall, and the living room entrance. The kitchen sat at the center of his unit. A bathroom off the kitchen led to the upstairs, right where Ronald was going. After twisting more than three dead bolt locks lining the door to open it, he headed up the dark stairwell, wood creaking under his sneakers every step he took. Just up ahead was another door secured with three additional dead bolts. Ronald turned the locks, releasing the metal bars from their hole to open the heavy wooden door. It dragged across the floor, sounding off a loud grumble, which is precisely why he was in no panic to handle the problem. If something were genuinely awry, Ronald would have heard much more than a buzzing alarm.

And there, Joe was strapped to a wooden chair. His ankles were bound to two of the legs, with his wrists tied to the arms of the seat. Even his head was covered with a white cloth bag. You know, the one that would hold the clothespins for the line. Attempting to escape, he'd tipped over onto the floor, setting off the alarm button under the leg of his chair.

Ronald walked over to the only cabinet in the empty room, pulling out a device that wrapped around his head to cover his mouth. He used the apparatus to distort the sound of his voice. "You almost made it, Joe. Bet you fought as hard as those little boys fought down at juvie. What's your mission statement? Do you know it? Juvenile correctional officers ensure the security of the facility with incarcerated minors by enforcing the rules and maintaining order," he informed him before swiping up a police baton from the corner of the room—one of those old nineteen sixties batons, an heirloom of his father's.

"Enforcing the rules." He terrorized Joe, jabbing the object into his battered rib cage. "Not your sick-ass fantasies."

Joe yowled at every shot that landed on his sweat-drenched, bruise-riddled abdomen. "Please stop," he whimpered.

"Maybe he's had enough," Ronald surmised.

"He hasn't had enough," Cecilia hissed, now standing over the top of him to see the pain up close. *"No, dear brother."*

"I have. Please. I've learned my lesson," Joe pleaded.

"Like little Mickey learned his?" Cecilia rebuffed, yet only Ronald could hear. *"There is no time for hesitation,"* she demanded, grabbing hold of her brother's wrist.

His head fell back, eyes wide, mouth just the same, while the vision maintained its hold.

Ronald spied Joe pushing the boy onto the cold cement floor of his solitary cell as he cried in protest. "Please, not again . . . What did I do? Why are you doing this to me?" the juvenile whimpered, recoiling further into a dark corner before burying his head in his knees.

"I thought we were pals, Mickey." Joe inched closer, removing his black leather belt.

"Had enough, dear brother?" Cecilia inquired, lessening her grip to allow Ronald to return from the heartbreaking insight.

Hard, rapid breaths foreshadowed the hateful glare that fell upon Joe once Ronald's head fell upright. The slight smirk made with a single side of his mouth told of the sinister deeds he'd anticipated exacting on his captive. He turned without a word, flipping a switch on the wall beside the door as Joe lay, begging for his life.

"Hey, man. Come on. Just let me go. I won't even tell anyone about this. I mean, why would I?" he pleaded, fingers jutting outward. "Goddammit, man. Let me go," Joe continued, choking down tears he'd vowed until then to restrain.

The then shamed corrections officer whined, all the while the house went on securing itself. Each open door in his unit slammed shut. First, the door to the room where they stood, then the door at the beginning of the staircase. Down through the bathroom, even that door slammed shut. Several bedroom doors, the additional three doors surrounding the kitchen . . . All slammed, one after the other. Of course, the front back and side doors were already closed. Still, reinforced locks on every door shut his unit down, all from the flip of his switch.

Next door, Gertrude leaped up from her chair in the kitchen, where she sat filling out a stack of official-looking documents.

"Oh my God, Auntie. What is all that racket?" She rushed through their side of the unit to ensure the safety of her elderly aunt.

Aunt May may have been pushing eighty, but she got around pretty good. And as far as wits went, she'd make you feel as if you were a ticket short for the ride at the county fair. Gertrude found her sitting in the living room watching an episode of Ricki Lake.

"Are you okay, Aunt May?" she huffed, concerned and winded.

"Are *you* okay?" Aunt May turned to her. "You look like your mama did when I threw that dart through the garage window when we were just little ole girls. It stuck right in her forehead." Her aunt faintly chuckled, recalling the event.

Gertrude gasped, covering her chest. "Auntie, that's a terrible story."

"Oh, don't ruin your bloomers. She lived, didn't she? You're here."

Gertrude rested a hand on her hip, letting out a sigh. She knew better than to put up a fuss with her aunt. "I guess you're right, Auntie. Auntie, what was all that commotion I heard?"

"Probably that boy next door, fixing up the house for his boyfriend or something," Aunt May answered before turning back to her show.

"Auntie, are you trying to fix me up with a gay man?"

May huffed. "I just wanted to know."

"Aunt May, that's not nice to experiment with people like that. What makes you think he doesn't like women?"

"I've never heard or seen one come to visit."

"Well, now, that's odd," Gertrude pondered the thought. *Maybe he can be my shopping buddy.* She shrugged her shoulders. "Looks like I'll have someone to show me around campus and go to the mall with."

"Have fun, sweetie," Aunt May bid her farewell with a wave of her wrinkled hand, not taking her eyes off the television. She loved her niece but didn't have time for someone interrupting her shows. Daytime television provided her excitement for the day—that and sitting on the porch, judging passersby.

As Gertrude hit the hallway, she heard music blasting from Ronald's unit. "Oh, brother." She rolled her eyes as if to say, what's next? "I'll have to get used to this too," she moaned, heading back to the kitchen to complete her work.

Meanwhile, Ronald busied himself with Joe's castration. A sedative he'd administered had taken effect almost immediately. His sight inside of that white cloth bag waned as Joe's eyelids became heavier each passing second, ensuring he wouldn't escape punishment. A bilateral orchiectomy would surely stunt his desires,

Ronald assumed. He had dragged Joe's body through the adjoining room, then into the attic. Two long, dark hallways ran alongside the stuffy space. Where Ronald had traveled took them behind the walls. A fluorescent light radiated off the exposed insulation along the walls, and the angled ceiling awarded the space a pink hue. There, Joe lay atop a row of thick, plastic, naked to the gills, suspended in the air by a steel-framed rolling table. A single tear dropped from the corner of his eye, running down his battered cheek as they closed a final time.

The clock on the nightstand read 1:00 a.m. when Joe's eyes opened. His body lay still atop the queen-sized bed as his gaze took in the scenery around him. Comic book drawings and posters decorating the walls stole his attention—he and his sons being into that sort of thing. After a few seconds, it dawned on him. *Oh my God, I'm home.* He lay in his very own guest room back at home. Safe in bed. *Was it all just a bad dream?* The evil officer thought maybe he'd dreamed it all . . . until he felt the achiness in his body as he attempted to get up. His torture had indeed happened. He'd been kidnapped, tied up, beaten, tortured, atop of being castrated. Joe went to move his arms. They were free from restraints, a fact that caused him to breathe a sigh of relief. But only for a moment before he winced from the pain in his groin as he attempted to move his legs, which, to his surprise, were free from restraints as well.

What am I going to do?

He thanked God that his wife and sons were staying at his in-laws for a couple of days. Joe knew he couldn't call the authorities. The last thing he wanted was for the real police to find out what he'd been doing down there at the juvenile facility, desires fulfilled at the expense of the young boys incarcerated there. At that moment, he decided to accept his punishment. After careful consideration, he concluded that he'd gotten off easy. As far as Joe was concerned, he was alive, and that was all that mattered. The castration he had undergone would eventually be brought to his attention. Only then would Joe feel the full weight of his transgressions.

Chapter 6

A Girl's Gotta Do What a Girl's Gotta Do

The sound of high-heel shoes clicking across the crumbling cement picked up speed as the crisp autumn air bit at her exposed ankles. Rochelle pulled at the edge of her tight, red minidress. The curvature of caramel hips caused the wardrobe malfunction. The fitted, white rabbit mink jacket she wore would keep her torso warm until she made it inside. She had pulled into the rinky-dink, two-star motel on Eight Mile Rd. to meet her prospect for the night. Being a secretary for Dr. Martyr wasn't exactly paying the bills. A fact that fueled the double life Rochelle had, in the past six months, taken up.

Forty-one. She counted, adding that time to the other times she had sold sex in exchange for money. As Rochelle stepped up onto the walkway, she noticed a note attached to the hollow metal door with the tarnished, brass number eight affixed to the front. That's where he instructed her to meet him.

"Gone to get ice. Make yourself comfortable," she read from the yellow sticky note before snatching it down off the door.

Rochelle inhaled deeply, then exhaled long, gathering her bearings. Having committed the act over forty times, she still had not gotten used to it. The pint of Crown Royal she'd guzzled down before arriving helped to settle her nerves slightly. She needed it for the mere courage required to commit the act. Rochelle didn't know the man she was meeting from a hole in the wall. But neither did she know the others. It was a risky side hustle, yet it was easy money.

A double-edged sword most would say. She twisted the knob, then went inside—the stench of mothballs and mold immediately filling her nostrils.

"What a cheap ass," she groaned as she slammed the door behind her.

Under low lids, Rochelle took in her surroundings. The thin, brown carpet had a large stain in front of the double bed. Peeling, vertical, orange and white wallpaper decorated the motel room. She turned on the small, thirty-two-inch box television atop the dresser, took off her fur, then sat on the edge of the bed. There was a rerun of *Jerry Springer* on the TV. Just as one of the women got up to swing around the stripper pole to the right of the stage, Rochelle's gentleman caller walked through the door.

She leaped up from the lumpy mattress. "What the hell are you doing here?"

"I'm here to be serviced," Arthur answered as he secured the dead bolt.

"I'm not about to sleep with you." Rochelle swiped up her jacket, covering her exposed arms.

Arthur frowned. "Correct me if I'm wrong. Are you not a prostitute? I mean . . . a call girl?"

"Regardless of that, I decide who I want to sleep with. I don't have a pimp," Rochelle rebutted as she attempted walking by him to leave.

He stepped in front of the door, blocking her exit. "You're not just going to leave like that, are you? What if I just want to talk? Can I pay for your time?"

"An hour, tops. And I want fifty dollars up front," Rochelle demanded, extending out the palm of her hand.

Arthur dug into the pocket of his jeans for the money she required, then handed it over.

"Have a seat. I won't bite."

Rochelle always felt something about Arthur was fishy. She just could never pinpoint his issue. Figuring since he wanted to chat, the mystery was about to be solved.

I could get used to getting paid to talk. "What would you like to discuss, Arthur?" Rochelle sat back down on the mattress.

"Why are you doing this if you already work a nine to five?" Arthur sat down next to her.

"It's not enough money for me to live on." Rochelle lowered her head in shame.

"What if I told you I'd give you sixty more bucks, and we still don't have to have sex?"

"And what would that entail?"

"Just let me look at it," he answered. His beady eyes thinned as he surmised what her response would be.

"You can look, but you can't touch."

"Can I touch myself?" he replied.

"The choice is yours." Rochelle took off her jacket, exposing the skin of her arms.

His manhood instantly started to rise. At least, he felt like it had. Arthur stuck his hand into his pants, not wanting to expose his semi-erect penis. He would have to work it over first, and even still, it might not fully extend.

Rochelle's skirt slid up her thighs as her legs opened. She pulled her G-string to the side so that Arthur had a full view of her naked lips. "You wanna see crème?"

"Yeahhhhh," he moaned, yanking on his member.

Rochelle stroked her little man in the boat with a few fingers on her right hand. Round in circles, she massaged until her head fell back in a liquor-induced state of ecstasy. "Oh yes," she moaned.

"Oh yes," Arthur tugged faster at his shaft. He was nearly there. Every bit he had stroked up was sitting at the tip.

"Oh, I'm gonna . . . Oh," she squealed.

He exploded just before her cries hit their peak.

By the time her eyes opened and head lifted, the mallet was crashing into the side of her head.

The blow knocked her off the bed, then down atop a row of thick plastic covering the floor.

Rochelle was out cold. She had taken the risk over forty times, the forty-first being her final. It was the last time anyone would ever see Rochelle alive, killed not by a stranger but someone she knew.

Chapter 7

Hearts Aligning

Ronald flung the plaid, flannel blanket from over the top of him to get out of bed the next morning at the sound of his doorbell chiming. He glanced at the clock on his nightstand beside the bed, displaying the time, 5:30 a.m. *She can't be serious.* He smacked his lips, a bit irritated with his early-morning visitor.

The stacked Styrofoam plates vibrated in Gertrude's unsteady hands as she waited nervously at Ronald's front door. *Maybe I should have worn my black shoes. No. They're heels. I can't be wearing heels all day around campus. My feet would be killing me by noon. I hope Aunt May's red flats look nice enough.* She caught the side of her bottom lip in her teeth, taking one last glance at her reflection in the window next to the front door. Her fitted blue jean skirt came just above her knock-knees, complimenting the curvature of her hips. She was sure to wear Aunt May's girdle underneath her tight, red, sleeveless cashmere tunic. Her necklace perched there between her luscious, lifted bosom would surely garner a few glances. Gertrude's hands began to steady themselves as her confidence boosted at the sight of her reflection. With one hand, she flipped her big, bouncing coils, then tugged at the bottom of her blouse, adjusting it to her liking. That's when it started. *Click, click, click, click, click.* Ronald twisted each lock.

She thought it odd he had so many locks to unlatch, but not enough to mention it. "Good morning, Ronald." She smiled, her teeth radiating brilliance.

As mentioned previously, he was a little annoyed. But as her smile fell upon him, he couldn't help but smirk. Not too much, yet, just enough to let her know he wasn't about to bite her head off for waking him so early.

"I figured I'd make us some breakfast to eat before we head out. Think of it as my way of saying thanks for showing me around. I even brought utensils," she said, lifting the plates just under her bosom.

"You didn't have to do that," Ronald remarked before opening the security gate. "I'm not turning down a free meal, though. So, what are we having?"

By that time, Gertrude had gained a full view of him standing there in nothing but a pair of white boxer briefs. His six-pack looked more like an eight. The ginger trail of hair running down his stomach beneath his bellybutton only made her more curious about what lay beneath.

Ronald noticed her pause. "Am I not decent enough? Because this is what you get when you wake me up at the butt crack of dawn."

"I'm sorry," she cringed, her chest sinking inward as her shoulders lifted—once again unsure of herself.

"Do I look that bad?" he asked, instantly relieving the embarrassment she felt.

Gertrude blushed. "You look like one of those guys in the magazine."

"Then why are you still out on the porch letting me hold this door open? Are you expecting some flies to join us?" he joked.

Gertrude rushed inside. "No flies. I hope you like bacon, eggs, and French toast. Aunt May made some cream of wheat with strawberries on top, but I'd rather not get that full since we'll be walking around."

"That's plenty. I appreciate it. I haven't had a good home cooked meal in quite a while." Ronald closed the door, securing only one of the locks. "Come on. The kitchen is right through here."

He led her through the living room to the kitchen, all the while she took in the décor. It was apparent to her he'd inherited the house from an older relative. *This place could use a young woman's touch.* "Hey, do you like shopping?"

"No. Not really." Ronald's tone was dry as if to say, why are you asking such a question?

He's definitely not gay. Gertrude pumped her hand with a clenched fist in celebration of his reply as she followed, nearly at the edge of his heels.

"Why?"

"Because I don't know where the mall is either."

"I'm guessing you'd like me to show you around there as well?"

"How sweet, Ronald. I thought you'd never ask," she remarked, beaming with pride as they took their seats at the old, wooden kitchen table.

"What are you studying to be, again? A politician?" Ronald poked fun at her.

Gertrude unwrapped their plates, sliding Ronald's across the table to him. "A chemical engineer," she answered off the back of a soft giggle.

"That's pretty impressive." He took a gander at his vittles in all their glory. "And this looks delicious."

"I'm the best cook in our family. That's living, anyway. . . ."

She's smart, pretty, and she can cook. What are the odds? He bit into a piece of bacon, convincing himself that dating would never work. Especially not with Cecilia's apparition there in the corner, staring at them. She'd been there with them all along, seething as Ronald continued to ignore her presence. Cecilia hated watching her brother enjoying the company of a stranger.

All this time, he'd been her doting twin brother, carrying out her every wish. Cecilia feared Ronald becoming fond of another. Where would it leave her? How could he continue to do her bidding if his attention remained focused elsewhere? Although Gertrude had only good intentions, she was a threat to Cecilia's very existence.

By the time the clock struck 7:00 a.m., the pair was perusing campus. Ronald showed Gertrude around the department of chemical engineering, the student center, even Williams Mall, where the undergraduate library was located. He figured she'd need to know where her classes were and where she could go to study in silence. She kept her eyes glued on Ronald as he pointed out the different offices in the administration building. It was the first time anyone, particularly a man, had cared enough to assist without her giving up something first. She'd been used on several occasions in the past, which Aunt May had put a stop to with her always keen advice. If it were left up to Gertrude's mother, may she rest in peace, her daughter would have lived most of her life a slave to a man's desires . . . barefoot and pregnant—as she'd lived until her death. Her mother had never even traveled outside the state of Illinois. Gertrude didn't want that for herself.

"So, what's on your mind, Gertrude? You've been letting me do all the talking. What do you think of the campus?"

"I like your hair. Who braids it for you?" She fingered one of the braids dangling atop his chest, ignoring his inquiry.

Ronald swallowed hard. She'd narrowed the distance between them to look him square in the eyes while he gave his answer. *Is this an interrogation?* He maintained his position, glare thinning as he surmised her intentions. "I braid it myself."

"I've never met a man that braids his own hair." Gertrude's brows lifted as she was indeed pleasantly surprised by his revelation.

"I didn't say it was easy, but it has to be done."

"You should let me braid it for you. I'm pretty good at it." She didn't want to be a slave to a man, but she certainly knew how to snag them. They often wanted to stay, but Gertrude wasn't having it once she realized the man didn't give back. She, unlike her mother, would kick them to the curb without haste.

"So, let me get this straight. You're studying to be a chemical engineer. You plan to plant a garden in the yard, go shopping at the mall, help me redecorate, *and* braid my hair?"

"Sounds like we're gonna be spending a lot of time together." She smiled, releasing her hold on his bushy braid.

"Hey, Gertrude. I see you're making friends already," her student advisor called out as he approached. He felt snubbed by her recent lack of communication. She'd all but blocked his emails.

"Oh . . . Hello, Chris. How are you?"

He smacked his lips defiantly. "So, yeah, why haven't you answered any of my emails?"

Gertrude looked at the ground as if ashamed to answer. Her gaze went up to Ronald, who quite frankly awaited her reply as well, then back to Chris. "Well, to be honest, you're a horrible student advisor. Your attention is devoted to those students who appeal to you visually. I can't allow myself to be subject to that neglect. I've found someone to advise me further. Chris, meet Ronald."

He disregarded the six-foot-four gentleman standing next to her and towering nearly a foot over the two of them. "Are you calling me vain?"

Oh, he's pressed like a panini. Gertrude sensed Chris's outrage simmering.

"You should be going. I'm sure you have other *students* to advise," Ronald chimed in, matching Chris's stern expression with one of his own.

His pink, collared, button-up khaki pants and loafers screamed nonthreatening. On top of that, the length of his high-topped fade failed to make a statement. Even so, it's tough to get a shorter guy to back down. Chris, on the other hand, had a position to hold. He wasn't jeopardizing his job as a student advisor by getting into a brawl. Not that he could take Ronald anyway. "You two have a productive day." Chris nodded, bidding them adieu.

"For a minute there, I thought he would make a scene," Gertrude whispered.

"You weren't too worried about him making a scene when you were calling him vain," Ronald chuckled.

"I guess I'm just prone to being honest."

"You should get going to class," Ronald remarked, dropping his smile along with the cavalier conversation out of nowhere.

Gertrude noticed the change in his mood but had no idea he'd spied his target Arthur coming up the hall.

"There he is, dear brother." Cecilia's apparition came into focus.

"What's wrong with your arm?" Gertrude grabbed hold of Ronald's wrist to ease its quivering.

It came almost immediately, his grasp onto hers, leaving Gertrude staring with concern. "Are you okay?" her voice softened.

He released his grip, prompting her to do the same. "I'm okay. I mean it. You should get to class. It's already 7:45," Ronald insisted, hoping his pleasant grin provided the assurance she needed.

Something was amiss. Gertrude couldn't pinpoint what it was that had shifted, yet she most certainly felt it. "I'll see you later, Ronald." She paused, then headed on her way. After a few seconds, Gertrude turned to see if he had been watching her leave. To her dismay, he'd disappeared. At least it seemed so. She didn't see him . . . not anywhere she turned. *Did I do something wrong?* Gertrude thought as she turned in disappointment heading off to class.

Having followed Arthur back out to the parking lot, Ronald watched him pull his work shirt out of the back-seat of his Nissan Maxima. For him to pin his subject down, he needed an address. The license plate he copied down on the small pad and paper he'd pulled from the breast pocket of his uniform shirt served to be the remedy to his dilemma.

Chapter 8

Take Nothing for Granted

That morning, Joe woke with shooting pains radiating within his loins. The medicine Ronald administered to sedate him had worn off almost completely. He sat upright on the bed, allowing his feet to feel the carpet beneath him. His arm clutched his abdomen, attempting to ease the achiness in his ribs. He thanked God for the feeling of the fibers between his toes, well aware that just hours ago, he was bound to a chair, beaten and dehydrated. Still, it hurt like hell. His battered ribs ached, swollen groin pulsated, and bruised cheek throbbed. *I've gotta get something to stop this pain.*

Joe stood up, inching his way across the room to slide into his house slippers. He planned on going to the drugstore to get something that would knock him out. Vodka and Tylenol PM, he figured, would do the trick. Dressed in the same jeans he was held captive in, Joe grabbed his car keys, then headed out the door.

Squinting from the beaming rays of sun impeding his vision, he cased the scene around him. The things Ronald had done to punish him remained fresh in his mind as he got into the car, flashes pervading his memory all at once.

The moment the bundle of wet cloth touched his abdomen, it all came into recollection. It grazed his skin, sending electric shock waves through his body. Ronald called it shock therapy. He had given Joe a choice as to

*the form of torture he would receive. From that moment
on, number one ceased to be Joe's favorite. It was as bad
as the drowning he had been subject to. Ronald dunked
Joe's head into the tub of water time after time, reviving
him only to submerge him again.*

Joe forced the disturbing memories from his thoughts,
started the engine, then sped out of his driveway, tires
screeching. He had even neglected to look before turning
out into the street. Just that quick, it was as if he didn't
care about his life. For that moment in time, his safety
was of no concern. Maybe he needed to feel in control,
strong, fearless. . . . Either way, the flippant gesture
oozed ungratefulness. The false sense of power dissolved
in his chest as he mashed his foot to the pedal to brake at
the four-way stop.

"What the fuck?" Pump, pump, pump. He mashed the
pedal repeatedly while swerving to avoid crossing traffic.
The minivan plowed right through the fire hydrant in
front of the house on the corner, sending a tower of water
shooting through the air. It was the tree that stopped
him—and sent his body flying through the windshield
toward it. The collision, Joe's head with the tree, killed
him on impact. That was the end of creepy Joe.

Down at the juvenile facility, Mickey could hear someone's boots coming up the hall. Trembling like a leaf, he
cowered in a corner, dreading the moment his visitor
would come into view. The sound of his keys jingling
could be heard as he inched closer to Mickey's cell. A
shadow finally revealed itself through the upheaval of
tears blurring his vision.

"Hey, kid. What's the matter with you?" the guard
inquired, concerned about why the boy cowered there in
the corner.

An instant sense of relief covered Mickey. He thanked God in heaven that it wasn't creepy old Joe coming to pay him another visit. With the sleeve of his shirt, the boy wiped tears that had since come popping out and running down his scarred cheeks. Not all the abuse he'd received was sexual.

"I'm okay."

"It's yard time. Are you not going out with the other boys?"

"Yeah, sure . . ."

Mickey got up slowly, then walked out of his cell and through the halls without seeing old Joe. He thought for sure once he hit the yard, he would be there, taking his pick of the juveniles out playing. But upon feeling the warmth of sunlight on his skin, he looked around, finding his surroundings absent of his abuser. Out of five guards roaming about, none were creepy Joe.

Ronald and Cecilia had done a good thing. At least, Mickey would see it that way.

Chapter 9

Gathering Intel

The lunch wave on campus had ensued, giving Ronald the perfect time to carry out his plan. Only then could he search Arthur's home without the possibility of being discovered. That is if Ronald was correct in assuming Arthur lived alone. He had done his due diligence to find out what he could from the license plate he'd copied in the school parking lot. After cutting the brake lines on Joe's car, Ronald had headed straight for the Columbus residence.

"Let's get acquainted, shall we, Arthur?" Ronald uttered under hushed breath as he picked the lock at the back door of the ranch-style home. If ranch style made it sound fancy, please know it was anything but. The one-level pigsty housed a swarm of gnats, the majority of which hovered over the pile of filthy dishes filling the kitchen sink. Ronald fanned the few around his face, shutting the door behind him.

He felt no change under his feet as he moved from the cement porch to the living room floor because the carpet had been pulled up, leaving the cement slab underneath exposed. Even though only a few of the bulbs in the light fixture illuminated when Ronald flipped the dingy switch on the wall, it was enough for him to see. Assisted by light shining through the tattered mini-blinds, he began to search for clues about the truth behind Arthur Columbus.

"Here, dear brother."

Just up the hall, Ronald spied Cecilia's apparition, pointing him in the direction of what it was he needed to see.

Down on Dwyer Street, the authorities were busy picking fragments of Joe's brain out of the maple tree in which they had been engrained. It was Detective Edward Barnes's first week in his position. The lanky bachelor maintained a fierce career focus as taught by his predecessor, who'd sadly met his end several years ago. The elation of graduating from beat cop carried him through his long shifts with gusto to uncover the truth. He held tight to the dream that his aspirations to become the first African American sheriff in his unit would be fulfilled one day.

Barnes examined the horrific scene while spectators loomed nearby, mouths agape as they surmised their versions of the tragic event.

With gloved hands, Drea Alanis, a female detective assisting him in the case, wiped a sample of the fluid from the pavement behind Joe's wrecked vehicle. She rubbed her fingertips together under her nose, testing its fragrance. "Detective, I think I have something. Smells like brake fluid."

"We might have a cold-blooded murder on our hands," Barnes proclaimed. It would be his very first time as lead on a murder case. "Let's get a sample. We're doing everything official on this one."

Detective Alanis, although under him in the ranking, had more experience as a detective on the force. Yet, because she was a transfer from Tarpon Springs, Florida, she had to accept the position under Barnes. Even though she felt completely out of her element at times, Detective

Alanis remained hell-bent on proving herself. The five-foot-five Greek American woman was the only one in her family to work on the police force, a fact that didn't make her father proud. He wanted her to find a nice man and settle down. But becoming attached was the last thing on her mind. Besides, first, she'd have to do something with her unkempt eyebrows and bushy brown mane. Either way, it would have to wait until the case was solved.

Joe Poser's murder had just become their number one priority.

Later that afternoon, Ronald cruised down Gable, his plans set in motion. He'd planned to go home, but upon glancing ahead at his house, he'd caught sight of Gertrude gardening in the front yard. She looked beautiful in her linen culottes and cheetah print bikini top. So much so, Ronald nearly hit the curb, turning at the corner just before his house.

Gertrude saw the last-minute departure he'd made. Her face flushed over in embarrassment. *Oh my gosh, I did say something to turn him off. He can't even stand to be around me. Maybe it was Chris. I hope he doesn't think I'm using him to make Chris jealous.* Gertrude feared the worst. She'd grown fond of Ronald in just the few hours she'd spent with him. His ignoring her while she lived right next door would be torture to her ego. Even though she felt saddened by his actions, it was because of Aunt May she continued planting the assorted tulips in the dirt lining the front of the house. Gertrude promised her aunt she'd give her some pretty scenery to look at while she sat on the porch. There was no way she was breaking her promise.

About ten minutes later, she noticed Ronald's van cruising up the street. *Just don't say anything, Gertrude.*

Let him talk to you. She coached herself on what to do once they'd come face-to-face.

Ronald pulled into the driveway, grabbing his bags before hopping out of the vehicle.

Gertrude was sure to keep her head down as if she hadn't noticed him there. He closed in on her, studying her attitude as she plowed the hand shovel into the soil.

"Here, put this under your knees." He pulled a square, flower-printed cushion from the plastic bag in his hands, handing it over to her.

Gertrude looked up at him, towering above. His frame shielded her from the sun's rays. The first thing she noticed was the tag. *Did he just go and buy this?* "You bought this for me?" she asked, brandishing a delighted smile.

"Well, I didn't want you to ruin your pants all because you want to make my yard look presentable," Ronald admitted.

"That's very thoughtful of you. Thank you, Ronald." Gertrude accepted the gesture of kindness, then proceeded to place the cushion under her knees.

"You're welcome. It's the least I can do. Do you need any help?"

"There is some dirt I need to be moved. It's kinda heavy, though."

"Let me open the garage. I have a wheelbarrow inside. I can move all the dirt you need."

A smile graced Gertrude's face as she watched him trek across the lawn—even more smitten than the first day she'd laid eyes on him.

Ronald unlocked the padlock securing the detached garage. No one who lived there actually parked inside. An old, cherry-red 1976 Chevy Caprice, however, did take up space in the windowless structure. The vehicle belonged to the late Mr. Doolally. His father kept his prize car in mint condition. Naturally, Ronald, being his only son and surviving lineage, kept up the tradition.

Like any other garage, it housed all Ronald's tools and gardening supplies. Yet, there beneath the shiny, red vehicle, something much more sinister loomed. Ronald passed it by, running his fingertips across the hood as he made his way to the corner where the wheelbarrow sat upright. As his hand gripped the worn wooden handle, Mr. Doolally senior came to mind.

Ronald turned, recalling the loud bang that sounded off when his father tossed the battered criminal through the side door of the garage.

The miscreant rolled across the concrete, unable to slow his momentum. So much so that he plummeted down into the dark opening, underneath the big metal lid propped up with a steel bar. What was hidden beneath the old Chevy had been unearthed that night. It wasn't often his father opened his "redemption chamber." The apparatus being privy only to those who didn't deserve instant death, those awarded the opportunity to redeem themselves. Mr. Doolally felt it imperative that the punishment fit the crime.

"Get your ass down there." He threatened his captive, who lay in the darkness atop the platform at the bottom of the cement stairwell.

Young Ronald cowered at the hate in his father's voice. Back then, he'd become frightened of him, well aware of what his old man was capable of. The 7-year-old little boy ducked behind the wheelbarrow, his heart pounding under the bones of his frail chest.

"I told you, didn't I?" Mr. Doolally pressed onward, having locked them all inside. On the heels of his prisoner, his stone-gray eyes adjusted as he trotted down

the dark, narrow, cement stairs, eager to do his due diligence.

Now, although fear had taken hold, curiosity won out. Young Ronald had to see what his father was doing down there in that eight-foot by fifteen-foot cement chamber beneath the garage.

The little boy crept from behind the cover of the wheelbarrow to tiptoe down the stairs. A light that flickered at the end of the steps shone against the concrete wall, illuminating his path down through the corridor, which encouraged him to continue forward. Young Ronald peeked his head around the corner, a witness to his father's deeds. He counted the holes alongside a Plexiglas box atop a steel rolling table, pondering what purpose they served. The more his bucked eyes took in the scene playing before him, the more his father's intentions became clear.

An iron trough filled with water sat alongside the men. Young Ronald wondered why the bad man wasn't screaming. That was until he caught a glimpse of the muzzle fitted around the stranger's head. It happened just as Mr. Doolally yanked his limp body up from the cold cement by the collar of his blue dress shirt, tossing him over into the Plexiglas casket of sorts. They locked eyes for a second, the obviously remorseful white-collar criminal and the impressionable little boy. Still, young Ronald didn't move a muscle, crouched there at the edge of the stairwell, safe from the glow of the flickering lantern affixed to the wall. He watched his father pull down the lid on the box, trapping the man inside. The ropes surrounding it, Mr. Doolally connected to a hook and winch suspended above their heads.

Seeing his captive squirm this way and that brought Mr. Doolally a great sense of authority. He brandished an unwavering smirk. His chest puffed with pride as *he cranked the Plexiglas casket into the air, then over above the trough of liquid.*

Initially, his father cranked it down slow, submerging his prisoner into the tub of cold water, inch by inch. Breaths that were, until then, short and panicked, shifted to deep and purposeful as the stranger anticipated his own drowning death. Mashing the muzzle against one of the openings drilled into the top, he tried desperately to keep his airway free from the flood of liquid overtaking his space.

He'd endure that process twenty times over for what he'd done. If his heart could bear it, he'd live to see another day. It was a decision left up to him in the end—to survive or not to survive.

Back then, young Ronald had no idea he'd one day be called to fill his father's shoes.

The realization pulled him from the daydream and back to reality. Ronald made efforts not to allow his feelings of regret to overtake him, knowing full well his sorrow would never go undetected. Taking Cecilia's presence into account proved beneficial, even in her absence. Deep down, Ronald felt she was always around . . . waiting to state her piece.

Chapter 10

Old Habits Die Hard

Detective Alanis called out to her parents as she crossed the threshold of their foyer. "Mom, Dad, I'm here."

"It's about time. We're in here," her irritated father answered from the dining room table, already having been waiting on their daughter to show up.

"I'll go and get dinner out of the oven since she's here." Mrs. Alanis got up from the table, then scurried into the kitchen.

"Hello, parents," Alanis greeted as she pulled open the door between the dining and living room.

"You're late," her father groaned.

"I love you too, *Patéras*." She kissed him atop his forehead. "Where is *Mitéra*?"

"She's preparing dinner now that her inconsiderate daughter has graced us with her presence."

"Oh, Patéras, you'll raise your blood pressure. You should calm down." Drea moved through to the kitchen to help her mother.

Mrs. Alanis stood at the stove tossing the salad, just having added the blue cheese crumbles and tomatoes. The moussaka sat cooling atop one of the stove's eyes. She could smell the eggplant and ground beef dish the moment she walked through the door. The traditional dish was a specialty of her mother's. Detective Alanis admired her mother, how well she kept herself up over the years just being there in the house. Her long, black mane stretched down her exposed back. The white linen dress she donned was something she only wore inside the house.

"Are you just going to stand there, or are you going to come over and help your mitéra?" her mother inquired without having even turned to see if she was there.

"I'd be happy to help," Drea replied as she rolled up her sleeves, proceeding to assist.

"Wash your hands, young lady."

"Of course." Drea went to do as her mother asked.

"Looks like your patéras is going to need more cons vincing," her mother remarked as to her father's state of mind.

"Is he still angry at me for not coming to All Saint's Day? It was ages ago, really," she complained.

"He's angry about more than that. Your being late today just dredged that memory back up. You know why your father is upset." Mrs. Alanis turned to her daughter, forehead wrinkled between her bushy brows.

"Tha perpei na pantrefteis prin pethano," her father yelled from the dining room. The term spoken in his native language meant, "You'll have to marry before I'm dead."

Drea finished washing her hands, then dried them off with the hand towel hanging on the cabinet below the sink before turning to face her. "I'll get married once I'm ready. I am certainly not in a rush. Did you know that 60 to 70 percent of officers' marriages fail?"

"Well, now, who told you to go be a police officer? Certainly, not your parents. You could always quit."

"All right." Drea threw up her hands. "I wasn't aware that I was walking into an ambush." She started to head for the door.

With pleading, blue eyes, Mrs. Alanis begged, "Please, don't leave," stopping her daughter in her tracks. "I'll keep your father calm."

"I would appreciate it. I kinda had a tough day today," Drea admitted.

"Well, help me get this food into the dining room, and you can tell us all about it."

Meanwhile, Gertrude proceeded to craft her creation. She kept her mind busy thinking about what she'd make for dinner. Aunt May had bingo that night with the ladies at Transfiguration's recreation building. The Catholic Church often hosted events to occupy the community. Bingo, carnivals, raffles, even State Fairs were held there on the grounds. There was no way May would be spending her Thursday night standing over a hot stove when she could congregate with like-minded individuals. Every elderly lady on that side of town would be in attendance, inkers for blotting and crossword puzzle books in tow for intermissions.

Considering her night alone, Gertrude hoped to eat her dinner with Ronald that night. *I hope he doesn't have any dinner plans.*

"All right. I'm all yours. What are my instructions?" Ronald pushed the wheelbarrow up the driveway in her direction.

His words were like music to Gertrude's ears.

After a long day of dropping fries and reheating chicken patties, Arthur strolled into the house, tossing his keys on top of the television before making his way to the kitchen to empty the contents of his bag onto the already-cluttered table. He took out the gnat spray, pulled the trigger, and began slaughtering the lot of them. Sure, washing the dishes would make more sense, but the way Arthur saw it, he'd already slaved all day at the fast-food restaurant preparing orders. Of course, he had no idea what actual slavery was like, but all he had to go off to form his opinions were his limited mind and experiences. Arthur loathed the job. He felt as if it kept him stuck, a captive of poverty. Yet, he blamed his financial situation on everyone but himself. Time after time, his bitterness and lack of effort had kept him from obtaining love, eventually allowing an ineptness to overtake him. An ineptness he'd allowed to manifest into a monster Ronald had recently come to discover.

After exterminating the hoard, he snatched open the bare refrigerator to grab one of the only things it housed beside a carton of milk, some cheese, along with a pack of frankfurters. The flat forty-ounce bottle of malt liquor from the night before would surely wash away his woebegone mood. Arthur twisted off the cap, then took several long swigs, gulping down a third of it as he stood in front of the opened fridge.

He hissed as he wiped the trickle of alcohol from his thin goatee with a swipe of his forearm, relishing its taste. *That hit the spot.* He made his way to his bedroom, placing his beer on the nightstand after taking another gulp. That's when his gaze shifted to the space beneath the bed. He proceeded to kneel beside the mattress, reaching his hand underneath to pull the cardboard box toward him. The moment Arthur placed the box containing his most precious belongings atop the gray comforter, a feeling of languor overtook him. Blinking lethargically, he had already begun to feel the effects of the malt liquor. However, there was the possibility that it could have been the sedative Ronald added to the bottle during his visit.

Even so, Arthur unzipped his pants, allowing his bulging member to poke through the opening. He was eager to be stimulated even before he had begun perusing its contents. Either way, by the time Arthur had opened his box of goodies and began pleasuring himself there on the edge of the bed, the sedative did its job. With his stiffened penis in hand, he tried shaking himself awake, but it was too late. Arthur's head fell back, taking with it the upper half of his body.

Chapter 11

Falling Hard

Meanwhile, Ronald and Gertrude admired their handiwork.

"Look at it, Ronald. It's beautiful, isn't it?"

The two of them, Ronald and Gertrude, stood on the sidewalk in front of the yard gazing at the colorful flowers.

"My mother would have liked it," he remarked, recalling how much his mother loved flowers. Tears nearly filled his ducts until he realized Gertrude's gaze had shifted from the landscape to his person. "Why are you looking at me like that?"

Gertrude cut right to the chase. "Would you like to have dinner with me tonight? Aunt May has bingo, which means I'll be eating alone. I hate eating alone."

"As long as you're doing the cooking, I'd love to. Should I come to your place, or will we be eating at mine?"

"Well, it's much easier for me to cook at my place. Besides, we have a dishwasher."

"Are you calling me outdated?"

"All right now, Chris. Jumping to conclusions must be contagious today."

Ronald chuckled. "You know I had to get you."

"You could always help me do the dishes if you'd like."

"I think I'll pass. I've done enough hard labor for one day. I'm looking forward to relaxing and eating a home cooked meal now that you've gotten me all excited."

"Any requests?"

"Do you know how to make goulash?"

"Do I know how to make goulash? I guarantee you haven't had goulash as delicious as mine. How about you come over around seven o'clock? Dinner should be ready by then."

"Sounds like a plan."

The two headed up the walkway to go inside—Ronald proceeding to his unit and Gertrude to hers.

Ronald had more work to do before he was due to be back in Gertrude's company. Without being sure of how much of the sedative Arthur had ingested, let alone if he'd drunk it at all, he was taking a risk going back there. If Arthur had ingested the drug and since recovered, he'd definitely know he'd been slipped a mickey. Not having drunk the beer at all would result in Ronald having to go about things the hard way. Either way, what had to be done would be. *Two hours should do it.* He committed himself to the time.

Ronald hurried to his bedroom to change, dressing in a pair of blue coveralls. A hood had been fashioned to the collar to help further conceal his identity if he was spotted at the scene. He grabbed his keys and a legal-sized clipboard with a few sheets of paper pinned to it. To avoid running into Gertrude on the way out, Ronald exited the back door, cutting through the yard to get to the driveway.

Alerted by the sound of his engine, Gertrude glanced out of the kitchen's bay window just as Ronald backed out. *Let's hope he's going to pick up a good bottle of wine.* She continued filling a pot with water to boil the pasta.

During the ride to Mr. Columbus's house, Cecilia's eerie presence perched silently on the backseat. Ronald could tell something was wrong since she'd refrained from uttering a word. The darkness around her eyes seemed even more apparent that day. Hostility oozed from the sullen scowl plastered on her face. Each time Ronald glanced in the rearview mirror, there it was, that scowling stare.

"Is that look directed at Arthur or me, dear sister?" Ronald asked, having noticed Cecilia's discord earlier that morning.

"I would never harbor any ill feelings toward you, dear brother." She masked her distaste for Ronald's recent choices with a sly grin.

He accepted the untruth, then mashed the gas pedal further to the floor, focused on Mr. Arthur Columbus. The short ride down the highway provided the time he needed to come up with a plan. By the time he pulled around the corner from Arthur's house, Ronald had a clear vision of how he would handle the situation. He hopped out of his truck with the clipboard in gloved hands, looking as if he were canvassing the neighborhood to check the electric meters alongside each house. To his surprise, he had yet to see a soul outside their home. No little girls playing double Dutch, no little boys riding their bikes. . . . As Ronald walked over the hopscotch diagram drawn in chalk along the sidewalk, he recalled a memory.

Back then, he and Cecilia were inseparable. They played along the walkway just beyond their front porch, Cecilia taking her turn to make it through the course. Her red Chucks hopped from one square to the next about the fractured cement.

"Step on a crack, you break your mother's back," young Ronald declared.

Cecilia stopped in her tracks, teetering on one foot, averting other flaws in the foundation. "Hey, no fair. That crack isn't even supposed to be there."

"Doesn't matter now. You stopped, so I win."

"You tricked me." Cecilia grimaced, flipping one of her pigtails behind her shoulder, then resting her hand on her hip.

"I'll race you for it." Ronald took off running.

Cecilia gave chase, maintaining a close distance. Every time Ronald glanced to his rear, his sister was on his heels.

"Time to kick it into overdrive," he yelled before shifting to increase his speed. It was an announcement he should have kept to himself. You know what they say, loose lips sink ships. With the uttering of his declaration, Ronald's plans were thwarted by the kick of his twin sister's foot. He'd gone flying through the air but only for a moment before his body crash-landed on the ground.

The sight of Arthur's home forced the not-so-fond memory to fade, bringing him back to reality.

"Hey, hey . . . Have a drink with me," the drunk man staggering up the block toward him insisted.

Ronald lifted his hand to let the man know not to come any closer. "Back up," he insisted.

"I just wanna have a drink with ya," the stranger staggered nearer.

A neighbor across the street came tearing out of her screen door. "Get in the house, Tony. You leave that meter man alone, or you'll regret it. Don't make me call the authorities."

"Ohhh, come on, Karen. I just wanted to have a drink with him," Tony slurred.

Karen defiantly waved her spatula in the air. "I mean it, Tony. You get inside your house and stop causing a ruckus," she demanded, quickly moving to close her housecoat as it undid itself.

"You're such a party pooper, Karen," Tony clamored, waving his hands flippantly in the air as he fumbled back up the street to his dilapidated flat.

The nosy, middle-aged woman griped but went to shut herself inside of her home. "Low-life scoundrel." She slammed the screen door, then the front door immediately after.

This is a disaster, Ronald thought. *Maybe I should just turn around?* His stomach felt uneasy. Second thoughts about going inside had just about won out when Cecilia laid her hands on him, sending his arm trembling.

"What on earth?" Karen blurted as she spied between the vertical blinds dressing her living room window. She thought Ronald's tremor odd, but the loud horn that erupted down the street stole her attention.

Another neighbor attempting to leave home blared their horn at Tony, who'd paused, chattering to himself as he blocked their driveway's exit. It took a few honks accompanied by angry words for Tony finally to move along. Once he had, Karen looked back, but by then, Ronald had disappeared completely.

Cecilia led her brother to the garage in the back. He took his time surveying the scene. Ronald had to find a way inside without breaking any windows. Walking around the structure brought him to a row of metal drums with tattered cans and broken glass scattered atop them. Aluminum cans, as well as broken glass, nearly blanketed the grass around the rusted drums. In plain sight, the revelation came to him in a flash. It wasn't just target practice. That's when Ronald pushed over one of the drums hoping the top would come flying off. To his dismay, they required more effort. He continued, thrusting the heel of his boot against each barrel one after another until all six were laying on the ground, every one of them still holding its seal.

The shed not fifty yards from there would hopefully furnish a tool needed to pry one open. After picking the padlock, Ronald managed to find a crowbar amongst the rubble of rusted tools.

That should do the trick, dear brother. Cecilia encouraged her twin as he tore by, determined to enforce her will.

Digging the thin end of the metal crowbar into a groove along the top of the barrel, Ronald used the weight of his body to pull back on it, his jaw bulging through clenched teeth.

Suddenly, out flooded a mass of disgusting liquid and dismembered limbs.

He coughed, gagging from the fetid odor as he backed off the horrific scene. Nearly losing his stomach's contents, Ronald choked back an upheaval of vile liquid forcing its way up to his esophagus.

"If you're gonna do this, dear brother, you need to see what it is he's done," Cecilia pressed him.

After a few forced, deep breaths, Ronald was tearing back toward the barrels. One after another, he pried off each lid. When he finished, there had to be body parts of at least a half-dozen mangled women in various stages of decomposition being eaten by gigantic maggots splayed about Mr. Columbus's backyard.

"Now, do you see, brother? He must be punished," Cecilia demanded.

Ronald turned to the house where Arthur lay. His dick, although softened, remained in his grasp.

Ronald entered the house through the back door in search of the man who'd viciously murdered all those women scattered across the lawn.

As his gaze fell upon Arthur, he thought about ending his life right then and there. Taking him back to the house, though, would allow him to take his time torturing him. Even so, something just didn't feel right. He'd already fulfilled his quota for the day, metaphorically speaking. Not to mention, he worried that Gertrude might see him return with Arthur's body. *Maybe I should just call the police. All the evidence they need is outside,* he reasoned with himself.

Ronald had made his decision. He was going to call the authorities and let them handle it.

"Where do you think you're going, dear brother?" Cecilia blocked his path out of the bedroom.

"There's no need for me to do anything here. There's no way he'll get away with what he's done. Joe was different," Ronald explained, passing right through the apparition.

Defying Cecilia's orders wasn't something her brother typically did. Instantly, she clenched his arm—completely forcing her will upon him.

And just like that, he transitioned. With bucked eyes and clenched teeth, Ronald tore through the house headed straight for the kitchen. It was there he'd found his weapon of choice. The wild-eyed avenger pulled a butcher knife from Arthur's kitchen cabinet, judging its sharpness. Then he stretched his neck from side to side, working out the kinks.

"It'll do," Ronald proclaimed before he darted off to commit cold-blooded murder.

Chapter 12

Second Chances

Detective Barnes was seated at the table in one of the local Coney Islands waiting for his number to be called. The lonely bachelor often ate at restaurants, preferring his food to be cooked, not burnt. He had yet to get the hang of cooking entire meals, washing pots and pans, and cleaning stovetops. Barnes had trouble even imagining himself doing anything other than being a cop. He ate, slept, and breathed justice. And though he was there to get a good meal, it was Barnes's duty that fueled him.

Barnes got a whiff of the filthy stench before looking up to see the fidgety man wearing the oversized jogging suit. He stood near the entrance, waiting for a waitress to assist him. Aware that he looked less than presentable, he tried to look civilized, hoping they would be willing to look past his filthy clothes and dirt-smudged face. His fingertips poked out the top of cheap cotton gloves meant to keep his hands warm on days that turned into frigid nights. The duffle bag on his back felt as if it weighed a thousand pounds after having lugged it around all day.

The vagrant had been on the run, going from city to city, even state to state, to get away from his past.

"You can seat yourself," the cashier announced over the public announcement system as she eyeballed the drifter-looking stranger. She was sure she had never before seen him in there.

He sat down in the booth, removed his mason jar full of coins from the pocket of his hooded sweatshirt, twisted off the cap, then began counting.

One of the waitresses approached to take his order, "Good evening, sir. Can I get you something to drink?"

The vagrant looked up, addressing her with the same kindness she had shown him, "Good evening, Sharon," He read the name etched on the lapel of her shirt. "I'll just have an apple pie and a cup of water. The pie is no more than three bucks, right?" He pushed through the quarters, dimes, nickels, and pennies coupled in the palm of his hand to ensure he had enough.

"How do you feel about corned beef?" Barnes chimed in to inquire as he approached. Even though the detective was dressed in his suit, he had put away his badge, being officially off duty.

"I'd say it's pretty good. I haven't had the pleasure of ordering it from this particular establishment."

"Sharon, can you put another sandwich on my order and an extra fry? We'll take it to go."

"Sure thing. An extra order of fries, another corned beef sandwich, and an apple pie." She jotted down the meal before leaving to process their order.

"Do you have a place to sleep tonight?" Barnes asked once the waitress was out of earshot, out of respect for the man.

It was apparent that he was embarrassed about his situation. He lowered his head. "I make my own way."

"How about I make a way for you tonight? I have the extra room."

"Why are you doing this?" The vagrant looked up at him through honest, hazel eyes.

Barnes took a seat in the booth, directly across the table from him. "'Redemption is something you need to fight for in a very personal, down-dirty way. Some of our characters lose that, some stray from that, and some regain it.' Joss Whedon said that."

"Why do you assume I need redemption?"

"Redemption is the action of saving or being saved from error, sin, even evil. You can't possibly feel as if you haven't experienced, at the very least, error. So, I'm asking, which one will you choose? Will you stray, let it fade from your existence, or will you regain redemption?"

What Barnes had put into perspective resonated deep down inside, compelling the vagrant to lay down his arms. "I wouldn't mind trying for the latter of the three," he admitted.

"I think I can help you with that." Barnes flashed a smile.

"I didn't catch your name."

"The name is Barnes, Edward Barnes." The detective extended his hand for a proper greeting, it being reciprocated without haste.

"My name is Richard, but people usually call me Bird."

"That's an interesting nickname. Why Bird and not call you Richard or Dick?"

"I'm by all accounts a hobo. I move from place to place, hopping trains. One day I might be in Michigan, the next, Illinois. Seeing me here and there, people began referring to me as Bird. It just stuck."

"If it's all right by you, I'm going to call you Richard."

It was one of the first times in years he'd felt respected. "That'll be just fine, Edward. I'd really appreciate that."

The lady at the counter behind the Plexiglas shielding tapped the bell. "Order up for Barnes."

Barnes and Richard got up from the booth, Barnes heading to the counter to pay for their order, while his newfound project, Richard, stood near the door.

After paying for their meals, Barnes turned to see Richard holding the door open for him. The simple courtesy showed potential. *He couldn't possibly be all that bad. How on earth did he end up in such a deplorable state?* "Thank you." Barnes stepped out of the restaurant with a plastic bag full of delicious-smelling vittles in tow.

"You're welcome," Richard replied with a smile, knowing he was about to get a fine meal and a good night's sleep.

Richard noticed but said nothing about the bulletproof vest he spied on the backseat as he tossed his duffle bag inside. *I hope he's not a cop just trying to arrest me.* The thought crossed his mind as he climbed into the front passenger of Barnes's Yukon. On the way to the detective's house, Richard relished riding in comfortable seats. Hopping from train to train often only offered as much as a crate or pallet to lie on. Richard saw no blisters on his bottom as a welcomed change.

Barnes stole glances at the stranger from the corner of his eye as he wondered what he was thinking. "If you don't mind me asking, how did you end up like this?"

"I don't mind," Richard replied as he gazed through the passenger window, preparing to recall his misfortunes. The stranger released a long sigh, a feeling of despair overtaking him.

"My life had been a constant struggle since I came home from the Vietnam War. Nothing was as I expected it to be when I returned to the United States. People threw trash at me. They called us subhuman. Accused us of going to war for a cause morally unjust . . . As if we asked for it. I was one of more than 2 million men drafted. It was the beginning of the end of my marriage. I went to war, married, came back single and homeless. On top of that, there was nowhere for me to turn. My government had used me and thrown me away. My people shunned me and called me names. I used to wonder why this happened to me, but after years of living it, I eventually came to terms with the fact that this is the life I was meant to live."

"Damn." Barnes shook his head, empathizing with what Richard had revealed. He remembered the war and how hard it was on many Americans, especially those who had returned from fighting. "I wish there were something I could say to make it better. Nothing could possibly justify what happened to you. The way you were treated isn't right. And although I can't make up for what the government, the people, and your wife did all those years ago, I can try to help you rebuild your life from here."

"You'd be willing to do that? Why? I'm merely a stranger to you." It had been so long since Richard had witnessed an act of kindness so selfless, he almost couldn't believe it. One could say he'd become accustomed to waiting on the other shoe to drop. Regardless of whether he believed it, he wanted desperately to. He'd been out on his own with no help for so long that he didn't even know how to react.

"You're my brother, and you need help. It's just that simple. I can see that you're a good person. Sometimes, people just need a new perspective to help them see the error in their ways. On behalf of America and its citizens, I apologize to you."

"That's very noble of you, but it's not necessary. It isn't your fault."

Barnes stopped at the flashing red traffic signal directing the four-way stop just a block from his house. "Do you believe that everything happens for a reason?"

"I don't know. I guess. I'm sure I picked that restaurant because you were there."

"I believe you walked into that restaurant for us to meet. You need help, and in a sense, I could use some assistance too. In other words, me assisting you will, in turn, help me. Going from place to place, you've encountered much. I'm sure you've developed a set of skills that are immeasurable for some. That's a gift in itself. From this moment forward, your life is going to change for the better. Are you ready for that?"

"I've waited more than two decades to hear something like this. I'm beyond ready," Richard professed.

Barnes pulled up to his three-bedroom bungalow, parking in the driveway behind his cruiser.

"I had a feeling you were a cop."

"Do you have something against cops?"

"Not the just ones," Richard answered.

"Justice is a matter of fairness that should always be determined by the individual. I'm always fair in my dealings. We all get what's coming to us. Lucky for you, it's a warm bed and a delicious meal," Barnes reminded him.

"There is no way I can repay you for your kindness."

"Seeing the shift in your life will be repayment enough. It will definitely take some work, but nothing good comes easy . . . except for this corned beef sandwich, of course," Barnes remarked, ending his response on a lighter note.

Richard's tummy growled as he took in the aroma permeating the vehicle. "Good. 'Cause, I'm pretty hungry," he admitted.

Barnes shut off his engine. "Me too. Let's get inside so that we can dig in."

Chapter 13

Date Night

Elsewhere, food and music provided a therapeutic release. . . .

"Never too much, never too much, never too much," Gertrude sang, sashaying over to the kitchen sink, where the metal strainer held the al dente-cooked macaroni pasta.

An aroma of garlic and oregano pervaded the two-family flat on Gable Street. Gertrude danced around the kitchen, singing along with the Luther Vandross classic as it played from the stereo in the living room.

She added a teaspoon of olive oil to the firm noodles so that they didn't stick together. She had prepared everything. She had fried the ground beef, the sauce sat warming, onions and bell peppers were sautéed, even the yellow and white corn she'd sliced off of the cob had been simmering. The only thing left to do was mixing the ingredients before she'd let her creation warm in the Crock-Pot. Dinner not only looked but smelled delicious. Gertrude had finished preparing their meal with an hour left to spare—time she'd use to get dolled up for her date with Ronald.

The steaming stream of water rinsed Ronald's blood-coated face running down his sculptured frame. He let his head fall back, allowing the hot shower to soak into his loose coils. It was that evening he washed away his worries and, along with it, the memories of what happened earlier at Arthur Columbus's house.

The fact that he had stabbed him over 100 times, ripping Arthur's limbs from his torso, would be a memory soon forgotten. When a stream of blood sprayed across his face, blurring sight in his gray eye, not even then did he stop the brutal dismemberment.

They were all memories Ronald was determined to forget just as he recalled them at that moment. Never again would he think or speak of them.

On the other side of that wall, in her own unit, Gertrude ran the loofa over her smooth, caramel skin, cleansing her temple. She thought it would be a good idea, just in case Ronald had a taste for dessert. Water rinsed her bouncing curls, stretching them beyond the center of her back. Its steamy temperature felt good on her skin. Yet, not as good as Ronald's hands, she imagined. Gertrude closed her eyes in anticipation of him touching her, running the loofa down between her soaked thighs. "Hmmmm," she hummed with delight, on the verge of pleasuring herself right there in the shower.

That's when the wall phone in the kitchen buzzed, halting Gertrude's me time and rushing her from the cleansing stream.

Aunt May was old school. Unlike most, she didn't have voicemail, which meant the phone rang until someone picked up. Gertrude rushed to the kitchen, the excess water dripping from her hair to the plush burgundy housecoat that covered her.

"Hello," she answered, snatching the phone down off the wall.

"I thought I was going to have to come over there early."

The sound of his voice had made her heart skip a beat. "You can come over anytime you'd like. Dinner is almost ready."

"I shouldn't be too much longer. I was calling to see if you needed me to bring anything?"

"A bottle of wine, maybe," Gertrude requested after a moment of brief hesitation.

"White, red, or pink?"

"Since we're having pasta, I think a white would be appropriate."

"White it is. I'll see you soon."

"See you soon," Gertrude responded as she leaned against the wall twisting the telephone cord around her index finger. "He's such a gentleman," she cooed to herself. The smitten young woman's walls were indeed coming down.

Not a mile from there, Transfiguration's recreation hall on Mound Road had a packed house. Fifty rectangular tables lined in rows filled the space. Each table seated ten people, and there wasn't an empty seat in the house.

Aunt May, being in her element, felt good to her soul. Bingo night had everything she needed for a good time: conversation, the chance to mingle with friends, as well as the opportunity to win some cash. A thin layer of cigarette smoke floating above their heads poisoned the atmosphere. The vast majority of those assembled were running through a pack of Slims sitting at their side. The crowd sat puffing and chatting while marking off key phrases in their crossword puzzle books as the brief intermission ensued.

"So, now I think she likes him. I told the child he didn't want none of what she had. You can't tell these kids a thing these days," Aunt May gossiped to her friend and neighbor, with whom she'd hitched a ride there, Peggy Avarice.

The 74-year-old widow with no children lived next to the abandoned lot. She'd lived in her house for over fifty years and naturally seen all the goings-on in the neighborhood.

Peggy snapped her neck, turning to face May. "Are you talking about that weirdo landlord of yours?"

"What makes him a weirdo? He just knows what he wants and what he doesn't want." May rebuffed, sliding her book to the side to place her ten bingo sheets out in front of her.

"That's not what I mean," Peggy quickly cleared up the misunderstanding. "I'm talking about the fact that he's always out there digging into the ground in the middle of the night."

"What is he doing out there?"

"One day, I saw him out there watering the flowers, and I asked him. I said, 'Hey, I saw you out here in the middle of the night. Were you burying something or digging it up?'" She motioned with her hands, adding animation to her claims.

"Ooohs," erupted from a few of the other players sitting at their table as Peggy had successfully garnered their attention, something her raspy voice usually did effortlessly.

"He told me he was outside building the foundation for a shed. Funny thing is he must have been building that shed for over a decade now. He was no more than 9 or 10 years old the first time I saw him out there digging." Peggy paused to puff her cigarette, allowing what she'd revealed to sink in.

"Why didn't you tell me this before?" May inquired, shocked her friend had kept such a thing secret.

"I had no idea you were going to push your niece into the arms of a crazy man."

"There has to be some explanation."

"Other than the fact that he's probably out there hiding something he doesn't want anyone else to see. What if his sister is not even buried at the cemetery?" Peggy protested.

"Why don't we find out is a better question?" Wilson Moral, a male spectator, chimed in.

"Now, we're talking," his old pal Grady Meek spoke up as he leaned into the table.

Following suit, May sat up, leaning in closer to the table. "Wait, what are we talking about here?" she quietly inquired.

Wilson flicked his thumb across the flint wheel of the lighter to ignite his Marlboro Red. "I'm saying we should find out if he's the kind of guy you want your niece to be hanging around with," he replied, masking intentions he would allow to surface in due time.

"I'll drive." Tom, another elderly man sitting nearby, chimed in, volunteering. The stoma at the front of his neck caused his speech to sound somewhat guttural. One would think that, along with the cancer he had contracted, it would put a halt to his smoking. It had done just the opposite. Tom was the type of man who refused to let circumstances determine the way he lived his life. He did what he wanted, whenever he wanted.

"Well, look who it is. Tom Swine. I haven't seen you in over a decade. I thought you were a permanent snowbird. When did you get back into town?"

"Just a few weeks ago. I thought it time I came home."

And just like that, the five of them had formed a gang: Peggy, May, Grady, Tom, and Wilson.

Chapter 14

Dinner Guests Arrive

Back at the house, Gertrude's doorbell chimed as she stood admiring her reflection in the mirror atop the vanity in the hallway bathroom. She twisted left, then right, checking to make sure her exposed back was adequately moisturized.

"Perfect." Gertrude blew herself a kiss, then furnished her reflection a wink before rushing off to answer the door. Her body smelled as if it had been dipped in coconut. Freshly washed coils bounced atop her shoulders, strands nearly intertwining with the spaghetti straps of her sundress as she trotted down the hall.

She paused upon reaching the front door, resting her hand on the knob. There, Gertrude took in a deep breath, forcing it out in one quick huff, hoping to quell her nerves along with its release.

"Wow. You look really pretty." Ronald admitted upon laying his eyes on the beauty he beheld. "I feel underdressed."

"Thank you. You look handsome as usual. I see you took your hair down," a blushing Gertrude remarked as her eyes devoured him, imagining how oiled he was under his black V-neck T-shirt.

Ronald's freshly trimmed goatee was lined up perfectly above his strawberry lips. The ginger coils dangling past his shoulders glistened from his shower. Not a trace of Arthur Columbus's blood remained.

"Are you going to let me in, or are we eating al fresco?"

"I've got to get better at this," she remarked, recalling the last time she had left him standing at the door. "Come right in." Gertrude stepped to the side, finally allowing his entry. "Would you like for me to take that off your hands?" she added, referring to the bottle of white wine in his clutches.

"I can open it. Just point me to your corkscrew."

"Come on. It's in the kitchen," Gertrude closed the front door, then proceeded to lead the way.

Ronald paused, not moving from where he stood. "You're not going to lock the door?"

"Oh . . . I didn't even realize I hadn't." Gertrude went back, twisting the lock. "There . . . We're all safe and sound. Come on," she brushed by him, caressing the back of his arm to usher him forward along with her.

The embrace worked. He followed, though determined to state his piece. "You should always lock your door. There are way too many bad people out here."

"I know. You're right, Ronald. Being from the South Side of Chicago, I should already be accustomed to it. I don't know what made me forget." She knew *exactly* what made her forget. It was the tall, handsome man standing beside her, regardless of whether she was willing to admit it.

"It smells delicious in here. Is that garlic bread?"

"It is, and it's just about ready." Gertrude rushed over to the stove with an oven mitt just as the oven alarm sounded. "The corkscrew is in the drawer behind you," she said, opening the oven, allowing the hot air to escape.

Ronald opened the wine, setting it inside the bucket of ice Gertrude had placed at the center of the table. Everything looked delicious—even Gertrude as she approached with a casserole dish full of goulash.

He leaned back in the kitchen chair, admiring her essence. *I could get used to this.*

At the same time, Gertrude inched closer, looking into his eyes. *I sure could get used to this.*

However, thoughts were quickly tarnished by surprise guests. . . .

"What's for dinner, kids?" Aunt May blurted seemingly out of nowhere.

"Aunt May," a startled Gertrude turned toward the kitchen's entrance. "I thought you were going to be playing bingo for a least a few more hours."

"Well . . . We got hungry, so I figured, why not goulash."

"Who's 'we,' Aunt May?" Gertrude reluctantly inquired.

"We thought you'd never ask." Grady popped his head into view of the kitchen entrance alongside Aunt May.

"Well, hello, there, Ronald," Peggy chimed in.

"The name is Wilson." Wilson nudged his way into the kitchen, cigarette hanging from his crooked mouth.

"Is that garlic bread?" Tom added, darting his head between the others to see.

"Looks like we'll be moving to the dining room table." Gertrude forced a grin, masking her disappointment.

"This should be interesting," Ronald murmured, reserving judgment toward Peggy. She'd rubbed him the wrong way ever since he was a little boy, and from the looks of it, the feeling was mutual.

Peggy stood glaring at him through narrow eyes. It was that very same gawp he had gotten a glimpse of that night she had confronted him as he dug barehanded into the soil and gravel of the lot next door.

It was nearly two o'clock in the morning when she spied him all alone. Young Ronald dug in a panic, sweat pouring down his face. "I'm coming, Cecelia," he grunted.

She snuck up on him. "Does your father know you're out here digging like some grave robber or are you burying something?" Peggy asked, startling him to pause. "I should march you right back across the street and let your daddy deal with you," the wrinkled hag threatened.

Out of nowhere, her husband, Russell, burst out of the front screen door onto the porch, nearly flipping over the porch railing. It would be the first time he'd cracked his head on the ground in a drunken rage. "Peggy, you get your ass in here," he yelled, standing upright yet wobbling left to right on his bare feet.

"Don't you ever come out here embarrassing me like that," she threatened with a wagging finger. The drunk woman charged at her husband, tearing up the porch, only to be knocked to the ground by a swift backhand.

"Get your ass up and get in here, or I'll show you who's boss," Russell demanded as he tore back into the house.

It was the first and only time anyone had ever confronted the out-of-sorts little boy during one of his night terrors.

But in the present day, it was time for dinner.

"Okay, everyone," Gertrude announced, "let's all go have a seat at the dining room table. Aunt May, if you'll lead the way, Ronald and I will be in there shortly with dinner, plates, and utensils for everyone. You guys just sit back and relax."

"Thank you, niece. You always were my favorite niece."

"Aunt May, I'm your *only* niece."

"I know," she smiled. "Come on, gang. Let's get ready for dinner." She headed out of the kitchen with her brood in tow.

Grady sucked his teeth, making sure to give Ronald the stare down before leaving the kitchen. The 78-year-old man had two granddaughters in their teens, so he was used to doing background checks on the boys they dated. Being skeptical of Ronald's intentions came naturally to Grady. Not to mention, he himself had been a bit of a hellion in his younger years.

"What the heck is that all about?" Gertrude whispered after their impromptu dinner guests cleared the kitchen.

"Do you think they are," Ronald paused, unsure if he should ask, "you know, high?" He painted a more vivid picture, lifting his pinched fingertips to his mouth.

Gertrude waved him off with a flippant hand gesture. "Ronald, no. My aunt May doesn't mess around with that stuff." Deep down, though, she wondered what the hell her aunt was thinking, showing up at home before bingo night ended and with a clan of other elderly in tow, claiming to be hungry.

"What about the rest of the bunch? They look a little rough around the edges," Ronald joked.

Gertrude finally relented, feeding into the notion. "The one with the cigarette, he's quite the character, isn't he? Is that a cowboy hat he's wearing?" she giggled.

"Didn't you see the boots? Fresh to death," Ronald added.

Gertrude tried her best to contain her laughter, shushing him in the same instance. "They're going to hear us," she whispered.

"Okay, let's get the gang some food before they tear up the place. You didn't happen to make dessert, did you?"

Dang it. Gertrude began kicking herself for not having prepared her famous banana pudding. "I didn't. I'm sorry."

Ronald hopped up from his seat. "No. It's perfectly fine. I actually have a batch of homemade cookies next door. I don't plan on eating them all myself, and this would be the perfect opportunity to share."

"Great. Aunt May loves desserts." Gertrude blushed, grateful she'd met a man so considerate.

"I'll be right back."

While Ronald headed back to his unit to get dessert, May, Peggy, Grady, and Tom all congregated around the cherrywood dining room table. Wilson stood nearby, pulling drags from his Marlboro Red as he eyeballed his reflection through the glass of the matching china cabinet against the wall. It housed a plethora of plates, teacups, and crystal figurines. Even an old-school photo of May seated in a wicker chair was among those on display.

"You sure were a young tenderoni," Wilson admitted.

He'd had a crush on Aunt May since the first time he saw her at the recreation hall. To his disappointment, May disregarded his many advances, content with being alone. Her husband, with whom she'd never had children, died in the Vietnam War. Aunt May had been single ever since. Her bedroom was always a shrine to her late husband, no matter where she lived.

Wilson's marriage took a nosedive after his daughters graduated high school. Both he and his wife had agreed they'd stay together as long as they had the girls, making the split amicable. His relationship with his girls never faltered because of it, a fact his grandchildren benefited from greatly. You could say he was the Bill Cosby of grandfathers, pre scandal.

Still, May didn't want anything he had to offer beyond friendship. "I was definitely a looker back then."

"Don't discount your more mature self," Wilson said, stepping closer, mashing the end of his Marlboro into the ashtray atop the table.

"Oh, put your britches out. We've got more important things to tend to," Peggy scoffed, secretly jealous of the attention Wilson constantly awarded May.

May could plainly see Peggy's jealousy, yet it didn't seem to bother her. She had no feelings for Wilson, so Peggy could have him as far as she was concerned.

Peggy leaned in, pressing her ample bosom to the table. "Now, how should we approach this?" she whispered, softening her voice as best she could.

"What are you guys in here whispering about?" Gertrude asked as she entered with two wicker baskets full of garlic bread sticks.

Grady finally chimed in, grabbing a bread stick from one of the baskets before it even hit the table. "That's for grown folks' ears, young lady."

"That's funny. Last time I checked, I was a fully grown adult."

"You betta check again," he mumbled with his cheeks full, devouring the tasty dough.

Gertrude rolled her eyes as she exited and returned to the kitchen, intent on not arguing with her elders.

Tom, who had at least waited for the basket to hit the table before digging in, finally offered his two cents. "This bread is delicious. She certainly cooks like a grown-up, that's for sure."

His admission prompted Wilson to partake in sampling the bread.

Chapter 15

A Special Ingredient

Next door, Ronald rummaged through the cabinets attempting to find a dish appropriate enough to house the batch of cookies. He had taken note of how much effort Gertrude put into cooking dinner. A tray that complimented her dinner décor was the least he could do.

"Look at you, making friends, dear brother. Am I invited to the party, or have you forgotten about me already?" Cecilia's apparition seethed in a dark corner of the kitchen.

Ronald continued his search, finding one of his mother's old silver platters in the cupboard, then began transferring the cookies from a plate onto it.

"How could I forget about you? You're my twin sister. I think it would be best, though, if you stayed home, Cecilia. There's no need for you to be there. Besides, I would really like to see these people from my own perspective."

"Of course, you do, dear brother. You always did like to see things through rose-colored glasses."

"I just want to eat dinner without having to anticipate hurting anyone . . . to be normal for a change. I'll see you when I get back. I won't be too long," Ronald responded before heading out to leave.

"Have your fun, dear brother . . . no matter how short-lived it may be," she threatened.

**

Back at May's, Gertrude emerged with the casserole dish filled with goulash, realizing one of the baskets of garlic bread had already been consumed.

"Looks like you guys are pretty hungry," she said, placing the dish at the center of the table just as the doorbell chimed.

"Who could that be?"

"It's probably Ronald, Aunt May. He must have locked himself out when he left to get dessert."

"We get dessert too? This is the best stakeout ever," Tom blabbed.

Peggy's mouth contorted—teeth clinched together upon hearing Tom's revelation. Luckily, Gertrude was out of earshot when he'd let it slip.

"If you guys don't pull it together, you're out of here. The *last* thing we need is for them to find out what we're up to before we get a chance to check this guy out," Peggy bullied the bunch.

Gertrude rushed to open the door. She couldn't wait to have dinner with Ronald. She had begun to warm up to the fact that Ronald would be having dinner with her and her aunt. It would give her a chance to prove to Aunt May that he wasn't gay. Although she would have settled for a shopping buddy, having him as her knight in shining armor would be much better.

"Thank God you're back," she confessed as she flung the door open. "You must have locked yourself out."

"What did I tell you? You should always lock your door," Ronald preached as he crossed the threshold, balancing the tray of chocolate chip cookies in one hand.

"Yes, I remember. Always lock the door." Gertrude closed, then locked it behind him. "Come on. I think the kids are getting rowdy. I love that platter, by the way," she tugged at his arm, pulling him along with her.

"Lover boy is back," Wilson blurted upon seeing Ronald enter the dining room behind Gertrude.

"I brought dessert." Ronald placed the platter atop the table.

Without hesitation, Grady reached for one.

Gertrude stood with her mouth agape. "You're not going to wait until after dinner?"

"I'm 78, not 7. You don't have to worry about me spoiling my appetite. I'm eating everything you put in front of me," he rebutted.

In complete agreement with what he had expressed, Tom and Wilson each grabbed a cookie as well.

"These are nice and soft." Wilson bobbed in an expression of its deliciousness.

Ronald took a seat next to Gertrude. "I assume those are better for your teeth."

Gertrude's hand atop his knee told him his comment came off a bit harsh. But at that point, something about Wilson just rubbed him the wrong way. Both furnished each other an occasional glance of skepticism through slanted eyes.

"Let's eat before the food gets cold." Gertrude attempted cutting through the tension emitted by their silent study.

Regardless of the energy, they were all famished. Each began taking his turn, scooping a healthy helping of goulash from the casserole dish, then adding it to his plate.

"So, Ronald . . . What is it you do for a living? If you don't mind me asking?" Peggy took her turn to interrogate him. He'd lived right across the street from her for decades, yet she knew little about his adult life.

"I'm a security guard."

"So that means you own a gun?" Tom inquired between bites.

"My father was a cop. We had guns around the house before I was even born."

"Then you should be all about obeying the law, right?" Wilson chimed in.

"Why do you ask? Are you intending on breaking it?" Ronald rebuffed his inquiry with his own line of questioning. By then, he'd surmised exactly what was going on. They were interviewing him for the job of Gertrude's man. A title Ronald wasn't quite sure he wanted, given his peculiar situation.

Tom chuckled, nearly choking on the lump of pasta in his throat. "Looks like he's ready for us, Wilson."

Wilson's brows wrinkled. He was tempted to press on with his line of questioning, but something in him had relaxed at that point. A matter of seconds passed before he had begun to chuckle.

"What's so damn funny?" Peggy scoffed, not finding the humor at the moment.

"Oh, calm down," Grady finally spoke up, a smile as broad and goofy as could be.

"Yeah, take a chill pill," Tom chuckled.

"Frankly, I don't see anything funny."

"You never do. You've had a stick up your butt since the eighties," Tom exclaimed.

The old men laughed as they continued to enjoy their meal.

Gertrude leaned in toward Ronald, whispering her thoughts, "What has gotten into these guys?"

He shrugged his shoulders as if to say he had no clue when in reality, his reaction was far from the truth. The cookies were the culprit. THC levels in the batch of chocolate chip cookies did exactly what Ronald expected. They'd dropped their guards—all except Peggy and Aunt May, who'd yet to have dessert.

"I saw you two planting flowers earlier today. They look good. Did you plan on putting more across the street at your sister's grave site?"

At that moment, all chuckles ceased. All eyes were on Ronald as they awaited his reply. He felt their eyes boring a hole into his psyche, surmising his next thoughts.

"Memorial," he said before taking a bite of his goulash.

"I'm sorry, I don't understand what you mean."

"It's a memorial, not a grave site. My sister is buried at Sacred Heart of Saint Mary's."

"Oh, do you plan on putting more flowers around her memorial? I saw you digging out there earlier this week. Late-night gardening, I assume?" Peggy's mouth twitched, anticipating either Ronald's complete blowup or breakdown.

He sat back in his chair, then let out a short sigh, having grown tired of Peggy's line of questioning. "Sometimes, it's the only time I have to get things done. Going to college and working are two full-time jobs that are time-consuming," he replied, playing it cool.

By that time, Aunt May figured Ronald could use a break. "How did your first day of school go, Gertrude?" she asked, shifting the focus from her niece's visibly dismayed guest.

"It was wonderful, actually. We got to campus an hour early, and Ronald showed me around. Being able to get to all my classes with ease was a load off my mind. No one wants to be late on the first day. It becomes a blemish on your reputation from the very start. Thankfully, I had Ronald, who was nice enough to help me out." Her hand caressed his thigh in appreciation of what he'd done for her.

The embrace did nothing to alter his now-soured mood. Every time Ronald and Peggy locked eyes, you could see a look of disgust oozing from each of them.

"Well, I, for one, would like to say, thank you, Gertrude. This is, hands down, the best goulash I've ever tasted. I'd love to get an invite again. Hopefully, we haven't been too much of a burden. We kinda crashed your date." Grady continued munching on his plate of vittles.

Gertrude smiled at the fact that Grady referred to her and Ronald's dinner plans as a date. Wishful thinking kept her from clearing up the misunderstanding. "You're very welcome. It was no bother at all. Right, Ronald?"

"Nah. Not at all," he responded in the driest of tones.

Gertrude could tell at that point something was amiss. Ronald's demeanor had changed completely. She worried they had ruined things for her.

"Ronald's going to show me around the mall this weekend. We'll have plenty of time to get acquainted, right, Ronald?"

He turned to look her in the eyes, his many other obligations coming to the forefront of his thoughts. "This weekend?"

Don't back out on me now, she thought. "I thought you said it would be okay?" she asked, noticing a hint of uncertainty in his tone.

Ronald couldn't say no. Gertrude's big brown, inviting eyes prompted him to cave under her will. "This weekend sounds great, Gertrude. How about Saturday? I have some things to take care of tomorrow."

"Saturday it is," she blushed, brandishing the brightest of smiles.

"Sounds like a gay old time," Tom mumbled, his cheeks stuffed with dinner.

Grady chuckled, being the only one who'd heard the comment.

Not seeing the humor in the situation, Peggy shot the two of them an evil glare—their chuckles becoming even more muffled under the pressure of her stare. "I've been meaning to take a trip to the mall. I could use some new clothes. I've been wearing these old garments for over a decade now," she said, turning her attention to Gertrude and Ronald.

Peggy's comment caused Gertrude's smile to wane. She didn't want anyone tagging along. The gang of elderly had already interrupted the dinner she'd planned. Within seconds, Ronald relieved the discord she harbored. Peggy tagging along was out of the question as far as he was concerned. "I hope you find what you're looking for."

"Would you two mind if I tagged along?" Peggy finally allowed the dreaded question to leave her lips.

"I would," Ronald spoke up without hesitation.

Gertrude scrambled to clean up his blatant response. "It's just that we have other things planned as well. Maybe next time, Peggy."

"I'll go, as long as you're driving. I've got some perks club coupons from JC Penney I could use," Aunt May chimed in cushioning the blow.

One way or another, they'd keep eyes on Gertrude and Ronald.

Peggy flashed a pleasant grin. "It's a date then."

"I'd like to come along. I'm supposed to be getting my granddaughter a gift for her birthday next week, and I have no idea what to get. I'm sure you two can help me pick out something she'd like," Wilson remarked, putting in his bid for time with Aunt May.

Quite frankly, Peggy had had enough of the men and their antics, but she couldn't decline since Wilson had to find a birthday gift for his granddaughter. "Fine. Whoever wants to go, we'll meet at my house on Saturday at noon. Don't be late."

The remainder of their dinner progressed without incident, although they all continued to harbor reservations about Ronald's intentions. Were they deadly or not so much? He was clearly interested in Gertrude, taking the notion that he was gay out of the equation. Still, Ronald wasn't in the clear just yet.

Chapter 16

Watchful Eyes

As the sun made its rise the next day, Karen stepped out onto her porch with a mug of freshly brewed coffee in hand. A pleasant grin graced her face as she closed her eyes, then took in a long whiff of the dewy air pervading the morning. That was until it hit her. Karen's eyes opened under wrinkled brows and contorted lips once she had gotten a whiff of the pungent stench coming from across the street. "What on earth is that smell?"

The stray dogs leaving Arthur's property clued her in about where the rancid odor was coming from. Down her porch steps, she trotted in furry pink house slippers and matching robe to find out what could possibly cause the foul funk lingering about her neighborhood. "You get out of here! Get!" she flailed her hand wildly, shooing off the strays as she approached Arthur's property.

The closer she got, the more sickening the smell became. Karen lifted the lapel of her robe over her nose, hoping to mask the funk. She thought about ringing his doorbell but harbored doubts he'd answer. Arthur had always been a private neighbor, one who preferred not mingling with the community around him. That, along with the fact that she once called him out for not maintaining his lawn, Karen knew she'd get little to nowhere with him. This had to be done without his permission. Even though her actions could be deemed as trespassing, she felt it was her duty. Besides, no one else on the block was nosy enough to care. Karen unlatched the gate, then continued into his backyard. She'd only made it a few steps until her house shoe pressed down on something gushy. *What the hell is that?* She looked down, lifting her foot from the ground. There it was—a fully formed, partially eaten human heart. She howled in horror, bolting from the scene. Karen couldn't get back across the street fast enough to call the authorities. Her robe flew open, putting her white, high-waisted panties on display. She clenched it tight to her chest, keeping it closed so that her large, sagging breasts didn't come flying out.

Thirty minutes later, detectives from the Detroit Police Department were canvasing the scene. Yellow crime scene tape sectioned off the property from front to back.

Detective Barnes stood with his arms folded, wondering what was waiting on the other side of that front door. If the backyard housed a buffet of waterlogged body parts, it couldn't be much better inside the home. "We're going inside first," he instructed Detective Alanis, who had already been vesting up.

"I'm ready. You vested?"

Barnes knocked at his chest, affirming her query. "Let's do this."

Both approached, shattered glass crunching under their shoes. By Barnes signaling, Alanis agreed to go left while he'd stay straight ahead.

He went directly up the front porch. Alanis decided to go along the front side, climbing the porch railings, then hopping over to gain access to a side angle. She waited there, gun drawn, cocked, and ready to fire.

He laid his fist into the thick, wooden door carrying its thudding sound through the house.

"Open up. This is the Detroit Police Department. If I ask again, I'm breaking the door down."

A few seconds passed before Barnes turned to Alanis, giving her the nod. At that point, she knew entry would have to be forced.

Barnes knew he could call the tackle team or get in inside themselves. He pulled his gun from his waist under his gray suit coat. It made him feel like he'd made it to the big time to be able to wear suits to work. To be perfectly honest, he thought of himself as kind of a badass. Many times, his "by any means necessary" tactics earned him stripes above the rest. Tactics he was about to exhibit then. Barnes smashed the butt of his gun against the single-paned glass window, shattering it to pieces. As Alanis approached, he continued knocking out the remaining shards of glass threatening to slice at them as they'd climb through.

Before climbing through, he reached and ripped down Arthur's raggedy miniblinds. "Now, we've got to come in and get cha."

He pointed his weapon, letting his eyes scan the living room. There wasn't a soul in sight.

Alanis tapped at his shoulder, seeing her moment to shine. "Let me," she whispered.

Barnes stood watch as she climbed through. She'd only been inside for a few seconds when the dead bolt unlatched. Then the front door swung open. "We're in." Alanis peeked her head out.

From the living room, they began their initial walk-through. Heading straight on through, they would get a glimpse into nearly every room in the house. They each pushed open a door as they approached, Alanis revealing what lay to the left of them, and Barnes, those on their right.

Nothing looked out of sorts. He barely had furniture in each room. Just a bed and a dresser here, a lamp and a futon there . . . that was until they hit the very last room, which happened to be in the middle. They had been headed right for it the entire time. Barnes twisted the knob, then pushed the flimsy door open. Blood. Everywhere they looked, they saw it. On the mattress, splashed along the flat, white-painted walls. Even as their shoes moved along the carpet, they could feel the squishiness of blood under their soles. The mirror atop the dresser also had been smeared with blood. But what there wasn't a body.

"What the hell happened in here?"

"A murder, of course," Barnes answered, continuing to survey their surroundings.

"Where the hell is the body?"

"Or bodies," Barnes added.

Arthur's body was gone. It had been carted off in the middle of the night. It all went down a little after 3:00 a.m.

The masked assailant crept through the neighborhood, almost making it to Arthur's house when a light illuminated several windows across the street, all of them belonging to Karen. The assailant launched a rock he'd found on the ground shattering the streetlamp above his head. Once she stepped out onto the porch, the assailant had blended in with the pole under the shattered streetlight.

"Is someone out there?" she called out into the darkness, not leaving the safety of her porch. "Is that you, Tony? If I find out you're out here loitering, I'm going to have to call the authorities." Karen browbeat the unidentified man.

The masked assailant stood still until she ducked back off inside her residence to shower and turn down for the night. Once the lights went out, the unknown perpetra-

tor pressed on. Directly to the Columbus house the perp headed, shattering every streetlamp along the way. An unlocked window in the back gave access to the home. After tossing the black duffle bag in through the window, the assailant climbed inside. The ax pulled from the duffle bag would be the only thing needed to break Arthur Columbus's body down to a transferrable size. A roll of plastic inside was used to cover the assailant. By the time it was all said and done, the room was covered in blood.

And so, the case had begun. Barnes and Alanis would first have to find out who lived there. Upon the two emerging, Karen stood at the border of the crime scene tape, rubbernecking left and right to see what she could see. "There's our answer right there." Barnes eluded to the nosy neighbor, clearly ready to spill her guts.

"Ma'am," Alanis called out to her as they approached, "you're the one who found the bodies, correct?"

"I am. I'm the one who called you," she spoke eagerly.

"Would you happen to know who lives here?"

"I certainly do. I know everyone on my block. His name is Arthur Columbus. He's a single, white male around 40 years of age. He works at the fast-food restaurant on campus at Wayne State University. What's the name of that restaurant?" She took a moment to search her memory bank. "Darn it. It's on the tip of my tongue, but for some reason, I just can't recall."

"Have you seen anything suspicious out here lately?"

As Detective Alanis continued to pick Karen's brain, Barnes walked up the street. He'd gotten as far as five houses down the block before shattered glass from the streetlamps became no more. Barnes took note, then headed back to his partner. By that time, there were officials everywhere . . . ambulance, police, even the coroner was on the scene. Karen, of course, rambled on.

"I have a neighbor named Tony. He lives down the street. He's always drunk, walking around in the middle of the night on other people's property, mind you. I had to get on him yesterday about bothering the meter man. I told him that man has a job to do and that he should stop harassing him. I believe it was him out here last night roaming about well after 3:00 a.m."

"What were you doing up at 3:00 a.m.?" Detective Alanis interjected.

"I'm always up late. I have trouble sleeping. It may be the Adderall my doctor prescribed me. Either way, I'm usually pretty alert."

"Is there anything else you can tell us, Karen?"

"You know there's a woman who lives about three houses down. She's always got her dog off the leash roaming the neighborhood. He's going to bite someone one day."

"Ma'am, you'll have to call down to the station for that. We're here to solve a murder," Barnes chimed in.

"I can do that," Karen affirmed, folding her arms.

"Thank you for your help, ma'am. If we need anything else, we'll be sure to call you. If you remember anything that could assist us in solving this crime, give me a call." Detective Alanis pulled her card from the pocket of her fitted, dark wash jeans, handing it over to Karen.

"I sure will. The boys in blue can always count on me," she went on as they left her standing there.

Chapter 17

High Hopes

Nothing decorated the room—merely a full-sized bed and dresser. Richard's eyes jutted open in a panic. *Where's my bag?* He sat up searching, as he'd assumed it stolen, not having realized where he'd woken up. A few seconds passed before it dawned on him. The bed was soft. Its sheets felt good on his skin. *This is where I'll be staying for a while.* He fell back against his pillow, allowing his rapidly beating heart to slow.

I wonder what we're doing today, he pondered as he sat back up to pull the plaid comforter from overtop of him. His mind shifted to the pie he'd saved from his meal the night before, assuming it would go perfect with a cup of coffee. He slipped his jogging pants on over his boxers, then headed for the door. The house was dark except for the space where windows provided natural light. Richard could hear the grandfather clock ticking at the other end of the hall. The sound of his steps creaking across the wood floor eventually drowned it out.

"Edward," Richard rubbernecked left, then right as he called out for the detective.

Richard, receiving no reply, relaxed his shoulders. His steps became more purposeful—eager to eat his pie in peace. The hungry stranger made a quick left into the kitchen, headed straight for the refrigerator. The first thing he noticed was the note taped to its door. Richard removed it from the clip, reading what the detective had scribbled with a Sharpie. *"Feel free to get cleaned up. Be back later."*

Richard looked around at all the things he could use as a source of entertainment to keep him busy after his shower. He couldn't remember the last time he'd sat on a sofa and watched a television show. The home personal computer in the library Richard remembered having glanced at on his way up the hall seemed altogether foreign. Regardless of which he'd choose, the first thing on the agenda was the warm apple pie he anticipated dancing across his taste buds.

After having his coveted apple pie, Richard washed his fork, tossed it into the dishrack on the sink, then disposed of his empty container. Even though all he wanted to do was rest his legs, Richard thought it best he showered first, in case Detective Barnes came home early. In the bathroom on the sink, he found a shaving kit with a sticky note attached reading, *Yours*.

"Nice," Richard remarked as he dug through the bag to see what tools he had at his disposal. The detective made sure he had everything he needed to begin again.

Steam from the hot water filled the bathroom as Richard washed dirt and grime from his body due to months of sleeping in shelters, hopping trains, and nights on park benches. He shampooed, then conditioned his greasy, knotted hair. It felt good to lather the hairs on his bushy chest.

After he cleansed his temple to his satisfaction, he turned off the water, then hopped out with the towel he'd snatched down from the steel rod above his head. He wrapped it around his waist, then used the hand towel on the sink to dry his shoulder-length hair. Strands that once looked brown showed to have been blond. Richard wiped the mirror with his hand towel, clearing it of the fog to reveal his reflection. Ruffling his hand through his beard, he decided it needed to go. So did his hair, for that matter.

He pulled the clippers from the bag atop the porcelain sink, then went to work on his profile. By the time he finished, his bob had become a buzz cut, and the beard on his chin trimmed down to a goatee. For the first time in ages, he looked into those baby blue eyes and was proud of the reflection he saw staring back at him. Although not yet the man, with Detective Barnes's help, Richard hoped to change all that.

Chapter 18

Shooting Her Shot

Just across the bridge at Hamtramck's border, the sound of crickets echoed throughout the block. Gertrude lay snuggled in her bed. Ronald in his. Aunt May, though, was wide awake and brewing a pot of coffee. Her show would be starting soon. *Maury* being the first of them. She couldn't wait to see who the fathers were. Anticipating the conclusion of the to-be-continued episodes always kept the old woman wanting more.

Until then, she'd watch the morning news on the thirteen-inch television atop her kitchen counter. The old woman hit the volume on the remote so that she could get a good listen.

In local news, tragedy strikes as decorated Officer Joe Poser is killed in a car crash, said to be the victim of foul play. Poser leaves behind a grieving wife and two young sons. We are all wishing them the best. They are in our prayers as well as the prayers of law enforcement. One of their own has perished, and they are working around the clock to solve this case. If you have any information regarding the murder of Officer Joe Poser, please contact the Detroit Police Department. A $10,000 reward is being offered to anyone with a tip that leads to the arrest of the perpetrator.

May turned the television volume back down. "Can you believe that, Henry? Violence has become the language we live by," she spoke to her late husband as if he were there listening. "These people nowadays have no regard for human life. It saddens me to know Gertrude will have to raise children in a world like this," she babbled on.

Gertrude peeked her head inside the kitchen, interrupting her monologue. "Umm umm . . ." she hummed. "That coffee sure does smell good."

"Come on in here, little girl, and get you a cup. You can keep me company until my shows come on. I was attempting to watch the morning news, but it's nothing but negativity, as usual."

"I'd love to keep you company," Gertrude replied before she lowered her voice to throw her aunt May a slight jab. "Then you can stop talking to your imaginary friend."

"Speak up, chile. You know I can't hear you."

"I said, who were you talking to?"

"When?" Aunt May poured her cup of joe.

"Before I came in, you were talking. Were you on the phone?"

"If you must know, I was talking to your uncle, my husband."

"Do you see him too?" Gertrude inquired, attempting to gauge how crazy her aunt had become.

"I'm old, chile, not senile."

Gertrude chuckled. "You can never be too careful."

"Silly, girl." May brushed off the comment. "So, enough about me. What's up with you and Ronald? Care to discuss it over breakfast?"

"I'd love to, Aunt May." Gertrude had been waiting for the open invitation to talk about Ronald. Her aunt was harsh but wise beyond her years; therefore, her advice was invaluable.

Ronald's eyes opened, squinting from the sun's glare coming through his bedroom window. It was time to get ready for class. Now that Gertrude knew how to navigate the campus, she didn't need to ask for Ronald's aid. There would be no piping hot breakfast being served that morning, something Ronald secretly wished for. Even though he missed it, it was nothing to sulk over, not as a grown man, anyway. He climbed out of bed, then headed to the shower, dreading the fact that he had to wash his hair again. Because the gang interrupted their dinner, he declined to stay afterward, so Gertrude braiding his hair had to wait. *Maybe she'll offer to braid it tonight,* he thought. It took him all of thirty minutes to shower and shave before he was ready to head out.

Upon opening the front door to leave, he spied a brown paper bag atop one of the stone columns on the porch. The words printed in a Sharpie read *Ronald To Go.* He grinned, imagining what she'd left inside for him. When he opened the bag, the aroma of maple sausage escaped with a light cloud of steam. *She made me breakfast, anyway.* Ronald pulled out the foiled sandwich, opening it up. Gertrude had made him a sausage biscuit with an over-easy egg on top. It was just what he needed. Avoiding the long line at Mickey D's that morning gave him more time to canvas the campus before he'd have to head to class.

Ronald waited until he got into his van before taking a bite of his sandwich. He hummed as flavor danced about his taste buds. He drove to school a happy man that morning, and with Gertrude on his mind, no doubt. She had accomplished the goal she'd set forth that Friday morning, securing a space in his mind. From then, all she had to do was garner a place in his heart, which happened to be a challenge Gertrude was well equipped to handle.

During Orientation Day, she met a couple of other girls she seemed to vibe with, cousins Brenda and Tiffany.

Tiffany was dark skinned with long, jet-black hair. She wore it in a wrap, which many of the guys found classy back then. A beautiful girl with a pretty, gleaming smile that could mesmerize a room full of gentlemen. Tiffany was all about the books. Finishing school was at the top of her list of priorities, much like her cousin Brenda. Most people would mistake them for twins because they were both dark skinned and had the same last name, their fathers being brothers. Brenda was just as beautiful, with long, thin dreads draped down her back. Neither of them weighed over 125 pounds, soaking wet. Still, they held their own.

The girls' energies meshed well. Gertrude liked nice girls who didn't have time for drama. That, alone, made pickins slim, and I'm not referring to the American rodeo performer. Regardless, she'd managed to find a pair of girls that pretty much stayed to themselves. The duo was their own book club. For the most part, they read crime, thriller, and mystery novels. They called themselves the Mystery Book Dames. Not only did Gertrude find that they matched her energy, but like the cousins, she loved reading books. Therefore, she made a perfect addition to their group.

That morning, Gertrude headed to the library first, where they'd decided, yesterday, they would meet up. She found them there lounging in plush leather chairs, both reading the same book by novelist and activist Barbara Ann Neely, *Blanche on the Lam*. The girls admired the fact that she'd created Shady Side, a community-based housing program for female felons in Pittsburgh.

"Hey, Queens. I see you're enjoying our selection of the month." They both looked up, the frowns on their worried faces turning upside down.

"Hey, Queen," the pair whispered in unison to not disturb any others in the immediate vicinity.

"You ready to head to class?"

They closed their books, of course, not before placing their bookmarks between the pages they were to return to.

"Let's go."

Together, they headed to class, chatting it up along the way with Gertrude walking between the two of them.

"Oh my gosh, there he is." She pointed discreetly upon seeing Ronald up ahead, crossing their path.

"The security guard? He's kinda weird. He never talks to anyone."

"I never thought he was weird. I just thought he didn't have a taste for girls. I mean, look at his hair. It looks better than mine," Tiffany chimed in, stating her piece.

"He is *not* weird. He's *not* gay. He's just a guy. A simple man who likes the simple things in life," Gertrude came to his defense.

"Girl, I guess. Whatever floats your boat. Just be careful. Guys these days seem only to want one thing."

"Ronald is definitely not like that. He hasn't even tried inappropriately touching me, nor has he even alluded to sex."

"You sure you got what he wants?"

"Oh, I'm positive," she smiled.

Brenda could see the glimmer in her eyes. Gertrude was smitten. "Don't give up the goods just yet. Hold out and make him appreciate it."

"Honey, I'm trying." Gertrude shook her head, doubting how long she could resist throwing herself at Ronald.

"I'm not settling for anyone unless he has a pocket full of cash."

"You and me both, little cousin," Brenda agreed.

"Well, he has his own house and his own car . . . more than one. That's got to count for something."

"Do your thang then . . . He never gave either of us a first look, let alone speak to us."

"He likes them thick and beautiful, apparently," Brenda admitted with a smile, nudging at Gertrude's arm with her elbow.

Gertrude blushed, delighted by its truth. "We're going shopping on Saturday. I don't know what I'm going to wear, let alone buy.

"We've got you, Queen. Don't worry," Tiffany professed.

"This should be fun. We get to do a makeover. Should we do it at your house?" Tiffany cooed. "Then we can get a better look into the life of Wayne State University's bachelor security guard."

Gertrude nodded in agreement. "My house would be perfect. I don't have a job yet, and the less gas I have to buy, the better."

"After this, remind us to help your broke behind to find a job. Independence is life, Queen. Remember that." Brenda would always "spit knowledge" out of nowhere. She prided herself in remembering choice learned phrases from books and whatnot.

"We should have lunch and discuss strategy," Tiffany chimed in.

Brenda rolled her eyes. "Girl, I swear you have a tapeworm."

Meanwhile, Ronald sat in a back row of the stadium classroom just up the corridor with his foot propped up on the seat. The instructor never bothered him much, knowing he handled the security and safety of students and staff. *I wonder what she's doing right now. I wonder what she's wearing today. She's such a great person. She'll make a man happy someday.* He started to think maybe he could be that man. It was a glimmer of a thought that lasted only a moment before the sound of *her* voice dashed his hopes.

"You really have taken a fancy to her, huh? You know there is no way you'd be able to keep your secret if you do. If you like her, dear brother, you'll leave her be—if you indeed care."

And live a life alone forever, right? Maybe that's exactly what I deserve for the crimes I've committed. Whether or not against the innocent, it's an injustice. It's my curse, isn't it, dear sister?

Cecelia heard Ronald's every thought, just as she did the others. *"You can have whatever it is you like. It's your life. You're free to live it as you see fit. Just remember, all actions have consequences," the apparition threatened before vanishing from view to simmer in her anger.*

In a huff, Ronald let out a heavy sigh, regretting the day his sister's apparition appeared to him—a thought he quickly forced from his mind for fear Cecilia would get wind of it. Ronald was trapped with her forever. If he were going to welcome Gertrude into his life, he would have to learn to do his duty while keeping her in the dark. Was that even possible?

Chapter 19

Searching for Clues

Down at the police station, the phones buzzed off the hook. Barnes and Alanis were held up in an interview room with a two-way mirror, going over the Arthur Columbus case.

"Forensics has been working all night on this. I contacted them early this morning. We should be getting results back about the identities of the women we found dismembered. They've already tested the blood splayed all over the residence. Forensics confirms the blood belongs to Arthur Columbus—a dead man. There's no way someone loses that much blood and is alive to tell the story," Detective Alanis rambled as she dug into a file on the table in front of her.

"His record shows him being arrested numerous times for voyeurism. Seems he was a habitual Peeping Tom. He was also arrested for groping women in the park. How this guy continued to get away with this time after time baffles me. If we only would have paid closer attention, those women would still be alive." She blamed the entire force for the tragedy.

"Look, Alanis, Detroit is a big place with over a million residents. There is *no* way we can catch every sick person out here. We try, but we can't prevent every crime. We'd have to be mind readers," Detective Barnes reasoned with his partner.

"So now it's up to us to find out who did it for us."

"You think someone killed Arthur Columbus and took the body with them?"

"That's exactly what happened, and I plan to find out just who our late-night vigilante is." Alanis slammed her fist against the desk.

Gertrude had waited all day for their powwow lunch between classes. She and the girls planned to eat al fresco downtown Detroit. They would get a chance to chat and talk more about her and Ronald. Although she valued her girls' opinions, she still was dead set on pursuing him. Gertrude just needed the skinny on Detroit men. She had Chicago cats down to a science if you asked her.

"So, what's on the menu, Queens?" Brenda asked as she pulled out of the student parking area.

Tiffany searched her purse, a shortage of cash becoming more of a reality to her. "We should just go to American Coney on Lafayette Street. They have the best coney dogs, and since Gertrude doesn't have a job, it won't stretch her pockets."

"Her pockets or your pockets?" Brenda mumbled under her breath.

Tiffany shot her cousin a dirty look. "Girl, I heard your subtle shade. Now, can we go get some reasonably priced lunch?"

Brenda didn't bother to respond. She felt bad for pointing out her cousin's financial situation in front of a third party. Sometimes, she took it too far. Then was one of those times. Brenda gave her attitude some silent self-adjustment. Although she couldn't say it aloud, her softer tone of voice notified Tiffany of the shift.

"I could actually afford to save a few coins. Coney Island sounds good." Brenda finally spoke up.

Gertrude hadn't even noticed the slight angsty moment between the two. She was busy daydreaming in the backseat.

They walked along the bar deeper into the restaurant for a table in the back so that they could talk as privately as possible in the busy restaurant.

A guy sitting at the bar spun around in his seat to observe Tiffany's movements. She noticed his interest in her but pretended she hadn't.

She had left him no choice but to come over and introduce himself. He walked over. "Hello, ladies. My name is Terrence. It's nice to meet you," Terrence greeted with his hands intertwined in front of him.

"Hello," the girls all greeted him pleasantly.

Terrence looked down at Tiffany sitting along the aisle. "Feel my shirt," he said.

Tiffany rubbed the tail of his collared button-up between her thumb and forefinger while Gertrude and Brenda gave each other the side-eye.

"You know what that's made of?"

"I don't know, rayon?" an unenthused Tiffany answered.

"Nah . . . That's boyfriend material."

The girls burst into a fit of laughter. Terrence had successfully broken the ice between himself and Tiffany, which was precisely what he'd intended to do.

"Can I talk to you for a moment privately?"

Tiffany looked at her cousin and friend for a silent yay or nay. Brenda, of course, shook her head no. Gertrude's expression, on the other hand, said, why not?

She hopped up from the booth. "Order me a coney dog with chilly cheese fries. Oh, and a water with lemon," Tiffany said, hoping the latter fancied her order up a bit.

"And that's what they would call a Detroit player or a wannabe Detroit player. She would ditch us as soon as we get to the restaurant. I swear that girl cannot sit still. Always switching up," Brenda griped.

Gertrude giggled. "Let that girl live."

"Anyway," she shrugged off Gertrude's comment, "speaking of switching up, what book is that hanging out of your purse? It certainly doesn't look like our book of the month."

Gertrude pulled out the book, flashing her the cover. "It's called *Lookin' for Luv* by Carl Weber. He's the best thing to happen to Urban romance."

"Girl, no wonder you're so smitten by this Ronald character. That book is getting you all worked up. Let me read it." Brenda playfully reached for the book.

Gertrude clicked her tongue against her teeth, snatching it back just in time. "I don't mind you borrowing it but not until I finish." Gertrude stuffed the book back into her big brown purse.

Over at the end of the bar, Tiffany sat with Terrence sipping lemonades as they got to know each other.

"So, you live with your twin?"

"Brenda's not my twin. She's my cousin. Our dads are brothers."

"You got a boyfriend?" Terrence inquired, looking her up and down.

"No, but neither am I looking for one."

Terrence chuckled, confident he'd be able to break through that barrier. He kind of liked the fact that Tiffany was playing hard to get. Most girls he'd attempt to take out jumped at the chance. He was skinny, but his bad-boy persona gave him a sort of swag the women on the more immature side of life were turned on by. He wore a nice outfit, from the wallabies on his feet to the button-up collared shirt. She had to admit, he was high yellow and packaged nicely.

"I'm not looking for a girlfriend either." Terrence thought two could play that game.

"Oh, really? So, you're just looking to hang out as friends? Is that why you called me over here, interrupting my lunch with my girls?"

"You have to start somewhere, right? If you never reach out, how can you establish a relationship?"

He doesn't sound like a knucklehead, Tiffany thought, already having begun tallying his favorable attributes. "I guess you're right."

"I usually am. But there's always room for improvement."

Tiffany smiled. "I like that. Room for improvement."

He seemed to be saying everything Tiffany wanted to hear. However, she didn't know if she was just interested in him because Gertrude was about to couple up with Ronald or because she really wanted to give someone the time of day. Either way, Tiffany wrote her number down on a napkin, then handed it over to the persistent young man.

Chapter 20

Torn between the Two

After school that day, Ronald headed straight home. If he didn't have to go to work or school, he usually stayed home for fear of having to punish someone. Because of that, he lived a leisure-deprived life. The time he'd spent with Gertrude had been the most human interaction outside of those places he'd experienced since his father was alive.

Ronald flopped down in a plaid sofa lounger tucked in the corner of his room, watching mysteries. He couldn't resist hoping Gertrude came by to bug him. Although he didn't actually see it that way, Ronald merely assumed she worried it did. With his feet kicked up and head tilted back, his eyes began to feel heavy. He was due a nap considering all the activity he'd had in the past few days.

Hours later, his eyelids drew open to the sight of the glitter-sponged ceiling above his head. A long sigh oozed from his parted peach lips. Ronald placed the palm of his hand upon his deflated chest, letting it rest there as the memory surfaced.

That day, the weather in Hamtramck, Michigan, was scorching hot. Some of the neighborhood kids had even decided to open the fire hydrant on the corner, sending a violent stream of water from one side of Gable Street to the other. They all played, taking turns dashing through it one by one.

Ronald sat on the corner nearby. He wanted to take his turn, but Cecilia hadn't made it outside just yet. The twins were around 6 years of age then and rarely did anything without the other. He wanted to make sure Cecilia would be willing to come out and play with the others first.

As usual, she was running behind. Cecilia rushed to stuff her feet into her red Chucks with one hand—the other planted firmly on the brick, stabilizing her position on the front porch, so she didn't fall over.

"Sweetheart, can you do me a favor and fill Sheba's bowl out back?" her mother called out to her, peering through an opened window in the living room.

"Do I have to?" Cecelia complained. "That stupid dog almost made me fall on my face yesterday. She won't sit still," the little girl whined.

"Honey, please don't make a fuss. Just use her leash," Mrs. Doolally rebutted.

Looking across the street, she could see the other kids laughing and frolicking about. Cecilia just wanted to get across the street as fast as she possibly could, sensing her twin's eagerness to join in.

"Yes, Mother," she digressed. Once her shoes were on, the little girl didn't wait for another second, leaping from the porch stairs, then down onto the grass below. She sprinted through the driveway into the backyard, where their German shepherd roamed free.

Ronald saw his sister disappear at the side of the house, deciding he'd take the opportunity to give her a scare.

Once Cecilia opened the fence, she made sure to push the latch closed. Otherwise, Sheba would be out frolicking in the water like everyone else. For the time being, she lay flat on the grass, tongue hanging from her open snout. Even for Sheba, it was a scorcher. Shade from the creepy apple tree provided her the only relief available since her bowls, both water and food, were empty. Usually, Mr. Doolally would have fed Sheba before he went to work in the morning. Unfortunately, he was working on a stakeout and hadn't been home in over twenty-four hours.

Sheba hopped to her feet once she spied Cecilia grabbing her food to replenish the bowl. Full speed ahead, she barreled toward the little girl lifting the seven-pound bag of food. Cecilia had her legs open and knees bent, allowing the bag to rest on her legs for support. Of course, Sheba saw the opening as an opportunity to slip right through. Forcing her broad head between Cecilia's knees sent the bag of food spilling out onto both bowls, covering them, along with the surrounding cement.

Cecilia gasped. "Now, look what you've done. Who's gonna clean this up?" She scolded Sheba, who at the time was paying her no mind. The starving pooch was quite content eating her vittles, whether they were served in a bowl or on concrete.

"Just wait a minute," Cecilia yanked at her collar, pulling her back from the mound of nourishment. But instead of putting her on the leash connected to the doghouse out back, the little girl dragged her pooch over to the garage, opening the side door, then shoving Sheba inside the hot, dark space.

"Stay," Cecilia demanded.

Sheba whimpered but lay down to submit, knowing exactly what she had done wrong.

That's when Cecilia poured the food that had toppled over into the water bowl back into the bag. Afterward, she filled it with cold water from the hose. "There. Now I can go play." She grinned before rushing back over to the garage door.

Seeing her feet through a small crack between the wood and the pavement, Sheba let out a few barks, requesting to be released, no doubt. Cecilia turned back, giving it a second thought as she looked at all the dog food still on the ground because of Sheba's rambunctiousness. I think I'll let her sweat a little, Cecilia concluded before bolting from the backyard, ignoring Sheba's insistent yelps, barks atop of howls for liberation.

Cecilia was gone in the wind, but Ronald had been there the entire time, watching from a hiding space along the other side of the house. That wasn't the first time he had been disturbed by his twin's actions, and it certainly wouldn't be the last.

He hopped the fence on the other side of the house to come into the backyard, headed straight for Sheba. Upon him opening the door, the faithful canine leaped onto the little boy, knocking him to the ground. Ronald giggled, knowing what was next. "Okay. Okay, girl. I gotcha. You're out now," he professed as Sheba licked the side of his cheek with love.

"That wasn't long at all, was it, girl?" he rubbed her sides, furnishing her a few light pats to send her off. "Go on. Eat your food, girl."

"I remember that too, dear brother." Cecilia's apparition appeared at the foot of his bed, ripping him from the daydream. *"Back when I was alive, free to be seen and heard. Free to live my life. Free like you,"* she pouted.

Before Ronald could respond, the doorbell rang, prompting him to spring up from his recliner. An unsuspecting visitor had come just in the nick of time. Ronald was all too eager to answer the door. The last thing he wanted to do was go down memory lane paved with guilt, which happened to be precisely where Cecilia was going.

His eyes lit up with delight upon opening the front door. There she was, holding up a wide-tooth comb and a jar of coconut oil.

"You ready for this?" Gertrude inquired with the most innocent, devilish smile he'd ever seen.

"You were serious."

"You thought I was kidding? We have a trip to the mall tomorrow. I came to tame that mane."

"Be my guest." Ronald stepped to the side, allowing her entry.

Chapter 21

A Love Connection

Gertrude had even gone to freshen up after school, changing into something more comfortable before she showed up. Her soft gray cotton jogging pants clung to her thighs. The gray V-neck shirt she wore showed just enough of her cleavage to be enticing, yet not enough to be considered inappropriate. To him, she looked perfect. He caught a whiff of coconut as her bouncing coils passed under his nose on her way inside.

He closed the door, locking a few of the locks behind her. Gertrude snickered quietly, thinking to herself it was a bit much. Besides, with a man like Ronald around, the last thing she was worried about was her safety. There was no doubt in her mind that he would protect her if need be.

"So, where are we setting up?"

"Where do you think would be best? What's the easiest position for you to braid in?"

"Can you lie on the sofa with your head on my lap? Would that be okay?"

"I can do that."

Gertrude made her way to the sofa in the living room, then took a seat right at its center, plastic crunching beneath her bottom.

Ronald let out a soft chuckle. "I'm a lot longer than that, sweetheart."

"Oh," she looked up, drinking in his six-foot-four height with her eyes. "Yes, you are."

"I don't mean to sound like a pervert, but it would be better if you got on the bed and just sat up against the headboard. It'll give us both more room. Plus, the television is in there. We could pick a movie to watch. I have a nice collection."

Gertrude stood up from the sofa, squinting her eyes as if to say she was surmising his intentions. "The bedroom, huh?"

Ronald put his hands up in surrender to her. "I mean, it's really up to you."

I thought you'd never ask, she thought. "I'd love to accompany you to the bedroom. Do you like murder mysteries?"

"They're basically the only movies I have to choose from. Follow me," Ronald replied, leading her to his bedroom.

Gertrude looked around as they crossed the threshold. She placed the coconut oil on the nightstand beside the bed, then proceeded to get comfortable atop the queen-size mattress. *This is going better than I thought it would.* She looked down, glancing at her bosom to make sure the girls looked inviting, even though she had no intention of them being exposed any more than they already were. Gertrude promised Tiffany and Brenda she'd make Ronald wait. Her confidence in the fact that she could had already begun to wane.

Ronald returned from the kitchen, having gone to pour them both tall glasses of lemonade.

"I see you're ready," he remarked, passing her glass to her before placing his atop a coaster on the nightstand opposite Gertrude.

"I am. Are you?"

"What movie are we watching?"

"How about a classic, like *The Shining?* Your hair will take a while."

"So Wacko Jacko is what you want? I've got you covered," Ronald affirmed as he headed for the television atop the dresser. Rows of VHS tapes lined the top drawer. He fingered through them, finding what she'd requested, then turned to look at her after inserting the video.

"Come on. I won't bite." Sensing his hesitation, Gertrude furnished her lap a few light, lie-hither taps.

Ronald crawled toward her, letting his head rest atop her plump thighs. Never mind the fact that Cecilia was sitting right there in the recliner where Ronald slumbered moments earlier, glaring at them with the most distasteful of stares. He didn't need to look at Cecilia to know she hated Gertrude being there. Ronald could feel the fear and anxiety his sister radiated. She made sure of it. Still, he refused to allow it to ruin his alone time with Gertrude. If he was going to entertain the fact that they might actually date, Ronald had to learn to control his urges around her. He had to be able to resist his twin sister.

"How would you like it? Would French braids be okay?"

"Beggars can't be choosy. As long as I don't have to wash it every day."

"Say no more. I've got you covered."

Ronald relaxed into her lap, pointed the remote, then pressed *play.* Even with Cecilia there grimacing, he felt nice. It was a niceness that, until then, he'd never experienced. *Can this be real?* An emptiness in him had begun to fill.

Gertrude made it to the other side of Ronald's head by the time she tensed up at the movie. No matter how many times she'd seen it, that particular scene creeped her out more and more each time she laid her eyes on it.

Little Danny rolled up the hallway on his tricycle when the evil twins appeared, stopping him dead in his tracks. "Hello, Danny. Come and play with us," the twins requested in unison.

"Oh my God, I can't watch this part." Gertrude shut her eyes. "Those girls are so creepy."

Immediately, Ronald thought of Cecilia. She was indeed an evil little girl. But if she was evil, did that mean he was evil too? All this time, could they have been wrong about the way they'd handled things? Was their justice an injustice? *Justice served cold, I'd say.* Ronald feared he didn't deserve the goodness Gertrude had to offer his life. Furthermore, he would rather not put her in danger. Not that any danger had ever befallen his home. For the rest of the night, he fought back and forth with his reservations about dating Gertrude. What would he do? They'd planned to go to the mall tomorrow, and since she was there, he'd gotten to thinking about dinner. It was looking like Gertrude would be his guest for the night or at least the evening.

Ronald rolled over to face her, his head still resting in her lap. Within seconds, she'd lost herself in his eyes. He recognized the look of absolute vulnerability, the way her brows lifted to meet at the center of her forehead as if considering the possibilities.

"Are you busy after this?"

"Not particularly."

"What's that mean?" Ronald huffed.

"I have things I could do, but I wouldn't mind canceling them to hang out with you."

Her revelation was exactly what he wanted to hear. "How about dinner? No interruptions this time."

Gertrude flashed that glowing smile, having then forgotten about the evil twins threatening little Johnny's demise. "I would love to. Are you craving anything in particular?"

"Do you like Chinese food? We could eat right here in bed and watch thrillers all night."

"I'm cool with that," Gertrude replied with a nonchalant shrug. *Oh my God, I thought he'd never ask,* she secretly gushed.

"I know the perfect place. It's about ten minutes from here, but it's worth the drive. You may have been there before. Yui Chan on State Fair Avenue. It's next door to Hood Book Headquarters in the city." Even though Hamtramck was its own small city, everyone knew whenever someone around there mentioned "the city," they were referring to Detroit.

"I've never been, but I'm not against trying it out. I love Chinese food. Do you think we could visit the bookstore next door while we're waiting for the food to be prepared? I'm kind of a book junkie."

"What's your favorite genre?"

"Crime, thriller, mysteries . . . That sort of thing."

Can this girl get any more perfect? The more Gertrude revealed about herself, the more Ronald fell for her. "That's my favorite genre too," he admitted.

"Stop lying. You ain't gotta lie to kick it."

"What?" Ronald didn't really understand the message Gertrude meant to convey. He simply wasn't that hip.

"You don't have to embellish about your liking thriller books just to bond with me. I like you just for you."

"Then like the fact that thriller novels are my favorite."

Gertrude became convinced of the truth as she peered into his brown and gray eyes. "I believe you," she spoke softly.

"Good."

"You ready to get these last five braids finished?"

Ronald turned back on his side, "Yes, ma'am."

Chapter 22

A Bond Forms as Another Breaks

Bang! The dresser drawer slammed as Tiffany went to toss another pile of clothes into the open suitcase atop the bed.

"Girl, you're either out of your mind or high to come in here acting like this."

Tiffany remained silent as she gathered her belongings.

"You don't even know this man, and you're going to move in with him? It makes no sense. Just to prove you can make it without my help?"

At that point, getting no response from her cousin had started to anger Brenda. She'd begun to feel disrespected. "Oh, I see why you're moving in with him. You're jealous. You're jealous that Gertrude is about to have a boyfriend while you're still single. God forbid someone couple up before you, right?"

Her revelation struck a nerve. "See, *that's* why I'm leaving. You always have something to say about everything. I swear you act like you're perfect. Nothing I ever do is good enough or measures up to what you do. And if I get anywhere near a title you claim to hold, you get defensive. I'm tired of living with someone who is in constant competition with me. What's funny is you never treat Gertrude like that."

Brenda scoffed. "Girl, ain't nobody gotta compete with you or nobody else, for that matter. I have my own.

My own house and my own car." She waved her hand flippantly.

Tiffany let out a long sigh. "You know what, Brenda? You're right. You have your own, and now, I'm about to go and get my own. No hard feelings. We're still the same. We just no longer live together."

"How are you going to move somewhere? You're barely getting hours at work. You can't live off what you make."

"Let me worry about that. I'm out of your hair now. No more cousin holding you back," Tiffany vented.

"I never once said you're holding me back," Brenda rebutted.

"Nah, you just pretend that's what it is in front of other people."

By then, Tiffany had gone back to pacing the floor as she gathered her things.

Brenda tried getting her cousin to calm down. "Why are you so anxious? Can't you sit down so that we can discuss this?" Brenda felt terrible for making her cousin feel inept. She could empathize with some of what Tiffany was saying. It was never Brenda's intention to push her away. The concerned cousin simply wanted her to do better, not realizing people grow at their own pace. All at once, the realization hit her. Sometimes, people can regress if pushed too hard.

She remembered her father's words. *People grow in their own time.*

After thirty minutes more of working on Ronald's braids, he and Gertrude were staring up at the menu board on the wall of the rinky-dink Chinese food restaurant. "I'm getting a number eight," Ronald called out his choice to the small Asian man behind the bulletproof glass.

Number eight was the sweet and sour chicken dinner. It came with shrimp fried rice, three fried jumbo shrimp, and an egg roll.

"Yum, that looks good," Gertrude remarked, having noticed it depicted there on the wall in front of them. "I'll have the same thing, please."

"Twenty-three, thirty-two. It be ready in fifteen minute," the man recited in the strongest Chinese accent they'd ever heard.

Ronald had ordered that meal more than a few times, so he knew how much it would cost without having to understand the cashier. He pulled out his wallet, handing over twenty-five dollars. "Keep the change, sir."

"Now, can we go look at some books?" Gertrude beamed with excitement.

Ronald was happy to grant her request. "Now, we can go get some books."

As they stepped across the threshold of Hood Book Headquarters, a woman sat behind the waist-high glass showcase stacked with full-lengths, novels, novelettes, even novellas. Hood Books was official. The store had an open floor plan, and everywhere they turned were books lining every wall.

"Welcome to Hood Book Headquarters. Is this your first time here?" a petite blonde with finger waves inquired as she closed her current read.

"It's my first time," Gertrude spoke up first.

"And you live here in Detroit?" the owner Michelle asked, shocked that they'd never visited previously. Frankly, she took it as kind of an insult. Her bookstore was legendary. And really, how much of a book buff could you be if you've never even been to the most popular local bookstore in town?

"Well, I live in Hamtramck with my aunt, but I'm originally from Chicago."

"Chi-town . . . Okay, cool." Michelle nodded.

"My friend here actually told me about your store. He's the one who's been here before." She looked up at Ronald to affirm her statement.

"I've been here more than a few times."

Michelle delved deep into her memory bank, attempting to recall if she had seen him before. "Yeah, I think I do remember seeing you before. You never talk much at all."

"I'm just here to buy books."

"Say no more. Look around. Holler at me if you have any questions. If you're into urban fiction, check out my collection, Ms. Michel Moore."

"Thank you. I'll certainly check it out. I'm always up for trying a new author. You guys have brilliant minds." Ronald stood staring in awe at the plethora of books along the wall behind her. After standing there in silence for long enough, Gertrude ran her hand across his back, gently reminding him of her presence. "Are you ready?"

Ronald looked down at Gertrude as if the pause were normal. "After you."

Gertrude gladly took the lead. She had no desire to find defects in her new love interest's character. It was one of many red flags she would ignore.

They arrived back at the Chinese food restaurant just in time, each with a bag of new books written by authors recommended by Michelle herself. The moment they stepped through the door, the cashier placed the large, brown paper bag containing their order into the square Plexiglas compartment. "Thank you. Come again," he waved them goodbye before retiring to the back to finish preparing other orders.

**

On the way home, hot food warmed Gertrude's lap. The tantalizing aroma of sweet and sour sauce made their stomachs growl in unison.

"Was that me?" Gertrude squirmed in the passenger seat, a little embarrassed that her stomach had ratted her out.

"I think it was both of us."

She let out a faint giggle. "Well, I'm glad it's not just me."

"I'm glad you decided to have dinner with me. Thank you for braiding my hair, by the way. It looks really nice. A lot better than when I braid it myself."

"It was my pleasure to do both." She smiled, basking in the joy his compliment furnished her ego.

The day had gone perfectly. Gertrude couldn't wait to see how the rest of the night would fair. *Fingers crossed . . .*

Chapter 23

The Catch

Barnes got back home that evening late. Even so, he remained committed to forging ahead with his plan. *The world needed soldiers. What better place to find them than in our fallen,* he thought, unlocking his front door.

Richard hopped up from the sofa as the detective come through the door. "You're home. I figured you'd be back before now. I made myself comfortable," he admitted, alluding to the movie playing on the DVD player, along with the plethora of snacks spread out across the coffee table.

"Don't worry about that. I kind of expected it."

"Thanks," Richard replied bashfully, still a bit embarrassed he had made a mess of the detective's coffee table.

"I see you found the shaving kit. The cut looks good on you."

"I really appreciate you. It means a lot."

"I told you, a whole new perspective. Hey, do you feel like riding somewhere with me? I'd like to show you something."

"Of course. Let me get my shoes and sweatshirt on."

While Richard went to get ready, Detective Barnes gathered the chips and salsa, a package of cookies, as well as the empty soda cans from his old wooden coffee table. By the time he'd put everything in its place, Richard stood ready and waiting near the front door.

"That won't happen again," he professed as Barnes emerged.

"I meant what I said. You're fine, but I appreciate you acknowledging it. Come on. Let's get going."

One the way there, Richard couldn't help anticipating where Barnes was taking him. He took a mental note of every corner they turned, every street they traveled.

"Do you believe the evil that men do will be punished?"

"I don't know. Before this happened to me, I would have said yes. But now, I just can't say. There are so many evil men walking this earth free to do as they please. All criminals aren't in the streets."

"I agree. Evil comes in many forms. I'd like to show you just a little of what I see every day."

Barnes took Richard down to the morgue at a local funeral parlor. Being an officer of the law gave him the liberty to walk through those tinted glass front doors as he pleased. He also knew the family that ran the establishment. They had laid many bodies to rest at Klein's Resting Place. Detective Barnes took Richard down to the basement where the bodies were stored. Stone walls lined the corridor of the basement. A set of metal, swinging doors brought them to the room for which they had searched. There had to be more than twenty sheet-covered corpses stored on tables. Most of them, Barnes knew personally, their story.

He walked over to one table, then pulled the sheet from over the top of a little adolescent boy. His lips were dark purple, flesh a hint of blue.

"Meet Jeffery. His stepfather beat his mother nearly to death. It went on for so long the boy decided one day he would protect her. Jeffery stabbed his stepfather fifty-two times with a swiss army knife his mother had given him for his birthday. They sent him down to juvie.

The investigation into his murder is still ongoing. There was a Goliath in front of this little boy, and he managed to channel his inner David so that he could save his mother. Who was there to save him, though? Who is going to right this wrong?"

Richard shook his head in sorrow for what had happened to the little boy.

Barnes covered him back up, then moved to the next corpse, which happened to be equally discolored. "This is Anastasia. A foreign exchange student from Russia. Turns out some of the guys on campus got angry because she refused to go on a date with one of them. They paid her translator to give her the wrong address to a party. When she got to the house, it was abandoned. They took her inside, raped her, strangled her, then left her for dead. The translator knew where she was yet refused to say a word. This girl's body sat in that abandoned house for two days until a man like you found her, then reported it to authorities. Wish we had more eyes like that in the world."

It was hard for Richard to look at her. In fact, he didn't say a word until Barnes covered her back up. He imagined the terrible fate she had suffered at the hands of those men.

The next cold, stiffened body he revealed belonged to that of Kenneth Prat. "Someone killed him in a barroom brawl that started because they didn't appreciate the fact that he was married to a Black woman. During the scuffle, one of the patrons picked up a broken beer bottle from the floor, then stuck it into his side. He bled out before the ambulance got there. Do you know out of fifty other bystanders, only one helped her attempt to cover the wound and keep him lucid?"

"I never understood hate like that. It's disgusting. Maybe years from now, it will be different. I can't imagine the year 2000 getting here and still dealing with blatant racism."

"What we need in the world are more people willing to stop things like this from happening."

"I never thought about being a cop. It's too late anyway."

"You don't have to be a cop to help. You just need cop resources." Barnes held his arms out, him being the resource he spoke of.

What do I have to lose? Richard thought, having seen his path clearly. "I think I'm starting to catch on to this redemption thing." He brandished a slight grin, not wanting to seem too excited in a room full of dead people. The former vagrant fancied thinking of himself as a hero. That kind of rush he hadn't felt since the war.

"I think we can go now." Barnes gave him a pat on the back, rousing a feeling of camaraderie between the two.

Chapter 24

Night Pursuits

During the wee hours of the night, Ronald and Gertrude lay together in a deep slumber. She looked comfortable hugging the pillow, an entire side of her face swallowed up by it. Soft, black coils fell over the top of her face. You could tell she had fallen asleep satisfied with the day's events. A waning moon illuminated the star-speckled sky that night, radiating a soft light into his bedroom window. The clock on Ronald's nightstand read 3:03 a.m. when his eyes sprang open, darting around the room as if he had no idea where he was or how he'd gotten there. He sat up, beads of cold sweat drenching his face. His short, panicked breaths only made it worse, threatening to rip Gertrude from her dreams, dreams filled with thoughts and scenarios, which all included Ronald, quite fittingly, the man of her dreams.

Only the man in her dreams was much different than the one rocking to and fro at the edge of the mattress. A vein running down the center of his forehead pulsated. Wincing from the pain radiating throughout his skull, he pinched the bridge of his nose between his bloodshot eyes, trying to quiet the voice, if at all possible. *"Help me, dear brother. Help me while there's still time! Don't let me die down here! It's cold, and I'm all alone. Please, brother, I need you."*

Cecilia's voice echoed throughout Ronald's fraught mind. It took every ounce of mental wherewithal he had not to scream. Still, he stretched his mouth wide as if it were bound to spill out. Not a peep, though. Even with the veins in his neck swollen, face flushed red, no sound emitted. He held tight to his therapist's words. *You must release it. Ronald, you must release her. As long as you harbor guilt over the death of your sister, the inner turmoil you're facing will never cease.*

Ronald dropped his head as he hunched over, elbows resting on his knees. *Smack. Smack. Smack.* He whacked the palms of his hands on the sides of his head in frustration.

"Yes, come on, dear brother. Release me." Her sinister voice demanded it of him, commanding Ronald's will by the time his head lifted. He peered up at the moon as if it were beckoning him.

He got up, moving about the room as if on autopilot, right past his slumbering date. Ronald exited the bedroom, slipped into his work boots at the front door, unlatched each of the dead bolts securing it, then headed out into the darkness.

"Release me. I'm here, dear brother."

He saw her apparition across the street, hovering above the spot where she met her end. Snatching up a shovel from the grass just below the porch stairs, Ronald tore off across the street to save his dear sister. Or at least he believed as much at that moment.

Next door, Peggy rolled out of bed, hacking as if she had inhaled a teaspoon of cinnamon and was about to meet her maker. The way she carried on, a lung was liable to come up if she didn't get to a glass of water as soon as possible. The closest sink was the bathroom next to her bedroom. She booked it, breasts dangling every which way under her Tom Petty T-shirt. The flannel pants she wore belonged to her late husband, Russell. He was a little on the abusive side, but so was she. Their arguments had resulted in tussling matches a time or two. That last one, though, proved to be more than Russell anticipated. Peggy didn't mean to kill her husband. It just happened suddenly. Alcohol coupled with arguments never ended well. That one, in particular, left Peggy a widow. Despite his demise, she fared okay, obtaining the house and his $75,000 life insurance policy.

When she finally made it to the bathroom, Peggy realized there was no glass on the sink. *Fuck it.* She turned on the faucet, then hunched over the sink to get a few gulps, hoping to tame the coughing fit. After several hard coughs, the spell passed. *I might as well pee since I'm up.* She groaned, flopping down on the cushioned toilet seat to do her business. That's when she heard it, the heavy breathing and grunting through the cracked window beside her. Peggy lifted it just a tad more, peeking out to see what she had already assumed.

There Ronald was in the flesh, digging as though his life depended on it. The hole he had excavated was nearly three feet deep already. *Ting.* He heard something metal hit the end of the shovel, realizing he'd found her. Ronald tossed it to the side in a panic, then dropped to his knees, from there, digging with his bare hands. "Cecilia," he whispered, pulling at the blue jean suspender strap he had discovered buried in the soil.

That's when his arm began to vibrate.

"I thought you said she wasn't buried out here," Peggy interrupted, having snuck up behind him.

Ronald turned his head slowly to see who it was standing there. "What are you doing out here?"

"Looks to me like you're digging up a body."

"I'm not digging up a body." He dug his hands into the soil, no longer feeling the strap of her overalls. It had vanished . . . disappeared as if it were never there in the first place.

"Then what is it you're digging up?" Peggy rebutted.

"I said, I'm not digging up a body." His tone hardened as he grabbed hold of the wooden handle beside him. With all his might, he swung around with the shovel, whacking her across the face with it.

Peggy's body fell over like a wet mattress. Blood oozed from her ear down into the dirt beneath her as Ronald continued digging his hole. Only now, it would need to be much deeper.

Chapter 25

The Need to Know

When Gertrude opened her eyes, alerted by the sound of running water, she glanced over at the clock. *It's 5:55 a.m., and he's already in the shower on a Saturday? Somebody's an early riser.* She saw it as an opportunity to look around. Maybe she would even be able to find something in the fridge she could make for breakfast.

The bedroom closet seemed to open a little more upon Gertrude noticing it being ajar. *Curiosity killed the cat, Gertrude.* She knew better, but on second thought, figured, what would it hurt? *He won't even know I looked.* That second thought was all it took for her to be convinced. Gertrude peeked her head out the door to make sure she could still hear the shower running before rushing back over to the closet door to survey what lay behind it.

She crossed the threshold of the large, dark space, feeling around for something to shed light inside. That's when she felt something tickling the tip of her nose. "Oh my gosh," she uttered in a panicked whisper, flailing her arms about. The nosy woman thought for sure she had walked into a spiderweb until she felt the skinny, metal, beaded string in her hand. "Thank God." She let out a sigh of relief, yanking on the string to brighten up the space. Just as she suspected, it was full of old clothes and boxes. But then, as she let her hand run across the clothes, she realized they weren't even his. They were his parents' clothes. Not a stitch of clothing hanging there belonged to Ronald. She gushed, finding it endearing he'd kept his parents' belongings. *He must be a family man.* Gertrude grinned at the thought. She equated his being sentimental toward his parents to Ronald being husband material. The notion one she tucked away as promising.

A big black chest sat on the closet floor, begging to be opened. It was one of those chests that looked like it could be filled with treasures. Gertrude assumed they would be priceless heirlooms. You know, school pictures, Mother's Day gifts made in grade school, maybe some old jewelry, or even an old letterman jacket. There was only one way to find out. She had to open it. Gertrude lowered to her knees to lift the metal latch but just when she was about to crack the lid, the water turned off.

Ronald stepped out of the steamy shower, free of soil, blood, as well as the skin and hair fibers from Peggy's body. He covered his waist with a towel, then with a swipe of his hand, he wiped a section of the mirror free of fog. The view of himself only lasted a moment before the mirror fogged up again. *What have I done?* Ronald wiped it away once more, staring in at his own soul seen through the windows of his eyes.

"You know exactly what you did, dear brother." The apparition appeared behind him amid the clouded bathroom as what he'd done came clearer.

Smack. The metal end of the shovel crashed into Peggy's skull, striking against her temple and knocking her out cold. Blood trickled from her ear down the side of her wrinkled neck, soaking into the collar of her T-shirt. A thud sounded off when her body hit the soil. Adrenaline pumping, Ronald panted as he stood over her stiffening corpse. "There's something fishy about you. I just know it. Ever since I was little, you've rubbed me the wrong way."

For her, Ronald dug a separate hole in the rear of the property lot. He dragged Peggy's lifeless body by the ankles across the dewy grass until he made it to the hammock between the two maple trees. It was the perfect place to put her body.

"Ronald?" Gertrude called out to him from the other side of the bathroom door.

"I'm almost finished," he answered, pushing the memory from thought.

"I'm going to go next door and get ready for our date later."

"I didn't wake you, did I?" Ronald worried she might have witnessed him coming back inside last night.

"I'm usually up pretty early. Aunt May is probably brewing a pot of coffee right now. She'll be expecting me to join her for a cup."

"Then you shouldn't keep her waiting."

"I'll see you at around one o'clock?"

"Sounds good to me."

"I'll be sure to lock the door on my way out." Gertrude snickered, poking fun at Ronald before heading on her way.

Chapter 26

Friends

"It's eleven o'clock, and I still haven't had anything to eat. Come on, Brenda. Just stop at one of these fast-food restaurants on the way there," Tiffany begged over the sound of her grumbling tummy.

"I'm not eating that crap. You sure love those horse meat patties."

Tiffany rolled her eyes. "What about some Chinese food?"

"Cats, dogs, and rats."

"Oh my gosh, Brenda. You think everything is bad for you."

"It is. Our meat is pumped full of chemicals and hormones."

"Well, I sure could go for a chemical burger and an order of hormone-injected nuggets."

"Let's just wait until we get to Gertrude's. She might be hungry too."

"Fine," Tiffany relented. "But if she isn't, I'm leaving to go get food myself if I have to.

Brenda glanced up at the street sign at the corner, "I think this is her street right here. Didn't she say, Gable?"

"Yup, Gable and Sobieski." Tiffany recalled the conversation vividly.

Brenda made a right, clipping her rear passenger tire on the curb.

"Let's make it there in one piece," Tiffany complained, clinging tight to the hand bar above her head.

"Huh," Brenda huffed. "I'm surprised you're still in one piece seeing you're mingling with the commoners, now."

Tiffany held up her hand in protest. "Brenda, I didn't come with you to get a lecture."

Brenda rolled her eyes at the flippant reply. "Whatever. We're almost there. She said it was the house across from the lot with the hammock and flowers."

"There it is, up ahead." Tiffany eagerly pointed it out.

"So, this must be the house." Brenda hung a sharp left into the driveway, tires squealing as they painted the cement on their way in.

Tiffany shook her head in disbelief. "I don't know how you managed to get a license."

"Says the person who failed her driver's test. If it weren't for me, you'd be on the bus," Brenda countered with a snappy comeback—a comeback that went unrefuted due to its validity. Tiffany had failed her driver's test more than a few times, so she had the least room to be critical of her cousin.

Brenda spoke up, breaking the awkward silence. It was apparent her comment had hurt Tiffany's feelings.

"So, he owns this place and the lot across the street?" Brenda turned, admiring the structureless property decorated with flowers. "Gertrude might be on to something."

"Hopefully, they have some food in there," Tiffany groaned.

"Only one way to find out." Brenda unbuckled her safety belt to hop out of the vehicle, prompting her cousin to do the same.

Inside, Gertrude thought it time she warned Aunt May about their incoming guests. She peeked into the living room where Aunt May sat immersed in gossip.

"I have some friends coming by, Aunt May. They should be here any minute. Please be nice to them."

"I'm always nice," Aunt May rebutted but kept her eyes glued on Maury. "As long as they don't come in here interrupting my show. Like the young kids say, we are good to go."

"Aunt May," Gertrude rested against the doorway between the living room and the hallway, "did you hear that on *Maury*?"

"In my travels," she shrugged.

"Travels? What travels, Aunt May?" At that point, Gertrude had found amusement in her aunt's replies.

"Get you some business, little girl. All up in my mix."

"Aunt May, you need to stop." Gertrude chuckled for a second before being interrupted by the doorbell.

"I'll make sure my friends aren't a bother, Aunt May." She rushed off to answer the door.

"Hey, girl," the cousins spouted in unison, eyes all aglow.

"Queens, I'm so glad you're here. Come in." Gertrude pushed open the screen door, allowing them entrance.

"So, what are we working on first, hair or outfit?" Brenda eagerly inquired, rubbing the palms of her hands together.

But Tiffany had other plans, which she didn't hesitate to make known. "Food," she blurted, before Gertrude could answer.

Gertrude pushed up alongside her. "Aww . . . You do look a little starved, sweetheart. I made some goulash the other day. You're welcome to some. I think there are a couple of cookies left too, which won't be for long. Aunt May really seems to like them, but I think she's trying to watch her weight. Let's go to the kitchen and get you fed."

By the time Tiffany finished the last bite of goulash on the plate, she had sat back on the sofa lounger in Gertrude's bedroom, pleasantly stuffed. "I'm so glad I didn't go to one of those nasty fast-food restaurants."

Brenda turned her eyes from Gertrude's bushy mane to shoot her cousin the side-eye. "Now, you *know* you were campaigning for horse burgers." She smacked her lips.

"Horse burgers?" Gertrude felt the need to chime in, even though she couldn't make eye contact with either of them with her head tilted. She knew if she tried to move, Brenda would likely get on her about not sitting still while getting her hair done.

"I'm outta here," Aunt May announced, standing outside Gertrude's bedroom door in her pink and blue tracksuit, ready to head off to the mall with the gang.

They all turned to look at her.

"You look nice, Aunt May."

Brenda and Tiffany chimed in to agree. "I like it."

While the girls boosted Aunt May's head about her choice of attire, the gang had pulled up across the street. Wilson, Grady, and Tom stepped out of their vehicles, all charging toward the porch. Peggy had instructed them to be there by noon. The time on Tom's watch read 12:07 p.m. on the dot. "Get ready for it, boys," Tom warned the others as their feeble limbs climbed the concrete steps.

They all paused at the screen door, the front door being ajar, causing them to pause. "Hey there, Peggy. You in there? The gang's all here. Us guys anyway," he hollered inside the residence.

Grady put his hands up to the screen, creating a binocular-like area for him to look through. The quiet inside seemed eerie to the point he shivered a bit. "I don't see or hear anything."

"She's got to be in there somewhere." Tom snatched at the brass knob to open the screen door. "Peggy, we're coming in. Hide your tits."

Something didn't sit right with Wilson about walking into a person's house without permission. "She might be in the backyard playing in the dirt. I'll check around back."

He made his way back down the stairs while the other two moseyed inside.

Everything looked to be in its place. The plastic on the sofa, the runners lining the hallway carpet, even the dining room table was set for six. The only light on in the house shined into the hallway from the bathroom.

"Peggy, you in here?"

Grady glanced left, noticing her purse there on the side table next. "She must be here. Her car's in the driveway, and her purse is on the table."

"Maybe she's over at May's." Tom suggested the alternative as both hesitated in the foyer just at the hallway entrance.

Grady started to head out before Tom even agreed. "Let's check over there."

Wilson emerged from around back after having surveyed the yard while Tom and Grady stepped out the front door.

"She wasn't out back. I'm assuming you guys didn't find her inside?"

"No luck. We're going to check May's," Tom replied, letting nothing stop his stride.

That was until he saw the flash of shiny pink material headed their way.

"What a sight to see." Wilson admired the sight of May as she drew nearer.

May had the smoothest caramel-toned skin he'd ever seen. The tiny freckle like moles that covered her cheekbones reminded him of a girl he dated back in grade school. Most women May's age had a short haircut. It seemed once women got past the age of fifty, they felt as if they had to chop it off. Bingo most nights looked like an audition for *The Golden Girls*. But not May. She had a long mane of thick, gray hair pulled into a ponytail that hung down to the center of her back.

"Like a fine wine," Wilson mumbled under his breath.

"Hey, where's our driver?" Tom shouted out before she could even make it across the street.

"She should be home. Her car is right there in the driveway." Aunt May pointed out the 1986 Ford Taurus Peggy had purchased after her husband's "accidental death."

"What the hell is going on here? Where's Peggy? She told us to be here at noon," Tom fussed.

"If she doesn't show up in fifteen minutes, we're leaving her," Wilson admitted with a shrug of the shoulders. All he cared about was the fact that May was there and ready for their unofficial day date.

"Did you guys check the entire house?" Wilson inquired, having become frustrated with Peggy wasting their time.

"We called out to her."

Unsatisfied with the answer Tom offered up, Wilson headed for her front door. "That's it. I'm checking inside. We don't have time for this."

Thirty minutes later and nothing. The gang all sat around the dining room table, Tom, Wilson, Grady, and May.

"Why would she leave her front door open and unattended for this long?" Tom asked, breaking the silence.

"Something ain't right about this."

It wasn't long before they called the police to the scene.

Ronald caught sight of the flashing red and blue lights from his living room window.

"They're looking for her body, dear brother. Let's hope you hid it well."

"They won't find it. I buried her deep," he murmured.

Chapter 27

On with the Show

That afternoon, the gang filed a missing person's report for Peggy, hoping to find out where she had disappeared to. Usually, they wouldn't allow a missing person's report to be filed, considering she hadn't even been missing for twenty-four hours. In the end, it was Peggy's age that was the deciding factor. Trying to stay optimistic, the friends decided not to cancel their trip to the mall. Tom agreed to drive, so they all piled up in his station wagon to head to Eastland Mall.

The girls remained oblivious about the goings-on just across the street while they helped Gertrude put the finishing touches on her looks. Brenda had braided the front left side of her head, pushing the remainder to the right, leaving her curls free. Her suede, heart-shaped, leopard print earrings complemented her all-black bodysuit and gold sandals. Her gold toe and fingernail polish gave off a metallic hue. She twirled left and right, admiring their creation. "I'm so glad I called my girls for reinforcements. I don't think I could have pulled this off myself." She smiled at her reflection, pleased with the results.

"I'm glad we could help. Right, Tiffany?" Brenda turned to see her cousin slumbering atop Gertrude's plush burgundy comforter. "Correction. I'm glad *I* could help."

"That food really did a number on her." Gertrude chuckled with delight. It made her happy to see someone so content after eating her cooking.

"We should get out of your hair so you can get going." Brenda nudged Tiffany's shoulder to wake her. "Come on, Tiff. It's time to go."

"Huh? What?" She woke startled, slobber leaking from the side of her mouth like a newborn baby.

"Dang, you were sleeping so good you're slobbering," Brenda cackled.

Tiffany wiped the excess spit from her cheek, her dazed expression lingering. "I don't know why I'm so sleepy."

"Girl, get up and come on. Gertrude has a date."

Tiffany yawned as she stood up, attempting to shrug off her sluggish mood. "Whew, chile, I'm sleepy. Let's go before I pass out again."

"As a matter of fact, it's about that time. I'll walk out with you." Gertrude showed them out, then proceeded next door as the cousins headed on their way.

"Have fun, beautiful." Brenda waved her farewell.

I don't know why I'm so nervous. Gertrude gathered control of her nerves, then knocked lightly at Ronald's door.

A smile graced his face as he opened the front door. "Look at you. Absolutely gorgeous," he admitted, taking in her beauty.

Gertrude couldn't help but blush. "I'm glad you think so."

"Oh, that's a fact." He stood holding the screen door open. "Come in. Let me get my shoes on, and we can get out of here."

She gladly granted his request. Gertrude waited in the living room, oblivious to the apparition glaring at her from the sofa, surmising her every intention. Still, as she stood there alone, something caused a chill to run up her spine. She ran her hands up and down her exposed arms, attempting to smooth the tiny goose bumps that had popped up out of nowhere.

"Do you need a sweater?" Ronald inquired, noticing her discomfort on his way back in.

"I'll be fine. Are you ready?"

"As I'll ever be," he answered.

The pair exited, Ronald making eye contact with Cecilia as he shut the front door in her face.

Resentment having reached its peak, Cecilia's eyes welled up with tears. She'd been discarded to the side once again, replaced by Gertrude, her brother's new-found love.

Chapter 28

Making Headway

For once in his life, things felt normal. Nothing about her caused him alarm. Ronald could truly be himself with Gertrude. Not having to worry about the true motives of everyone around him was nice for a change. He was finally experiencing something he would be eager to tell his psychiatrist about. A date with a girl he felt connected with was a big step in the right direction. At least, he was sure Dr. Martyr would see it that way. Ronald couldn't wait to tell her. For once, he wanted her advice about what he should do regarding his new love interest.

"Perk up, guys and gal, the subjects have arrived," Tom announced as he spotted Ronald's conversion van rolling through the mall parking lot.

May, Wilson, and Grady all sat up at attention, spying through the windows of Tom's station wagon.

"That's them, all right," May confirmed, keeping her eyes glued on Ronald's vehicle.

Wilson, sitting alongside May, rolled his window down, allowing a fog of cigarette smoke to escape into the air.

"They're going in through Macy's. Let's get out and head them off," Tom suggested prompting them all to unbuckle their safety belts.

***

Meanwhile, Ronald picked the closest parking spot he could, which happened to be more than a hop, skip, and a jump away from the entrance. They couldn't have expected anything less, choosing to go to the mall on a Saturday.

The look of excitement on Gertrude's face conflicted with Ronald's expression of overwhelming. He hadn't thought things through before agreeing to go on such a busy day. The scene was like the first day on campus, multiplied by two. But unlike the mall, on campus, Ronald held authority. He was just a tall guy cloaked in jeans and a plaid, collared, button-up at the mall. His Rockport loafers certainly wouldn't make anyone feel intimidated in the slightest.

Gertrude turned to him, noticing the look of bewilderment on his face. "Are we going inside?" she inquired modestly, hoping he hadn't changed his mind.

Ronald snapped out of the trancelike state, giving her his full attention. "Let's go," he replied, instantly shutting down the engine.

Inside, Tom and Grady covered the entrance near the shoe department. The aroma of chocolate cookies and caramel cakes pervaded their nostrils. The pastry station near the entrance attracted its fair share of patrons, Tom and Grady being among those headed that way. May and Wilson covered the entrance to the Men's section.

Quickly turning her back, Aunt May held a shirt up to Wilson's chest as if to measure how stylish he'd look draped in it. The last thing she wanted was for her niece to see her there, watching them as if they were children.

They waited for the two to pass by before trailing them up the escalator to the Women's department.

Although in their minds they were stealthy, Ronald had noticed May and Wilson there lurking as they passed by them. He caught a whiff of the tobacco stink lingering on Wilson's person. The smell was unforgettable when coupled with the Old Spice he'd applied after his shower that morning. Ronald smelled that same stink just days ago at dinner. It was just as strong then as it had been that night at Gertrude's house. *They can't seriously be following us. And her Aunt May is going along with it? I guess I just can't be trusted.* Ronald shrugged off the propensity to feel wronged in some way, finding reasoning in the fact that he was indeed a killer.

For the time being, he'd allow them to follow him around. Besides, they weren't doing anything wrong, simply shopping. Maybe even dinner and a movie later. Ronald remained determined not to let anyone ruin his and Gertrude's day together. The more time they spent together, the more he knew Gertrude had come into his life for a reason, to show him a different way of living finally. One like his parents had.

Ronald recalled how loving his father was to his mother. It gave him comfort to remember how his father doted on his mother until her very last breath. To have someone love you so unconditionally had to be a blessing. Fond memories of his parents' relationship gave his father's reputation the polishing it needed.

Back when he was alive, everyone thought of him as a hard-ass. There was no leniency when it came to criminals. He was the toughest kind of cop. Some would even say they thought he was racist. That was until they found out his wife and children were of African American ancestry. It shocked most people to hear his family was of mixed race. Mr. Doolally had gone as far as breaking ties with his mother to marry Margaret Louise Buckman, Mrs. Margaret Louise Doolally.

Mr. George Doolally fell in love with Margaret the moment he laid eyes on her.

It was one of the hottest days of the summer back in August 1967. Most of the Black residents within the city of Detroit remained on edge, rocked by the riot that ensued on Sunday, July 23rd. The Twelfth Street Riot was among those bloodiest between residents and law enforcement. Margaret, a 20-year-old librarian at the time, sped down Charles Street on her way to work. She'd taken the position at the Knapp branch library next to Cleveland Middle School, it being a place familiar to her throughout her adolescence. The location was less than four miles from her house, yet Margaret always managed to get to work with just a second left to spare. She mashed her wedges down to the gas pedal, hands at ten and two, with her chest up close to the steering wheel.

Officer George Doolally, about five years her senior, took note of Margaret's race car driver pose as he pulled up alongside her. He intended to get her attention, then motion for her to slow down. The speed limit was thirty-five miles an hour on that street, and her speedometer read well over forty. Considering the brewing tension, he thought it best he let her off with a warning. Margaret stopped at the light by Laskey Park, head darting left, then right in anticipation of the light's conversion from red to green.

That's when he saw the leak and the faint steam cloud coming from under the hood of her vehicle. George sounded off his siren until she locked eyes with him.

"You should shut that off. You're leaking coolant pretty bad," he shouted from his driver's-side window.

Gertrude shook her head in disagreement with what he'd brought to her attention. The foreboding expression on her face spoke of her suspicions of him being a "dirty cop."

"What do you mean no? Your car is leaking antifreeze," George rebutted.

"I don't believe you," Margaret yelled back before taking off at the green light.

"What on earth is wrong with this girl?" George chuckled. At this point, he was amused by the fact that she'd completely disregarded him. To add to Margaret's defiance, she'd picked her speed back up into the forties.

Being the helpful civil servant, George decided to follow her to make sure her car didn't overheat. When they finally pulled into the library's parking lot, Margaret hopped out fast to rush inside behind the safety of the establishment's doors. During her mad rush, a small yellow wallet dropped from the side pocket of her wheat handbag.

George scooped it up off the gravel, waving it in the air. "Slow down. You dropped your wallet," he demanded in the most nonthreatening voice he could muster up.

Margaret checked the zipper along the side of her purse, realizing it had been left unzipped. Seeing no other choice, she stopped in her tracks. Her shoulders slumped, foreseeing what bullshit excuse he was about to offer up to detain her.

"Did I do something wrong, Officer?" She turned to him in frustration.

"I don't know. Did you? You sure do seem like you're in a hurry."

"Does that automatically equate to me doing something illegal?"

"I didn't say that."

"You implied as much." One of the reasons Gertrude preferred not to stop was because of her propensity to question the law.

"I'm assuming you were in a hurry because you were speeding. And, well, you speeding just so happens to be illegal." George appreciated her attempting to match wits with him.

Margaret stood in silence, not having a justifiable rebuttal for his reply.

"It wasn't my intention to treat you like a criminal. I simply wanted to make sure you got to your destination before your car overheated." George broke the silence.

"There's nothing wrong with my car," Margaret professed, just as a shooting cloud of steam escaped her radiator.

"You're right. That looks perfectly normal."

Unable to hold back her emotions, Margaret covered her face, only to sob into the palms of her hands. The part-time librarian didn't make enough to cover car trouble.

When she cried, George wanted nothing more than to wash all her worries away. He didn't even know Margaret, but every fiber of his being told him he wanted to. "I can probably help you out. I know a little bit about cars," he admitted, hoping to extinguish her worries.

And that's how their journey began. Within a year, the two of them were married and expecting the arrival of their baby boy, Ronald.

If only Ronald could give Gertrude a life like his father had given his mother, he pondered. One where they could genuinely be happy. Gertrude certainly believed it so. The way she looked at him made him even more convinced as he allowed himself to become lost in her enchanting stare. Ronald had become so immersed in their conversation that he'd almost missed Cecilia standing there at the end of the mall corridor. He'd caught glimpses of her in the spaces between passing shoppers, something beckoning her in its direction.

"So, where to next?" Gertrude asked, noticing his attention shift from her to that which lay in the distance. Awaiting his reply, she studied him.

Her words had fallen on deaf ears. Every sound within his earshot had become inaudible. There was one thing he heard loud and clear. *"Follow me, dear brother. I'll show you the way,"* Cecilia coaxed.

After a few more seconds went by without a word from Ronald, Gertrude took hold of his arm, wrapping hers around it. "Come on. Let's go." She ushered him onward at her side, hoping his odd behavior would pass. *Maybe this is what my girls were talking about.* She tried connecting the dots as they strolled casually down the mall corridor through the crowds of people. Once they picked up their pace, Gertrude realized she was no longer leading.

Unbeknownst to her, a little pale, dingy fingertip determined the direction of their stride. It was quite possible Gertrude would finally see just how strange Ronald could be. The couple rounded the corner by the Pretzel Stand, and there they were. A host of vandals snatching sneakers, clothing, and jewelry from outside store displays as they passed them by immediately garnered Ronald's attention.

He paused but only for a brief second before springing into action as he'd come up with a way to foil their plan.

The sports shop was running a special on rubber dodge balls, two for five bucks. Ronald took a twenty-dollar bill out of his pocket, handing it over to the store attendant, who'd joined the onlookers in the hall to witness the spectacle unfolding before them.

Twenty dollars bought him eight balls—eight balls Ronald whipped at the miscreants with great speed and accuracy. Sure, he'd tripped several of them up, even caused a couple of them to tumble over, assisting the mall cops in the capture of four out of six of the fitted baseball cap-wearing hooligans. Even with their combined efforts, four of them managed to make it to the exit at the end of the corridor, then out of the mall doors.

"Oh my God. Ronald? How did you know? *Did* you know?" Gertrude inquired, baffled by his seemingly stellar intuition.

"Of course, I knew. You could hear the raucous noise from around the corner," he answered nonchalantly, taking note of the escaping thieves' attire. He thought it odd one of them was wearing a D.A.R.E. shirt, which stood for drug abuse resistance education. To think a D.A.R.E. student would be causing such mayhem didn't seem right. They had to be imposters.

Gertrude shrugged. "I guess I wasn't listening hard enough." Regardless, she couldn't help but wonder how the heck he heard anything over the chatter of the other shoppers.

That aside, he'd shown great courage stepping in to help. It turned her on the way he'd whipped those balls through the air, hitting his target. Soon, the oddities of the situation faded into the background. All that mattered was the tall, handsome, courageous man at her side, hopefully soon to be in her bed. If she had even an ounce of reservation left in her, it had been completely drained after that moment. The squishy feeling between her thick, caramel thighs told her so. Gertrude's loins yearned for Ronald's touch more than ever, kicking her mind into overdrive. Right then and there, she began formulating a plan to bed him.

Chapter 29

Things Get Complicated

The top of the door knocked against the bell, alerting the liquor store clerk of his next patron as they came through the door. One donned stonewashed jeans and a tie-dyed T-shirt, the other wearing jeans and a black D.A.R.E. T-shirt. Both sported fitted baseball caps, brims low to conceal their profiles somewhat.

Wilson Moral looked up, then back down at his paper, paying the young adults no mind. Much of the time, he tried his best to mind his business. He'd taken on the part-time job to fill the time during his lonesome days. His grandchildren certainly appreciated the impromptu gifts it allowed him to award them. He intended to put in no more than six hours a day, four days per week. That's it. Ring up a few customers and go home.

So far, the night had been slow on a normally high-traffic evening. Saturday was when everyone headed to the liquor stores to stock up for their get-togethers, celebrations, and whatnot. The way Wilson saw it, the fewer customers, the better. He didn't want any trouble, which was something he unfortunately encountered regularly. The clock struck 10:23 p.m. His shift had gone smoothly the entire four hours he'd been there. There were a few times Peggy crossed his mind. Where was she? And why'd she stand up the gang like that? Both questions would go unanswered. For the rest of the night, at least.

His customers were busy filling their book bags with energy drinks, sodas, and malt liquors in the back near the coolers. They'd already hit up the toiletry aisle, snagging tissue, lotion, toothpaste, and a few other essentials.

Ding-a-ling. The bell rang once more, and in walked Ronald cloaked in a navy-blue jogging suit. He kept the hood of his sweatshirt up, letting his loose braids hang down in front of his shoulders. The aroma of rotisserie smoked Red sausage and beef hot dogs hit him when he crossed the threshold. Fortunately, Ronald had already eaten dinner; otherwise, he would feel inclined to partake in the rolled concoction of spare animal parts. His lack of vanilla cream soda, a drink that paired perfectly with his apple pie, brought him there that night. Ronald was big on desserts. It was a dish his mother prepared after every dinner. Even if they ordered out, which was rare, Margaret made sure she had something at their humble abode to satisfy one's sweet tooth.

It'd become a habit for Ronald to take in his surroundings. He always had to be ready for the evil in men. Cecilia had proved that to him time and time again. The man behind the counter holding the *Ebony* magazine open in front of his face was clearly uninterested in the fact that a customer had just walked through the door. Ronald shifted his attention to the large round mirrors attached to the wall along the ceiling. That's when he saw the pair looting the refreshments. He remembered their distinct clothing and hats. Ronald couldn't tell whether they were male or female. Frankly, it didn't matter. They were the same ones wreaking havoc at Eastland Mall. Now, they were getting their rocks off at a corner store. Ronald assumed they were a bunch of excitement junkies—a bunch of punks, really. Choosing to carry out the melee in such a public forum had to be solely for attention.

They got away with it before, but Ronald vowed they wouldn't a second time. With a smirk plastered upon his face, he emerged from behind the Better Made chip stand just as the stranger in the D.A.R.E. shirt lathered their hands with the stolen lotion. The other stood choosing between two types of malt liquor in search of their alcohol content.

The moment they saw him with that smug expression on his face, they knew they'd been found out. Both took off down the aisles, separating unintentionally. Ronald gave chase, dodging can goods, macaroni boxes, and vegetable oil along with any other groceries the D.A.R.E. misfit decided to launch at him.

Ding-a-ling. The guy in the tie-dyed shirt was out the door first. He waited for a second across the street behind the cover of the big blue mailbox.

Shit, what have I done? This is all my fault. I should never have gotten her into this. His worry compounded as he willed his companion in crime to come out that door.

Ding-a-ling. She came sprinting out the doors. She was going so fast that her baseball cap flew off, sending her long, wrapped hair flying free.

It's a girl. Taken by surprise, Ronald slowed his speed just a little. With the force at which he barreled toward her, he was liable to mow her down. *I can't hurt this girl.* He fought with his morals. Every fiber of his being told him not to hurt her. But there was another part of him that refused to be silenced. The part of him that said she deserved to be punished spoke to him right on time.

"Make her pay, dear brother. Make her pay." A seething Cecilia hovered nearby, imploring him to do his duty.

Is that what this is all about—making them pay? What did she do? Steal some petty items? Cause a ruckus? Does this warrant her death? Ronald fought with his duty to enforce Cecilia's will as he chased the female on to an I-75 overpass. He intended to grab her and make her see that what she'd done was wrong. He hoped to convince her never to do it again. That's when it all changed. The scene around him shifted from an overpass to a dark alley. A rabid dog suddenly appeared at their heels and seemed to want nothing more than to rip the woman Ronald was chasing to shreds. The bloodthirsty hound caught up to Ronald disregarding him as he ran at his side. It was the girl he wanted.

The frightened girl kept up her speed but glanced back once she heard them within arm's-reach of her. Ronald threw his arm into the air, blocking the canine's bite as it leaped toward her. The woman's foot caught the edge of some lifted concrete, catapulting her through the air, then to the ground. Just that quick, his mission turned from capturing her to saving her life. Ronald grabbed the snarling beast by the collar, flinging him back through the air. Push back from the weight of the animal knocked Ronald to the cement. He reacted without hesitation, forcing the girl back against the dumpster behind him as he attempted to subdue the wild animal that had charged back in their direction. They were nose to snout, Ronald and the canine. He fought mercilessly, taking bites to the forearm and hands. The girl's body pushed back, attempting to give him the leverage he needed to fight from their position.

Then she shrieked, nearly rupturing Ronald's eardrums. The effects being a loud ringing that refused to subside. That's when the scene shifted to reflect the reality of their situation. They weren't in an alley at all, nor was there a vicious dog attacking them. Ronald's arms were free of bite marks. No scuffs or scrapes covered his hands. It was as if he'd imagined it all. He sat up on the edge of the concrete curb along the overpass, letting out a deep sigh. *What's happening to me?* He had begun to question his sanity.

"Help me!" she screamed.

Ronald sprang up at the sound of her cries. "Where are you?" He looked around for any signs of her.

"Please, don't let me die," Tiffany begged as she hung from the side of the bridge.

Ronald leaned over the edge, gripping the metal railing as he peered into her sorrowful, dark brown eyes.

"I didn't mean to hurt anybody. They were just groceries. Please," she stated her final plea.

It was then that the lotion she'd applied to her hands in the store did its job. The slip was slow and painful for Tiffany, knowing the entire time she was doomed to plummet to her death. There was no way Ronald could reach her, even if he were willing to. Besides, it was him who had pushed her off the bridge in a crazed panic. Cecelia made sure, one way or another, he would fulfill his duty.

From that day on, Ronald would have to bear the brunt of killing one of Gertrude's dear friends. Not only did he have to worry about the murder, he couldn't help but wonder who'd witnessed the frenzy between him and the shoplifting couple.

Just then, he heard it . . . Tiffany's partner in crime calling out for her in the distance.

"Tiffany, where are you?" he cried out as he made his way over the bridge.

"If she's bad, he's got to be much worse, dear brother. Wouldn't you agree?" Cecilia's narrow, crusted, purple lips whispered at the base of her brother's ear.

"Tiffany, can you hear me?" the voice echoed as it drew nearer.

His breaths escaped hard and deep. Sweat marked the pits of his tie-dyed T-shirt. *Smack, smack, smack.* He hit the side of his face, trying to slap some sense into himself. But he was a moment too late.

"My God. Tiffany! Tell me where you are," he cried out.

That's when an arm coiled around the five-foot-nothing man's head, squeezing firmly on his neck.

"Let me go. What are you doing?" he whimpered, attempting to tussle against the six-foot-four frame his back crashed against.

Those were the last words Ronald allowed to leave his lips. Tightening his grip, he dragged the man across the concrete. One of his black sneakers came off as it scraped against the curb. Ronald did have enough heart to choke him into a dead sleep before he flung his body over the bridge and down onto the train tracks, next to Tiffany's corpse.

He'd gotten it over with as fast as he could. It wasn't that he wanted the man to suffer. Ronald's decision was more out of survival. The last thing he wanted to do was go to jail. Once Tiffany was dead, he had no other option than to kill her companion.

Chapter 30

The Call

Moments later, the call came over Barnes's dashboard CB radio. He sat parked in front of Peggy's residence, filling out his missing person's report. She'd yet to surface, leaving her front door still wide open. Because her vehicle, keys, and purse were there at her residence, Barnes opted not to shut her front door. Instead, he hung around, hoping she would soon resurface.

"Barnes, do you copy?"

"This is Barnes. Go ahead," he replied, snatching up the handheld speaker.

"We received an anonymous call in your area regarding a man chasing a woman across the bridge on Mt. Elliott near Mound. Are you still in the area?"

"I'm actually right around the corner." Barnes shifted his squad car into drive, then sped off to assess the scene. "Have Hamtramck police been notified? I don't have time to argue about turf."

"Sir, just like the one you're at, they gave it up. I believe it's too close to the border for them," the female officer on the other end responded.

"Well, I'm almost there. Over and out."

Ronald's conversion van passed by Barnes on his left just as he turned on to Harold Street. The two briefly locked eyes, furnishing each other a nod. Up ahead, streetlamps sporadically lining the edges of the bridge illuminated as he rounded the corner onto Mt.

Elliot. Barnes flipped on his own spotlight affixed to his driver's-side window to get a good glimpse of what might be lying there in the darkness. It had been an otherwise peaceful night. Not a soul on the bridge in either direction. He took his time inching his way up the bridge. That's when the small bottle of travel-size lotion in the middle of the street caught his eye. Barnes stopped the cruiser, threw it into park, then hopped out with his Maglite, leaving the driver's-side door ajar.

He crossed over into the beaming rays of his head-lights to look it over. It wasn't until he lifted his head in contemplation that he saw the black sneaker nestled there next to the curb, not six feet from where he stood. About six more feet sat the edge of the bridge.

Barnes clicked on his light, shining it in that direction. The only logical thing for him to do would be to look over the edge, but first, he had to make sure there was no one around threatening to push him over once he'd gotten there. He did a 360-degree turn, illuminating the area around him, finding nothing—just the sound of crickets competing with the buzzing street lamps and an occasional barking dog.

He took his time looking on the other side of the over-pass, scanning the scene behind him one last time before he finally glanced over, shining his flashlight below. There was nothing. Nothing out of the ordinary anyway. Just the train yard and a few abandoned cabooses.

Barnes huffed, even more perplexed by the shoe and lotion bottle. Even though no crime looked to have been committed, he gathered up the shoe and lotion as evidence, just in case.

The sun rose, glistening against the dew, revitalizing the grass Sunday morning. Barnes lay reclined back in his seat. A black cat leaped onto the hood of his cruiser, waking him from a deep slumber. He groaned, lifting his seat upright to find Peggy Avarice's front door ajar.

He let out a long sigh. The cases were piling up. He was used to it. I mean, it was the inner city, but whenever a case involved someone elderly, it hit a soft spot for him. His mother passed away, suffering from dementia. In the end, she forgot how even to feed herself. A feeding tube provided her the only nourishment at the time of her death. He hoped Peggy didn't suffer the same illness. Barnes feared she'd wandered off and gotten lost. The city was vast. Finding her would be like finding a needle in a haystack. He got out and shut the front door to her house before leaving the scene.

"Where is she? I can't believe she's not home yet," May complained as she spied Barnes's cruiser pulling off from Peggy's residence.

"Aunt May, what are you doing up so early? I don't smell any coffee brewing."

"Do I look like a barista to you?" Aunt May snapped at Gertrude out of frustration of her gal pal being missing.

Even without an explanation, Gertrude could see the worry overtaking her aunt. Whenever she wasn't watching talk shows or soap operas, she had her eyes glued on mysteries, which often contributed to Aunt May fearing the worst.

"I'm sorry, Aunt May. You know I didn't mean it like that. Would you like me to make the coffee? As a matter of fact, I am making the coffee. You just relax," Gertrude replied as she rushed off to brew the pot of joe. The sound of her house slippers sliding across the wood floors worked more than a few of Aunt May's nerves.

"And what did I tell you about picking up your feet when you walk?" Aunt May carried on, not letting up on her.

"Whew, chile," Gertrude mumbled under her breath. *She is really tap dancing on my nerves today.* Of course, she'd never in a million years say that out loud. Gertrude had the utmost respect for her elders. It was one of the characteristics that made her Aunt May's favorite. "Thank you for reminding me, Aunt May," she called out so that her aunt could hear her from the kitchen.

Defused for the moment, Aunt May shifted around in her recliner in front of the television, switching on the news.

Gertrude stood over the kettle of water she'd placed on the stove. Her mind focused on one thing . . . Ronald. She thought about how gorgeous his skin looked when the moon shone into his bedroom window, causing the glow about his cheek. She'd enjoyed their time together watching movies and relaxing in bed. Most guys would have made a move on her, but not Ronald. He was a true gentleman. In recent days, he had proved to Gertrude that chivalry was indeed alive and well.

Out of nowhere, the wall phone in the kitchen buzzed, startling her from her thoughts. The pleasant grin on her face dropped as if she knew the news on the other end would leave a dark cloud looming over their day. She certainly didn't want Aunt May to be the one to answer it, so she rushed over to the phone, being sure to pick up her feet along the way.

"Hello." She pressed the cordless phone to her ear.

"Gertrude, have you seen or talked to Tiffany?" Brenda blurted on the other end of the receiver.

Gertrude could hear the subtle panic in her voice. She'd seen last night what Aunt May was watching on the news. The melee Tiffany and her newfound friends had caused was the evening newsbreak. Brenda thought maybe she'd be hiding at Gertrude's. No one would ever think to look there.

"I haven't seen her since you guys did my makeover on Saturday."

"Oh my God. Gertrude, we need to talk. Not on the phone, though. In private," Brenda implored.

"You're welcome to come over here. Aunt May won't bother us. She's not really in the mood to talk anyway. Mrs. Peggy is still missing."

"I'll be there in about thirty minutes."

"Drive safe," Gertrude responded before ending the call.

She leaned back against the wall, hanging the receiver up overhead. Gertrude couldn't help pondering where the hell everyone had disappeared to.

Meanwhile, the liquor store owner, a short, chubby Middle Eastern fellow, had forbidden Wilson to leave. He wouldn't have the "all clear" to go until they reviewed the store cameras in efforts of finding the identities of the vandals who'd ransacked his establishment. He'd worked hard to earn money to purchase him a convenience store in the United States. There was no way Nadi Salem would let anyone get away with desecrating his legacy.

"What are you doing here all day, man? Reading magazines while my store is being torn apart?" Nadi interrogated as he leaned over Wilson's shoulder.

Wilson lent him no response but continued to fast-forward the VCR's cassette tape to the day and time in question.

"Here it is. This is when he comes in." Wilson pressed *play*.

The video's resolution was awful. On top of that, the tape glitched every fifteen seconds or so. They could tell

Ronald was wearing a blue jogging suit, but his face was unrecognizable. Nadi noticed that the unknown vandal in the blue sweat suit had confronted the other two amid their five-finger discount shopping spree.

"Wait a minute. Go back. Rewind the tape to when the baseball cap-wearing misfits walked in."

Wilson complied with his boss's request, rewinding, then restarting the video when Tiffany and her companion arrived. The two of them watched as the couple entered the store and began filling the bookbags over their shoulders.

Nadi stood upright as the enlightenment provided by the glitchy video set in. "The guy in the blue wasn't stealing."

"Yeah, he was trying to apprehend a pair of thieves," Wilson chimed in.

Chapter 31

Family Ties

Fifteen minutes later, Brenda was tearing up the porch steps at Gertrude's, having sped up the highway the entire ride there. She pounded at the screen door before ringing the doorbell more than a few times.

Within seconds, the door flew open. "Girl, pick one. You know Aunt May is in here watching her shows." When Gertrude answered, Brenda panted, pacing the porch in deep contemplation.

"Is everything okay?" Gertrude frowned upon noticing the worry plaguing her friend.

Instantly, Brenda's eyes welled with tears. "I wish I could say it was, but I can't. I don't know where Tiffany is, and I'm afraid wherever she is, she's in big trouble."

"Come inside and tell me what's going on. Maybe I can help."

Brenda entered the house. "I don't know if anyone can help at this point," she cried.

Gertrude rubbed her hand across her friend's back, attempting to ease the turmoil boiling inside. "Please, don't cry. Just calm down. Let's go to the kitchen, so we don't disturb Aunt May. She's not in a very good mood today, either. Her friend Peggy is still missing in action."

"That seems to be the theme, lately," Brenda sourly remarked as she followed Gertrude to the kitchen.

"Have a seat and tell me what's really going on."

"I don't even know where to start." Brenda took a seat at the table.

"Start from the beginning. I'll make you a cup of coffee."

"I don't even know if I should drink coffee as amped up as I am right now."

"How about some tea? I can even put a shot of auntie's whiskey in it." Gertrude pulled the bottle of bourbon from the cupboard showing it off.

"Yes, please. Maybe a shot will calm my nerves."

"What is it that's got you all panicked anyway?"

"It's Tiffany. Ever since she met that guy a couple of weeks back, she's been gradually changing. A few days ago, she moved out, claiming not to need me. Tiffany swears she can make it on her own, but ever since she's been with him, she's been hanging around with his group of hooligan friends we had lunch with. That's why she was so hungry the other day. I don't think she's spending her money on the right things. Hell, I can't even verify she's still working. The temp service she works for sends her on different jobs, so I have no idea what location she's working at. I can't call her because they don't have a phone at his house—if he even *has* a house. She's probably been lying to me about that too. I just don't know what to do or how to talk some sense into her."

"So, you're worried because you haven't talked to her since yesterday, and you think she's with her boyfriend? There's got to be more than that bothering you. You were practically in tears when I opened the door," Gertrude responded, sensing there was something Brenda was leaving out.

Brenda let out a long sigh. "Did you see the news this morning?"

"I didn't. Why? What's going on?"

"A group of hooligans ransacked the mall yesterday."

Gertrude took in a deep breath. "I know. I saw them when I was there. I couldn't believe it. And I thought Chicago was bad. . . ."

"Tiffany was with that group. I saw her with my own eyes."

"No way. Tiffany wouldn't do something like that," Gertrude protested.

"I used to think so, but after seeing it, there's no way I can deny it."

"Oh my God. She's going to get in so much trouble. Maybe that's why you can't find her. She's hiding from the police."

"I have to find her, Gertrude. I need to make sure my cousin is okay. I promised always to protect her. She's like a sister to me."

Gertrude brought over the cup of tea, setting it down on the table in front of Brenda. "Do you know where the boyfriend hangs out?"

"There was this one house I dropped her off at one time. I think I have the address written down on a piece of paper somewhere in my car."

"Well, we definitely shouldn't go alone. Would you mind if I asked Ronald to come with us for protection?"

Brenda's eyes lit up with hope. "Do you think he'd be willing to?"

"I'm sure he wouldn't have a problem. Let me make Aunt May's cup of coffee. Then we can both go next door and ask."

"Thank you, Gertrude. I really appreciate your help. Lord knows I can't do this alone."

"You don't have to thank me. That's what friends are for."

Chapter 32

Lover and a Fighter

Next door, Ronald tossed and turned in bed, attempting to wake himself from the dream he'd found himself trapped inside.

Young Ronald stood at the corner, the sun beaming down on him and his sister, Cecelia.

"Where are you going? You know we're not allowed to go around the corner alone."

"I'm never alone, dear brother. You just stay here in case Mom comes outside looking for us."

"If Dad finds out, you're going to get in big trouble," he yelled in a last-ditch effort to keep her from going.

He had tried, even though he knew his words alone couldn't stop her. Cecelia was always a curious child who explored where she chose.

Her brother watched her drift across the street, then around the corner, only this time, his dream took him along with her. For the first time, Ronald could see where Cecilia had run off to that day she'd left him standing guard.

Cecelia skipped down Dwyer Street on her way to the corner store. She had saved up five cents for some penny candy, which she preferred not to share with her brother. Usually, they wouldn't leave each other's side, but there were times Cecilia wanted to be on her own due to her brother's Goody Two-shoes' nature. If he had known about her finding the nickel in the couch and deciding not to tell their parents, Ronald would surely have spilled the beans. So, Cecelia saw no other choice than to go at it alone.

"Slow down there, little girl. Where are you rushing off to?" the man with the white hair and hole in his throat remarked as he lounged on his porch swing.

Cecilia stopped in her tracks—the sound of his voice causing her pause. She turned to him in wonderment. "Why does your voice sound like that?"

"It's cancer," he replied as he lit his cigarette to take a drag.

"Are you going to die?" Cecelia asked innocently.

The stranger twisted the edges of his mustache, flashing her a sly grin as a cloud of smoke escaped his mouth and stoma. "We all die, little girl. Eventually, we're all called back to the station."

"You mean heaven?" Cecelia asked as her arm had begun to quiver.

"Wherever your station is, little girl. Why is your arm twitching like that?"

"I'm not sure. It only does it sometimes. My momma always says it's just my nerves acting up."

"Would you like some candy? I have some in the house there by the door. My grandchildren left it here, and I don't eat candy much. I like a different kind of sweets."

Cecilia practically cringed at his words. "I really shouldn't take candy from strangers," she rebutted.

"But I'm no stranger. I'm your neighbor. Besides, it's right there on the dining room table. As soon as you step inside, you'll see it. Go on. Step inside. It's right there for the taking," he coaxed.

Something about him told Cecilia not to trust him. She was on her way to the store to buy her own candy anyway. There was no need to eat his grandkids' so-called stash. "Thanks for the offer, but no thanks." Cecilia waved, then hurriedly went on her way.

The convenience store was at the end of the block, only about ten houses down. She made it there in less than five minutes, purchased her five tootsie rolls, and was on her way back in a flash. Yet, by the time she was halfway up the block, she had consumed every sweet morsel and still wasn't satisfied. Her little eyes scanned the block, noticing her new neighbor friend had walked up the street to talk to the couple who lived on the opposite corner. He'd left his front door open, which, back in those days, people tended to do. All I have to do is slip inside and grab it from the table, just like he said. Cecelia mulled over the thought for a few seconds before she decided to go inside.

She climbed up the side of the porch, then hopped over the railing, making her way to his door behind the cover of his tall hedges. Once she ducked inside, the aroma of cotton candy permeated her nostrils. "Yummy." She rubbed her tummy, imagining how delicious the smell would taste on her tongue.

Albeit the lights were out. Rays of sun beamed in through spaces in the open vertical blinds showing her the way forward. Cecelia's stone-gray eyes scanned her surroundings. She had never been in a neighbor's house before. The layout was much different than theirs. Brown shag carpeting covered the floors from the living room through the dining room and then up the hall into other bedrooms. The couch was void of plastic, unlike the one in her parents' living room. Cecilia ran her hand across the row of bobblehead sports celebrities that decorated the bookshelf. Then there it was in all *its glory—an entire sandwich bag of tootsie rolls. Just as her hand moved to grab the bag, his shadow loomed over her.*

"Go on, take them."

Cecelia turned to face him—her arm vibrating so constantly she had to grab hold of it. "You can have every one of them. All you have to do is do me a favor."

"You didn't ask for a favor when you offered them before."

"That was before you broke into my house. I was not home, yet you waltzed right in. In fact, as I came inside, you were stealing. You could get into big trouble for that. Stealing could land you in jail. Juvenile for little girls . . . So, do we have a deal?" He extended his hand for what he assumed in his wicked mind to be a fair shake. Instead, she stomped down hard on his foot, then took off deeper into the residence. He almost snagged her by one of her suspenders until it snapped loose, giving her the opportunity she needed to slip away. Much like her parents' home, a door led to the basement just off the kitchen. She tackled the stairs running as fast as she possibly could to get away from his long strides.

The panicked little girl reached the bottom of the stairs, searching frantically for the back door. "I know it's here. It has to be." She nearly burst into tears. But there was no time to stand there crying. Cecilia knew it because the smaller his shadow got as he barreled down the stairs toward her, the closer he got to her. It was either face him or the unknown. She darted left into the big, open space, headed for the furnace. The little girl was desperate to find anywhere she could hide and have time to think of a way out.

"Daddy, please, come save me," she cried quietly, tears drenching her face.

Suddenly, the lights went out. Fortunately, her body was small enough to squeeze between the back wall and the furnace. She figured if she could barely squeeze through herself, there was no way he would get to her. Cecelia tried her best to calm her breathing. She didn't want him to hear her hiding there.

With her arm clutched tightly, the little girl squeezed her eyes shut. If I don't see him, I won't panic, she told herself. The hand that reached in, lifting Cecilia off her feet, then snatching her from the crevice, had done so with so much force, it nearly snapped her neck.

Ronald's view into his sister's experience began to fade further away, back up the basement stairs, through the kitchen and dining room, then out the front door. All the while, all he could hear were his sister's screams.

He woke from the nightmare, eyes wild, forehead drenched with sweat. Was it real? Ronald asked himself. Had Tom Swine sexually abused Cecilia?

Chapter 33

The Hero

The doorbell chimed, interrupting his train of thought. That's probably Gertrude, he presumed. Ronald hopped right out of bed, headed to the front door.

Brenda turned away when he answered in his white boxer shorts, too bashful to take it all in. Gertrude snickered, "Were you expecting me?" she smiled.

"Actually, I figured it was you. No one else visits me." Ronald held open the screen door. "Come on inside. I'll go put some pants on."

He ducked back off into his bedroom, reemerging cloaked in a navy-blue jogging suit. "You can look now," he said to Brenda, who had lowered her head when he came into the room.

She picked up her head to greet him properly. "Hey, Ronald."

"Hey. So, what are you ladies up to?"

"We were wondering if you could go with us to see if Tiffany is at her boyfriend's house," Gertrude spoke up, getting it over with.

"You ladies need security?"

"Yeah, sort of." Gertrude nodded in affirmation of its truth.

"No problem. When will you require my services?"

"Now," Brenda finally chimed in.

"Now?" Ronald quickly gave it some thought. He had intended to find out where the remainder of the miscreant pack lived, either way. Brenda was about to serve them up on a silver platter. "Okay. Let me get myself together. You know, wash the cold out my eyes. . . ."

Other than the humming sound of her tires running across the road as they sped up the freeway, it was all but silent during the ride there, each of them allowing their thoughts to occupy them. Brenda worried her cousin had done something to destroy her reputation irrevocably. *What would that mean for the rest of Tiffany's life?* she thought. She had seen the struggles of criminals attempting to reform their lives after, unfortunately, falling into the trap of committing illegal activities. Much of the time, it was easy money that enticed them. Brenda never thought her cousin Tiffany would ever succumb to this. She gripped the steering wheel tighter as she fought back the tears.

Ronald, on the other hand, worried about whether he could keep his secrets from being unearthed. Not only did he have to worry about the authorities, but Gertrude was becoming more immersed in the situation with Tiffany. In addition to that, Wilson, Grady, Tom, and May keeping an eye on him had become a concern. If Tom had done the things Ronald dreamed about, him being a good man to Gertrude would be the least of the gang's worries.

Gertrude could think of nothing other than the strapping, courageous gentleman sitting behind her. The fact he had agreed to come made her feel like a mound of melting butter. She hoped Ronald would be willing to sop her up. As her view through the passenger window changed from brick highways to dilapidated houses, her mind shifted to that of their mission. Gertrude realized then she had been selfish beyond belief. All that time, they'd been focused on her and Ronald's relationship or lack thereof. *Maybe if I had not made myself and my life such a priority to others, Tiffany would have never been in this situation. Was I just not listening?*

"How come she didn't tell me?" Gertrude finally spoke.

Brenda cleared her throat, resisting the urge to get choked up. "She probably doesn't want you to think less of her. Tiffany is determined to do it all on her own. I guess she feels like people think she needs me to stay afloat. She's trying to prove a point, but instead, she's ruining her life."

"There's got to be something we can say to convince her to come home."

"Trust me. I've tried everything. That guy she's dating, Terrance. He's a complete degenerate. He and his friends . . . I'm surprised you couldn't tell."

Brenda made a left at the street she remembered dropping her cousin off at the last time she had seen her. "Speaking of degenerates," she stared them down, recognizing the two young men that stood out in the front yard of the run-down flat with the dandelion-infested grass.

Brenda parked in front of the house next door, breathed deeply, then let it out in a long sigh. "What am I going to say to her?"

"I should go see if she's even here, first," said Ronald.

Brenda instantly rebutted, saying, "Maybe, I should go with you since they'll recognize me."

"I think you should stay in the car," Ronald reiterated his stance with eyes glued on the pair as they stood clowning around.

The lanky con man with the classic finger waves jogged back and forth along the crumbled sidewalk, reenacting how he had evaded mall security. He concluded the story by popping the collar of the Ralph Lauren plaid button-up he was wearing, then dusted off his loafers that matched . . . all being stolen goods.

Daryl and Joey were proud thieves, already conspiring about when they would strike next. Although Joey was one of the ones who had gotten caught by security, the police let him off with a warning. They figured he was just a punk kid trying to fit in. The authorities assumed he had succumbed to peer pressure, as they often did. He had never once been convicted of a crime yet had participated in well over a dozen. Smooth, milky skin, short, black hair, a naked baby face, and icy-blue eyes gave him a "boy-next-door" kind of look. After his first few times of being released with a warning, Joey caught on quickly. He knew all he had to do was play that role.

"Man . . . It was crazy, D. I thought I was going to jail for sure this time, but you know the kid found a way out," he bragged, wearing a wife beater and a pair of jeans. The sneakers on his feet were dusty since the goods he'd grabbed during the snatch and grab had been confiscated during his detainment.

"Yeah. You got away with your freedom, but you still dusty, homeboy," Daryl teased.

"That's okay. I'll be on top again soon. They can't stop my shine." Joey rubbed his flat belly as if to say he was hungry.

Daryl sucked at his overlapping two front teeth before spinning the toothpick hanging at the edge of his mouth with this tongue. "You hungry? I made those hot sausages with some eggs. There's enough for everybody. We'll just have to figure out dinner."

"Who is homeboy rollin' up? You know him?" Joey inquired, noticing Ronald headed in their direction.

"Naw. He could be the boys for all I know," Daryl answered, immediately brandishing a mean mug.

"I'm looking for my cousin, Tiffany," Ronald spoke up as he drew nearer, extinguishing their skepticism.

"Oh, you're related to Tiff. She's cool peoples," Joey remarked, believing Ronald's lie as fact.

Daryl was not so welcoming. Even if Ronald were related to Tiffany, he still didn't want him there. "Yeah, well, Tiffany ain't here."

"Would you happen to know where she is? My uncle is really worried about her. We just want her to come home."

Daryl crossed his arms. "Yeah? Well, like I said, she ain't here. And we don't know where she is, either."

"What about Terrence? Maybe he knows where she is," Ronald offered up more of what he knew, hoping to get him to lay down his arms.

"He ain't here, neither." Daryl spread his feet apart a little as if to say he was standing his ground on the matter.

"Could you call him?"

"Could you call him?" Daryl snapped back.

"Hey, fellas"—Joey stepped between them—"chill out. There's no need for things to get out of hand." He attempted to quell matters. He couldn't fight anyway, so it was best he kept things copasetic.

"Look, Terrence doesn't have a phone, and we haven't seen him or Tiff at all today. You should probably check somewhere else."

"I'll do that," Ronald replied, not taking his eyes off Daryl, who, in return, continued staring him down as well.

Brenda smacked her lips, her impatience having grown. "I wonder what they're saying."

"I don't know, but whatever it is, I have full confidence that they can talk like adults and come to a helpful conclusion. Ronald is, hands down, the most levelheaded man I know," Gertrude bragged with a smile. The smile and look of admiration on her face as she admired Ronald, however, slowly faded as the scene before her played out.

Daryl thrust his finger at the side of Ronald's head, threatening violence.

Ronald's reaction was instant once he felt the man's dingy fingertip at the edge of his head. He grabbed hold of it, twisting it back until the bones in his wrist fractured.

The kick he thrust into Joey's stomach with his foot sent him butt first onto the ground and out of his way.

Daryl howled in agony, his body bending back, then over in submission. Still, he refused to go down without a fight. He threw a haymaker in Ronald's direction but a second too late because the left hook Ronald had launched landed before Daryl could make contact. The bridge of Daryl's nose crushed under the pressure of his punch. The moment he hit the ground, blood that previously trickled from his flared nostrils had begun streaming. Daryl saw no other choice than to flash the 9 mm in the waistband of his jeans.

"So that's how you want this to go?" he threatened, spitting blood at Ronald's feet.

By then, the girls had both rushed over, prompting Daryl to conceal his weapon with the bottom of his bloody shirt.

"Stop! What's going on? There's no reason for this," Brenda pleaded. "We're just looking for my cousin. We don't want any trouble."

"Y'all way past wanting." Daryl stood up. He and Joey both dusted themselves off.

"Look, we'll just leave," Gertrude chimed in. She touched Ronald's arm, calming his hard breaths. "I think we should get out of here."

He took his time backing off with a devilish smirk still plastered on his face. Ronald left without a word under the gaze of Daryl and Joey's hateful stares.

"I can't believe they tried to jump you like that," Gertrude fussed as they all piled back into Brenda's vehicle. "Are you okay?" She turned to look at him.

Ronald flashed her a grin. "I'm just fine, Gertrude. What about you? You seem a little shaken up."

"I'm okay if you are."

"Then all is well."

"Let's get out of here." Gertrude turned to Brenda, who already started the car.

She shifted into drive, then skirted off. "I'm really sorry about this, Ronald. I didn't think it would come to this," Brenda apologized.

"I knew what I was signing up for when I agreed to come along. I'm a grown man who makes his own decisions. You're not to blame."

Even though she didn't find her cousin, Ronald's admission made her feel a little better. The last thing she needed was to feel guilty about something else.

Their ride home, much like the one there, was a quiet one. Brenda worried about her cousin's safety. She hoped the consequences from the confrontation would not fall upon her cousin.

Gertrude, on the other hand, had been turned on all the way. Her body burned intensely with a desire for Ronald. Sure, the fight had rattled her, but in hindsight, she realized Ronald was magnificent. Seeing him take charge like that, knocking his opponents left and right, turned out to be an aphrodisiac. Her body burned so hot that Ronald could smell the aroma of her perfume getting stronger.

Like a lion stalking his prey, his eyes surmised every breath she took, along with each movement of her limbs.

It was then Ronald decided he would have her in his bed for more than a thrill.

Once they pulled back up at the house on Gable Street, Ronald said his goodbyes, then got out, leaving Gertrude and Brenda to talk. The moment he was behind closed doors, he had begun pacing the floor with one thought plaguing him. What would he do about Daryl and Joey? Back and forth, Ronald wore down the living room carpet. Then the epiphany dawned on him, right along with the realization that Daryl had spit blood and saliva onto his shoe. Ronald grinned in contemplation of his next move.

Chapter 34

A Passionate Release

It was nearly midnight when Ronald exited the back door of his home to get to the garage. When he'd looked out of his living room window fifteen minutes before, he noticed Brenda's car still parked in the driveway. Because he preferred to remain undetected, he thought it best that he traveled under cover of darkness. There was a switch along the wall he'd flipped on his way out, shutting off the porch and garage lights. The only witness to his crimes would be his sister, should she decide to show herself.

Ronald locked himself inside the garage, where he had the Chevy lifted to access the room beneath his feet. He traveled that dark, narrow stairwell, it now having a battery-powered lantern hanging on the wall above the landing. Ronald snatched up the light on the way to three standing refrigerators along the cement wall. The first one he opened housed the corpse of Terrence, aka Tiffany's boyfriend. Straps across his chest, waist, and legs held the body in place. Ronald looked down at his feet. One, of course, missing a shoe. "Let's see who fate is smiling on." He knelt, pulling the shoe off Terrance's stiffened foot. To his surprise, his dead adversary wore the same size he did. That alone was confirmation enough for Ronald that his plan was meant to be carried out.

***

"See you later, hon. Get you some sleep and call me tomorrow." Gertrude waved Brenda farewell as she backed out of the driveway. That's when she heard the garage door open, then close again. She couldn't see anyone there in the darkness, but she, of course, assumed it was Ronald, or at least she hoped so. "Ronald," Gertrude called out to him as she walked further into the abyss, it darkening the closer she crept. "Ronald, is that you?"

"Is that you?" he answered, wrapping his arms around her, then lifting her into a soft, passionate kiss.

Gertrude couldn't see Ronald, but she could surely feel him. His erect penis pressed against her thigh. The warmth of his breath on her neck as he nibbled beneath her ear made the moisture between her legs run down her inner thighs. He gently pressed her against the house. "I think you're ready," he said, lifting her legs around his waist.

"I am," Gertrude whispered at the base of his ear just as she tasted its lobe.

Just as he started to take her inside, Gertrude's words stopped him in his tracks. "Out here is fine."

Ronald had never fornicated outside before. Moreover, he gained no comfort by being so exposed. God forbid Aunt May look out the window and catch a glimpse of her niece's bare caboose in the air. Instead, he opted for an equally exciting option. He carried her over to his conversion van. The bed in the back had already been laid out for Tiffany and Terrence's bodies. Ronald gently set her down, then slid her linen pants down past her ankles. Gertrude kept her eyes on his as she eased her bottom back to allow him to lie on top of her. She had waited so long to allow him access to her.

At last, him running his hands up her caramel thighs, then along her torso to grab at her voluptuous breasts had become a reality. The river between her thighs flowed for him, and although they couldn't see much of each other, her hands could feel the ripples in his stomach, much like the muscles in his pecks. She wrapped her hand around the back of his neck, then pulled him in to her to taste her lips. Ronald eased into her smiling mounds as he caressed the side of her face. The rest of their garments came off in seconds, and so ensued the night they had been waiting for.

Ironically, his suspicions were spot on. Aunt May spied out of her kitchen window as Ronald's van sat rocking. "That boy and his weird music." She shook her head with disapproval, then rushed off to search for Gertrude. She'd left the front door wide open when she walked Brenda out but had yet to surface. "Well . . . She can ring the doorbell if she's out there. I ain't letting all my cool air out," Aunt May complained, shutting the door, then locking the dead bolt.

Monday morning in class, all Gertrude could think about was her escapade with Ronald the night previous. She fiddled with her mechanical pencil as the professor passed by her going on about the day's lesson. She'd instantly felt the warm sensation between her legs become ever more intense as her daydream drowned out the sound of the teacher's voice.

Gertrude could practically feel his lips on her neck, his hands caressing her nipples, even the strength of his arms when he lifted her bottom to straddle his waist. Everything he'd done that night he had done with pre-cision. Ronald made her feel appreciated, sexy, wanted, and, more importantly, cherished. Gertrude couldn't wait to see him after school. She wondered if she had crossed his mind as much as he had hers. Had she performed well enough for him, she wondered. It certainly had been a long time since her garden had been deflowered.

The professor tapped his knuckles on Gertrude's desk to get her attention as he moseyed on by. "This part will be on the lesson, Gertrude. You may want to pay attention," he reminded her.

Gertrude nodded, adjusting her position in her seat as if that had transformed her into a model student. Her mind, however, stayed fixed. Fixed on her new man, and if he even considered himself as much.

Knowing Ronald had been watching her for the last five minutes from the window on the door of her classroom would undoubtedly have boosted her confidence. He took in her beauty, notably the way her cheeks dimpled when she smiled. Even something as small as the way she would twist her ringlet-like coils around her forefinger when she was in deep thought didn't get past Ronald.

He noticed everything about her, and that which he wasn't aware of, he planned to find out. When her class was over, Ronald waited by the door for her to exit. As the students filed out of the classroom one by one, he came face-to-face with one of his most recent nemesis, Joey. You'd think once they locked eyes, Joey would be running scared, but it was quite the contrary. He furnished Ronald a smirk that told Ronald everything he needed to know at that moment. It told Ronald they then knew where to find him. And if they knew where to find him, that put Gertrude and Brenda in danger as well. His reckless behavior had, for the first time, endangered someone close to him. Ronald knew it was up to him to rectify the situation. He shot Joey a smirk back so that he knew Ronald wasn't rattled. Although the look made Joey nervous, he had confidence in the fact that a squad would be behind him.

Gertrude noticed the stare down as she walked out of the classroom. "Oh my God." She cringed at the sight of Joey face-to-face with Ronald. She'd never even noticed that he was one of her classmates. Above all, she hoped they didn't start fighting right there outside of the classroom.

Joey had other plans, though. "I'll be seeing you around," he menaced, eyeballing Ronald before turning to Gertrude to reveal the name he had captured that day. "Gertrude, right?" he stated before strutting off, feeling as if he had gained the upper hand.

Joey couldn't wait to get home and tell Daryl that he'd seen the guy who'd ambushed them while they were standing in the front yard. That's how *they* saw it. Ronald had ambushed them. Knowing where he worked was exactly the intel needed to carry out their evil plan. Joey and Daryl were out to prove to Ronald that he had messed with the wrong group of friends. Joey darted off the bus as it came to a complete stop on the corner of the block. The chill spot was just up the street, and Daryl was already there.

Unlike his comrade, Daryl didn't attend college yet benefited from the perks that came along with being Joey's friend. He bussed tables at Capers, a local family-owned steak house in Detroit. Daryl had gotten the gig when he was still in high school. The managers paid him a pretty good salary for a busser back then. Nine dollars an hour, plus getting a fair share of the waitresses' tips kept his pockets full in high school.

Fast-forward four years later, his pay had only gone up one dollar. Yet, by then, Daryl had amassed an undying dedication to the owners of the business. It all but killed his will to progress in life. Sure, he got up and went to work, but he had nothing to show for it. He didn't even enjoy his job. It made him angry, jealous, and, much of the time, a party pooper. If you had a dream you wanted to be crushed, all you had to do was mention said aspiration to Daryl. He'd surely dash your hopes.

Every so often, his friend would give him a call. All he had to do was find good enough merchandise, then make the drop. That's how he'd bought the chill spot. Calling it his house would be more appropriate if he had more than a couch, a love seat, and television in the living room. The rest of the house was void of furniture.

Just as Joey's sneakers hit the porch step, Daryl pulled up in a utility van. He honked to get his attention.

Joey turned, looking out toward the street through beaming rays of sunlight. Quickly throwing his hand up across his eyebrow, shielding his blue eyes from the sun, Joey focused his eyes to see. "Is that you, Dee? How'd you get a car?" He rushed over to see it.

"Bro, whose car is this?" He leaned into the open window resting his arms on the door.

"Don't worry about that. We're driving it for now."

Joey nodded his head in agreement. "Well, check this out. Guess who's in one of my classes?" He paused with his eyes glued on Daryl, awaiting an answer.

Daryl smacked his lips, already agitated. "I don't know, man. The fuckin' tooth fairy? Just tell me."

"Gertrude," Joey replied, completely brushing off Daryl's negative nature.

"And who, may the fuck I ask, is Gertrude?"

"Remember homeboy who handled us in the yard the other day. He had two broads with him. One of them is Gertrude. I think it's his girlfriend or sister or something. He was staring into the class today, watching her."

"First of all, I didn't get 'handled.' We got ambushed."

"Well, let's get the crew. We've already got the whip. We can ride down on him."

"I'm not telling nobody else about what happened," Daryl barked. There was no way he'd ruin his reputation by admitting one guy beat him up.

"So, what are we going to do?"

"All right, check this out. I have a pickup and a drop to make. In fact, I think I know just the merchandise to collect for my next payoff." Daryl had hatched a plan that would kill three birds with one stone.

Chapter 35

Plotting Revenge

While Daryl and Joey were busy ironing out the details of their plans, Ronald thought it best he finds out a little more about his "friend" he'd had the run-in with outside of Gertrude's chemistry class. Back home, he had access to the school's computer and security system. All he had to do was pull up the list of students in the class, then cross-reference the name with those assigned school badges. If he was a student there, he had to have an identification badge.

A few clicks followed by a minute of scrolling, and Ronald had found his man. Joey Acolyte, a 20-year-old sophomore from Birmingham, Michigan. He looked him over to make sure it was indeed Joey. Blue eyes, dark brown hair, skinny baby face—there was no doubt in Ronald's mind. He'd found his next victim.

"He looks guilty," Cecilia hissed in her brother's ear.

Ronald kept his eyes fixed on Joey's image. "He is guilty. And he's going to pay."

Late that afternoon, Ronald rolled up the street on his way to pay Daryl and Joey a visit. He liked to survey the land before rushing in. On the way there, something caught his eye. He rolled right past it a million times before but had never connected the dots. It was the same station wagon that was parked at Peggy's house. Tom's station wagon was parked there at Laskey Stadium with all the children running about, playing softball, tag, even jumping rope. But what was Tom doing there? Ronald guessed he was up to no good, so he pulled into the parking lot of the recreation center to find out. The urge to kill him had already manifested. It was just a matter of looking him in the eyes and seeing the truth.

As Ronald got out of the car, he could see Tom there helping one of the little girls tie her shoe. The white short-sleeve shirt with the emblem affixed to the breast pocket told Ronald he must have been part of the staff or, at the very least, a volunteer. He walked up, noticing Tom's hand run down the little girl's naked calf before tying her shoe. All Ronald could see there in front of him was Cecilia being taken advantage of by the very same man that had abused her in life.

Ronald ran up as fast as he could, launching his boot forward into Tom's face, knocking out his top row of teeth and painting his uniform shirt crimson. Or at least that was the image that had played out in Ronald's head as he slowly approached, arm trembling. He wished he had knocked Tom's entire head off. But he had to consider that there was a hoard of children in the vicinity. Subjecting them to a blood-and-guts murder would be a crime against their innocence. Ronald wouldn't dare do that.

"You should go and play now," he instructed, standing directly behind the girl with the pigtails and blue jean dress with suspenders.

Tom looked up at Ronald, trying not to assume the worst. *How could he know anything?* he thought.

"Go on, sweetie pie." Tom tapped her frail little arm, ushering her away, then struggled to get to his feet. "Can you help an old guy up?" He held out his hand for assistance.

To which Ronald huffed in defiance, "I'm only going to touch you one time, and now is not that time."

Tom struggled to his feet, showing more courage. "What are you going on about?" he snarled.

"'Sweetie pie.' Is that what you called my dear sister?"

"I don't know what you're talking about. You're crazy just like Peggy said, ya know that? You need some help. I didn't touch your sister."

Tom tried storming off from the conversation, but Ronald wouldn't hear of it. He grabbed him tight around the bicep, pulling him in closer. "I know what you did to Cecilia that day she snuck inside your house to get candy."

Tom's eyes jutted wide open. He couldn't believe he'd been found out after all these years. He was nearly in the grave. Still, he was getting around good, even living life as he wanted, no matter how sick and twisted a life it was. Tom couldn't allow his good name to be ruined, not to mention the potential to go to prison. He knew he would never survive there.

"I told you, boy, you need some help. Now, turn me loose before I have to call some of my constituents over to assist me in removing your sorry ass from the premises." Tom tried snatching away once more; still, Ronald wouldn't turn him loose.

"I'll be coming to steal some candy, Tom. You should leave the door open for me," he threatened before finally releasing him.

Tom couldn't get away from there and to the safety of the other volunteers fast enough.

Ronald watched him slither away, knowing his time would soon come.

Everything was starting to make sense to him. He thought back to a time he assumed the affliction had already taken place.

Chapter 36

Innocence Stolen

One scorching summer afternoon, Ronald and Cecilia moped, stuck inside cleaning the mess of toys they had scattered about the Doolally residence. They scooped them up little by little, mood sullen from having to complete the arduous task.

"The longer you take to pick them up, the longer you'll be stuck inside," Mrs. Doolally advised with a wagging finger.

Her twins frowned but continued their daily chores.

"Can we go swimming once we're done picking up our mess?"

"Ronald, sweetheart, your father hasn't had time to clean the pool. I'm sorry. You and your sister can run through the sprinklers in the yard."

"Anything would be better than sitting in the house all day," Cecilia groaned.

Ronald peered through the curtain to see the other neighborhood children outside playing tag. "Let's just get it over with so that we can go outside and play like everybody else."

"Fine." Cecilia reluctantly agreed but picked up her pace.

Tidying up took them about an hour or so. Afterward, the twins got into their bathing suits, then trotted outside.

"Stay in the backyard with Sheba," Mrs. Doolally *instructed as they tore out the side door headed for their backyard.*

"Don't worry, Mama. We'll stay in the yard."

Outside, Ronald set up the sprinkler while Cecelia waited alongside the house for her brother to let her know it was safe to turn on the hose.

The little boy twisted on the sprinkler nozzle as tight as he could. "You can turn it on now," he announced, hopping up off the grass from a kneeling position to run out of the stream's range.

Cecilia approached in a hurry. "Let's race."

Catching her off guard, Ronald took off toward the fence. When it came to him and Cecilia racing, he always needed a head start. "Come on, slowpoke."

Making it to the fence seconds ahead of his sister, Ronald boasted it would only be the beginning. "I'm taking the title today," he professed.

The twins raced across the lawn, hopping through the sprinklers time after time. No matter how many, though, Cecilia remained the victor. Both panted, their drenched auburn curls glistening in the sun.

Sheba lay on the sidelines under the shade of the big tree, her tongue hanging from her mouth out onto the grass. She had watched them darting back and forth yet never mustered up the energy to join in.

"Tired of me beating you yet?" Cecilia asked.

Ronald popped a squat near Sheba, caressing her head with the inside of his wrinkled palm. "This is stupid. We should be swimming right now, instead of running through a sprinkler," he complained with a frown, more so downtrodden because of his losses as opposed to not being able to swim. Then to his delight, he saw it driving by. The swim mobile in all its glory beckoned.

The huge truck pulling a pool behind it often cruised through the inner city, allowing children to swim who didn't have the privilege of having their own pool. It traveled from block to block in intervals of thirty minutes, awarding the children the experience.

"It's going around the corner! If we go now, we can catch it."

Cecilia's chest sank inward, her shoulders upright. "Mama said we have to stay in the yard."

Ronald could tell what he had proposed made her uncomfortable, but there was no way he was going to keep losing against her at racing. "Since when did you become a Goody Two-shoes? It's just around the block. What's the big deal? Are you afraid of the big kids that live around the corner?"

"I'm not afraid of anyone," she rebutted.

"Prove it."

"Fine," she agreed. "We should take Sheba with us so she doesn't start barking when we leave."

"Good idea." Ronald hopped up, then proceeded to grab Sheba's leash from the side of her doghouse out back. "We'll tie her to the fire hydrant so that she doesn't run off."

Ronald fitted Sheba with the leash while Cecilia kept lookout just in case their mother emerged.

"Come on, girl. Wanna go for a walk?" Ronald attempted to rile up the unenthused pup as he attached the leash to her collar.

Out of nowhere, the bedroom window in the back of the home lifted. Mrs. Doolally popped her head out, checking on her twins. "Are you two having fun in the sprinkler?"

"I beat Ronald five times already," Cecelia admitted excitedly.

Her mother smiled softly. "You two are always in competition. Can't you just play without there being a winner or loser?"

"Somebody has to lose," Cecilia admitted.

"What makes you think so?"

"Dad said we can't all be winners."

"Well, your dad should have also told you that sometimes you have to lose a lot in order to start winning." She looked up, giving her boy a wink.

Ronald cheesed, somehow feeling better about the fact that he had failed epically.

"You two have fun, and remember to be kind to each other. Someday, when your father and I are gone, you'll be all each other has." Mrs. Doolally closed the window on their awed expressions. Neither of them ever wanted to consider losing their parents.

Ronald broke the silence first. "Come on, Cecilia. Let's go. Mom will be back to check on us in about thirty minutes."

They rushed out of the gate barefoot, straddling the fence along the alleyway to avoid the sharp rocks threatening to slice the soles of their feet. Sheba trotted alongside them, tail wagging.

They made their way around the corner to Dwyer Street, and there it sat parked in the middle of the block. "There it is, Cecilia. The swim mobile," Ronald exclaimed, dashing up the street ahead of her.

"Ronald, wait for me."

"Come on. You can keep up any other time," he rebutted, continuing to rush that way.

Cecelia lagged behind. The entire time, her eyes were glued on the house where the swim mobile had parked. Her lids widened as the man with the hole in his throat came out on his front porch to see what all the commotion was about.

Other children dashed up the block to climb up, then into the mobile pool.

The gentleman sat down in his wooden rocking chair, watching the children frolic about.

Her eyes started to well up with tears until she saw what he had begun glaring at so intensely. His eyes studied the little boy as he wrapped the dog leash over the fire hydrant next door.

Cecelia darted toward him. "Ronald, let's get in," she urged, tugging at his arm.

"All right. All right, I'm coming. Stay here, Sheba. Be a good girl," he instructed the patient pup.

Cecilia turned back, grimacing, in hopes her expression was threatening enough for Tom to look away.

The entire time swimming in the four-foot-deep contraption, all she could think about was all the things he had done to her. Those heinous acts he had committed that she could never reveal haunted her every day since. Anger that festered began brewing as screams erupted from the other children splashing about.

That's when another little boy splashed Cecilia in the eyes with a wave of water. "Hey, stop it," she screeched, wiping the water from her stinging eyes.

By the time she had regained her sight, the little boy had turned to splash other unsuspecting children. Without another thought, she leaped up halfway out of the water, bringing her hand down atop his bushy Afro, forcing him under the water. Cecilia held the boy there as he struggled to breathe. He tried snatching her hands away, but she had a good wad of his hair clenched tight in her fist. It wasn't until Ronald witnessed what was going on that the incident veered from the path of imminent danger.

He swam over just in time, grabbing her by the arm. "Stop it, Cecilia. What are you doing?" Ronald implored.

"He splashed me in the eyes on purpose," she explained as she released him from the death hold.

The boy came up, taking in a deep heave of oxygen. "Are you crazy? You could have killed me!"

"Come on, Cecilia. We're going home," Ronald replied, not wanting the dispute to go further than it already had.

They never talked about the incident after that, nor did their parents ever find out they had ventured around the corner.

In Ronald's mind, there was no doubt that Tom had committed horrible crimes against children, including his twin sister.

Chapter 37

Protecting What's His

Across town, Brenda and Gertrude stopped to have gyros for lunch on Woodward Avenue. Brenda was still pretty upset that Tiffany hadn't contacted her or come to the house. She started to consider the fact that maybe her cousin was hiding out from the police. "What if I never see her again?" Brenda feared as she bit into her sandwich, Ranch dripping down the side of her mouth.

"Girl, you can't have a shirt full of tears and Ranch," Gertrude remarked, reaching across the table to hand Brenda a napkin.

She accepted the offering. "I know. I'm a mess. I just don't know what to do without Tiffany in my life. All this time, they thought it was her that needed me, but, in fact, it was *me* that needed her. I just wish she would come home or at the very least call. I just need to know she's okay."

"I hope she calls too, Brenda. I sure miss her crazy butt."

They both chuckled a little, hoping for the best. Still, their smiles dimmed almost immediately.

"Don't worry, Brenda. She'll call. Just give it some time for the heat to die down."

Gertrude consoled her friend, having no idea that Daryl and Joey had walked through the doors.

The two men squeezed by other waiting customers to take a seat at the counter.

"That's them right there, ain't it?"

"Yeah, the one with the dreads is Tiffany's cousin."

"Well, Tiffany's the reason this bullshit fell on our doorstep, so guess who's going to pay the price first?"

They sat staring at the girls as the waitress walked up to deliver menus to them.

It was around eight o'clock at night when Ronald rang the doorbell as he stood on the front porch. In seconds, the door flew open. Gertrude didn't want whoever it was to ring again and risk waking Aunt May, who remained wound up over Peggy's disappearance. Gertrude had to make her a pot of chamomile tea just to get her to fall asleep.

"Ronald, what are you doing here? I wasn't expecting you." Gertrude fluffed her hair, hoping her curls weren't too frizzy.

"You don't have to do that. You like beautiful either way."

"Thank you," Gertrude replied, holding open the screen door for him. "Come inside."

Ronald did as she requested, wiping his feet on the mat as he entered. He kept his hands stuffed in the pockets of his jeans.

Gertrude's eyebrows wrinkled. "Are you nervous about something?"

"Why would you ask that?"

"You wiped your feet on the mat for one, and for two, your hands are in your pockets. You look bashful. So, what is it?"

"I think you should stay at my house tonight."

"Really? What brought this about?"

"We can talk about it once we get next door. Come on. Grab some pajamas. I'll wait right here," he instructed.

"Sir, yes, sir," Gertrude answered with a salute.

"I'm sorry. I didn't mean to boss you around like that. What I meant to say was, I'd love for you to stay the night with me."

Gertrude blushed. "I'd love to stay the night with you. I'll grab my things, and we can be on our way."

"Hurry up," he said jokingly.

"Boy," Gertrude sang, shaking a warning finger at him as she trotted off to do just as Ronald had instructed.

On her way by the kitchen, the phone rang. Gertrude snatched the cordless phone up off the wall. "Hello," she spoke softly as not to disturb her aunt.

"Hey, girl, it's me," Brenda answered on the other end of the line.

"Hey. What's going on? Have you heard from Tiffany?"

Brenda lugged the bag of garbage up the driveway with one hand while she held the cordless phone to her ear with the other. "No." She huffed in frustration. "Unfortunately, I haven't. I just wanted to call you to say thanks again for lunch. I really needed that. It helps to have someone to vent to."

She cooed. "Anytime, Queen. That's what I'm here for. We've got to help keep each other's crown straight."

"Tell Ronald I said thank you as well. He really went over and beyond by going with us. I just wish those guys were more helpful. Nothing but scum is what they are."

"I got *yo'* scum, bitch," a voice whispered as the hand with the dingy, worn, black sleeve wrapped around, covering her mouth to silence her. The trash can fell to the ground, spilling out smaller bags onto the driveway.

Brenda's heart pounded as her bulging eyes welled up with tears. Once they focused on Joey's face, she knew her chances were slim to none. She tried screaming, but Daryl's grip was so tight it nearly pushed some of her teeth through her closed lips. The phone in Brenda's hand was her only out. She swung an arm back over the opposite shoulder, cracking him atop his skull. Once, twice, then a third and final time before he was able to contain the blows.

His surroundings got hazy before Daryl had his fainting spell, which didn't matter because the moment he'd released her, the grip of the pistol in Joey's hand came crashing down against Brenda's head hard enough to knock her out instantly. He let the cordless phone hit the ground but caught her body as it fell.

"Can't damage the merchandise, Joey." Daryl winced from the pain as he tapped lightly at his forehead to check for signs of blood. She'd done a little more than penetrated the flesh, but it wasn't leaking by any means.

"Hello, Brenda? Are you there?" Gertrude called out from the other end of the telephone.

Daryl picked it up off the ground and, with gloved hands, placed it near but not on his ear. He let her call out to Brenda a few more times before hitting the power button to disconnect the call.

"I don't know what happened," Gertrude remarked as she hung up the phone.

The perplexed look on her face instantly spoke to the protector inside Ronald. "Maybe she got upset and decided she didn't want to talk anymore."

"You think so? I'm sure she's fine. Call back. See if she answers."

It made her feel better that Ronald wasn't making it seem as if she were exaggerating. Ronald truly cared, and Gertrude loved that about him.

She picked up the phone doing just as they'd discussed. Three times, in fact. Each time the phone just rang, then switched over to voicemail.

With a concerned expression, Gertrude turned to look Ronald in the eyes. "She's not answering."

"Let's ride by there. Come on." Ronald threw up his hand, ushering her to come along.

"Are you serious? That wouldn't be too much trouble? Or too intrusive on our part?"

"It's called being a concerned friend," Ronald rebutted, quelling her fears of being too much.

Gertrude rushed to his side, wrapping her arms around him as she leaned into the safety of his chest. Ronald embraced her, rubbing his hands across her back. It comforted him to know she needed him. That had been a compulsion of his since he was a boy. Dr. Martyr, his psychiatrist, had told him it was because of his inability to save his sister. Cecilia needed him, and he'd failed her. The incident created a need to be needed, a compulsion to save. It was his pleasure to ride by Brenda's house.

It took them about half an hour to get there. As they pulled into the driveway, the headlamps of Ronald's vehicle illuminated the bags of trash in the driveway. The mess was there, but no Brenda. "Is her side door open?" Gertrude rolled down her window, noticing the front wasn't.

"I don't know." Ronald shifted the car into park. "Let's go see," he instructed before popping off his seat belt.

They got out of the car, stepping over and between the bags of garbage. That's when Ronald's foot kicked it across the pavement. It was Brenda's cordless phone. Both looked at each other, equally concerned.

"Where the heck is she, Ronald?" Gertrude immediately began to panic.

"I don't know, baby. Calm down. We'll find her." He tried quelling her anxiety.

Gertrude tore off toward the side door. The screen was closed, but the main door had been left ajar.

Ronald rushed up beside her as she snatched at the brass handle to go inside. "Let me go first," he demanded, bringing her charge to a halt. "Just in case there is someone other than Brenda inside," he explained.

She thought the action noble of him. Gertrude was more than happy to step back, allowing her man to lead the way.

Moments later, a police squad car pulled up to Brenda's residence. They didn't know where she had disappeared to. They simply knew something wasn't right. Brenda had vanished just like Peggy and Tiffany.

Chapter 38

Opening Up

Gertrude sat, worried sick. Her shoulders slumped; her eyes drooped down along their outer edges. The light in her eyes had dimmed. She took the officer's card after they'd been questioned there at the scene, then turned to walk back to Ronald's car. He held his arm around her until he'd helped her into the van after opening her door. Gertrude was speechless the entire ride home. She gazed in silence at the waxing moon and scattered stars. *How can there be something so beautiful in a world that is so broken?* Her eyes glazed over.

Ronald stole glances at Gertrude from the corner of his eye. How can something so beautiful exist in a world so evil? he asked himself silently. He watched the hope drain from her resolve, wishing he could do something. But, quite frankly, at that point, Ronald had more important things to worry about. The fact that Brenda had disappeared was not a coincidence. He had to figure out how he'd keep Gertrude safe from the same people who were responsible for Brenda's disappearance.

Once they had returned home, Gertrude got out, following Ronald up the porch stairs.

"I'm still staying with you, right?" she inquired sheepishly.

His face softened. "I wouldn't have it any other way." Ronald unlocked the door, allowing Gertrude to slip inside first. "If you don't mind, I'd like to take a shower before I lie down. It's been a long day."

"I don't mind at all. Go ahead and wash up. Maybe I can find a movie for us. There's no way I can fall asleep right now."

Ronald locked the many dead bolts lining his door, one after the other.

"Why do you have so many locks?" Gertrude blurted inquisitively, unable to hold her tongue.

Ronald turned to face her. "The boogeyman doesn't knock. He slips right in when you're sleeping." He stepped closer. "Or washing little Billy in the tub. He comes when you least expect it. When your guard is down . . . Jogging up the pathway in the park with your headphones on. Not a care in the world . . . *That's* when he comes for you."

Although his reply wasn't what she'd expected, Gertrude understood what he'd meant by it. Considering everything that had happened with Peggy, Tiffany, and Brenda, she agreed they should take every measure possible to keep themselves safe.

Gertrude heard the shower water turn on as she fingered through the movies on the dresser to find one she thought they would both enjoy. The smitten young woman could hardly wait for her freshly cleaned king to be at her side. It was all she could think about, finding refuge in his arms.

Out of nowhere, that closet door creaked open, yet again, beckoning her closer. This time, Ronald had just gotten in the shower. Surely, she would have time to learn at least a little more about him while he lathered up.

Gertrude succumbed to temptation, heading right back to the mysterious chest in the closet. She kneeled in front of it, then squeezed the button, popping the latch to the side. To her surprise, it worked like a charm. *I can't believe it's that easy to open.* The curious young woman grabbed the first thing she touched. A photo album coated with a layer of dust was the first memory she had unearthed. Gertrude wiped her hands across the picture behind the plastic casing on the front to reveal their happy little family. Mr. and Mrs. Doolally depicted standing with 4-year-old Ronald and Cecilia out in front of the house on Gable Street captivated her.

She gushed at their precious family moment, eager to dig deeper into his past.

Gertrude flipped through more photos, each picture looking happier than the last. That was, until the little girl seemed to vanish from the endearing memories. The smiles of her remaining family had dimmed, their pos-tures sulking. Each photo looked more serious than the last. One of the photographs looked to be merely a pile of gray gravel stones. Gertrude flipped to the next page. Her eyes jutted in horror. A woman's corpse dangled from a rope tied to a metal post. It was the same woman in all the pictures with Ronald. Disturbed by the gruesome image, she read the caption on the old, fragile newspaper clipping, *"Buried Alive A Tragedy."* The picture of the property on the paper looked familiar to her. She had seen it just a moment ago, Gertrude recalled.

"A tragic accident on the border of two cities. Six-year-old Cecilia Doolally crushed to death at an impending residential site," she read further.

Something was different about the picture before. It looked like a Polaroid of the actual grounds where the little girl died. Before, wildflowers and a hammock decorated the property. Gertrude turned back to the photo, examining its details. As if it had appeared out of nowhere, she saw it. Cecilia's little fingers sticking up out of the pebbles.

Gertrude threw her hand up over parted lips, masking her shock. *What am I looking at? What kind of sick person keeps photos like this?* She tried telling herself there had to be a rational explanation for it . . . an explanation she'd soon hear since Ronald had just snuck up behind her.

Gertrude turned to face him, having felt his looming presence behind her.

"What are you doing with that?"

She stood before him with a look of fright in her eyes.

Ronald could tell her trust for him had begun to diminish.

"I'm sorry. I had no right to go through your things. I was just trying to know a little more about you."

"You do know you could just ask. I actually enjoy our conversations." Ronald reached for the album, and Gertrude flinched. His heart sank. He couldn't believe her reaction. "Why would you pull away from me like that? Are you afraid of me?" Ronald asked in the calmest voice he possibly could.

"I'm sorry. I didn't mean to—I'm not afraid. I promise. Just a little confused."

"Can I have the album back?" Ronald extended his hand. Gertrude handed it over to him, that time without hesitation. "What is it you're confused about?"

"Why do you have pictures of dead people in your photo album?" Her eyes moved to the book in his clutches.

He silently walked over to the bed, plopping down on the mattress. He rubbed his hands over his face in frustration. There was no easy way to tell Gertrude the story, and hell, quite frankly, he simply didn't have the desire to. If at all possible, the last thing Ronald wanted to do was lie to Gertrude. As he thought about it, he realized that was only the beginning. She'd eventually find something else, which would compel her to ask even more probing questions—the worst being, what had driven him to murder.

Ronald swallowed hard before opening the floodgates. "The woman hanging in the picture is my mother." He opened the album to the exact page depicting her death. "She committed suicide when I was a kid," he confessed, allowing Gertrude to get a good look at the photo. He remembered the nightmare as if it were yesterday.

It was three years after Cecelia's death that it happened. Young Ronald strolled up the sidewalk. Sheba was out front as they strutted up the street on their daily walk. Any neighbors standing nearby dispersed for fear of judgment from young Ronald and his faithful pooch, his reputation around the neighborhood having changed over the years. It seemed not a kid within a three-block radius of his home stepped out of line. Young Ronald enjoyed his newfound power. Not a person would dare challenge him. It remained one of the many benefits of his father being Sheriff Doolally of the Detroit Police Department.

The moment young Ronald had made it to the corner of his block, he could hear her calling out faintly. "Help me, Mommy. Please, help me." The voice sounded just like his twin, Cecelia. He picked up the pace, Sheba, still out front, leading the charge. Ronald finally made it to the yard, not having heard the cries for help a second time. Maybe he was mistaken, he concluded. There were times when he'd seen things unexplainable. Young Ronald trekked up the driveway, then through the fence into the backyard. The moment he closed the gate behind him, Sheba broke away, giving chase to a squirrel roaming out back. The canine barked viciously as she took off after the trespassing squirrel.

"Sheba, come back. I have to take off your leash," Young Ronald demanded, then waited there a moment for the faithful pooch to return. Suddenly, her barking transitioned from barking to whimpering. That's when he took off to see what was wrong with his best friend. White linen sheets and wool blankets hung on the clothesline behind their garage, making it difficult to see what Sheba was pawing at behind the sunbaked laundry. Young Ronald came closer, lifting the sheet to duck behind it. Turns out, laundry wasn't the only thing hanging on the line. Mrs. Doolally dangled by her neck, stiff as a board. His mother's house shoes slipped from her feet, leaving her pastel yellow manicured toes on display.

"Mommy! No! What did you do?" he screamed, attempting to lift her body from the rope tugging on her neck. "Oh no, Mama. Please, don't go. Don't go, Mama," he begged, sobbing into her wildflower-pattered housecoat.

Ronald held back his tears, not wanting to break down in front of Gertrude. Instead, he turned the page to the picture of Cecilia's exposed fingertips.

"The girl under the rocks is my twin sister, Cecilia. My father was the police sheriff at the time, and he'd been to hundreds of crime scenes, seen hundreds of corpses. For some reason, he believed that the soul of the individual is captured in the first picture taken after their death. He found the first pictures taken of my mother and sister's deaths and kept them here with him." Ronald closed the album. "That's why you see these gruesome photos here before you." He looked up at her, wondering what she thought of all he had divulged.

Chapter 39

The Chase Is On

Sleep that night was a tad uncomfortable. For Gertrude, it was because she had gotten caught snooping and caused Ronald unnecessary pain by asking him to unearth traumatic memories. She lay there with her eyes closed in silence yet fully awake. *How can he trust me now? Stupid Gertrude . . . Why can't I just mind my own business? I had no right to go through his things.* Gertrude silently chastised herself.

Ronald felt uneasy for fear of the collapse of his and Gertrude's relationship due to the traumatic memories he had drudged up from his past. He worried they were too much for Gertrude, too fast. Anticipating it would soon be over between them, Ronald rolled this way, then that, trying to get comfortable enough to drift off to sleep. To make matters worse, he pondered Brenda's whereabouts. What really happened to Brenda, and was Gertrude doomed to suffer the same fate was a major concern. He couldn't bear her simply disappearing from his life. There had to be something he could do.

Sitting in a parked car, staked out down the street from Ronald's house, was none other than that which he feared—Joey and Daryl. There to carry out the next phase of their plan, the two waited for the perfect moment.

"You think they're sleeping yet?" Joey turned to Daryl in the driver's seat of the van.

They'd been sitting outside the residence since following Ronald and Gertrude home from Brenda's house.
Knowing the area well, Daryl was able to lag further
behind when tailing the unsuspecting couple. He himself
had grown up on St. Louis, only two streets over from
Ronald's.

Daryl glanced down at his wristwatch. "Nah. Let's give
them some time to have sweet dreams. We'll sneak in
on them when they least expect it. Once they're sleeping,
snuggled warm in their blanket, feeling safe and sound,
that's when we'll get inside." Daryl snickered, assuming
what their fate beheld. "It'll be their last night together.
Hopefully, he gets him some."

"Get it while you can 'cause we're about to take it," Joey
remarked excitedly. "Thanks for letting me in on this
deal. I really needed the cash for school."

"I don't know why you do this anyway. You could be at
home living off Mama and Daddy."

"It ain't in me to be what they want me to be, to act like
they want me to act . . . I'm me, and that's all I can ever
be." Joey shrugged as he peered out the windshield for
any signs of movement in the Doolally house.

"You're my homeboy, either way."

"You trying to back out on me moving into the house?
I'll carry my own weight. Don't worry about Joey. I put in
work."

"Let's hope the 'merchandise' pays well," Daryl mumbled, then sucked at his teeth.

Joey pointed toward the lot on his right. "What do you
think that is?"

"I don't know. It looks like a memorial or garden or
something. All you need to know is it's something we
shouldn't be focused on right now," Daryl reminded him,
doing a quick course correction.

Out of nowhere, they spied the living room light illuminate.

Ronald rushed out the front door, then tore down the porch stairs on his way to the garage. By the time he opened the door, Gertrude was pushing through the screen door, searching for him.

"There she is. We should grab her now," Joey exclaimed.

Daryl motioned with his hand for Joey to tone it down. "Chill out, man. All in due time."

"Ronald? Ronald?" Gertrude called out to him as she crossed the threshold of the driveway. "What is he doing in there?" she said as she'd caught sight of the light in the garage.

He rearranged tools and whatnot to gain access to the space under his shelves, where he had stored the family's luggage. Ronald also needed keys. If he and Gertrude were going where he'd made up in his mind to take her, they would need access. He snatched the keys down off a nail in the wall.

"What's going on, Ronald?" Gertrude interrupted, seemingly having popped up from a deep sleep. She eyeballed the luggage at his side. "Are you going some-where?"

"I thought you were sleeping."

"Surprise." She held her arms outstretched. "What's with the luggage?"

"We can't stay here. I have a bad feeling about it. I think we should just go away for a few days and allow things to cool down." He wasn't sure if he was more panicked about her possibly leaving him or if it was the truck he had seen parked out in front of his house since they'd returned home.

"Ronald, where would we go? And do you really think it's that serious? What do you suppose will happen?"

"Come on, let me show you something." He ushered her out of the garage with him.

Meanwhile, Daryl and Joey waited for them to re-emerge from wherever they'd ducked off to. As the couple rushed up the driveway, suitcases in hand, the criminals slid further into their seats to not be discovered by the couple.

Ronald glanced over at the van, eyes only. The last thing he wanted was for Gertrude to be even more frightened. He led her back into the house, closing, then locking the door behind them. Gertrude tagged along as he rushed back to the bedroom, where he took out the album once more. "Do you see this picture?" he asked, opening it up to show her a photo of him, his sister, and parents. The vacation photo showcased them all smiles, modeling their swimsuits. "The cabin in the background belongs to my family. Well, to me now, since I'm all that's left."

Gertrude took a good look. "Is that where you want to take us? How far away is it?"

"It'll take about four hours to get there. Will you go with me?" He stared deeply into her vulnerable eyes.

"There's no other place I'd rather be, Ronald. What about Aunt May, though?"

"Leave her a note. Pretend you're on a girls' trip. That way, she won't worry about you," Ronald offered up the excuse.

Gertrude agreed, feeling it was a good idea. "I'll go write the note."

The last thing Joey and Daryl were expecting was for Gertrude and Ronald to resurface within minutes, luggage still in tow. The men watched as the lovebirds seemed to linger on the porch for a moment. "What the hell are they doing now?"

They finished up whatever they needed to before taking off to load into Ronald's conversion van. He watched the wicked men through his rearview mirror as he drove off into the night.

"Damn it. Do they ever sit still?" Daryl griped as he started his ignition, taking off in pursuit.

For most of the drive there, Gertrude slept. The car ride helped to ease her tensions. She felt safe with Ronald. The fact that he was taking her away made her feel even more protected. Her sleeping, Ronald saw to his advantage. It gave him time to think about how he would handle the situation at hand. He wondered what Joey and Daryl's endgame was, even though it didn't matter. His endgame meant neither one of them who had come to challenge him would walk away. All the reinforcements he needed glared at him through stone-gray eyes via his rearview mirror. She'd been there the entire time regardless of whether Ronald chose to acknowledge her. *"We'll make them pay, dear brother."*

Her words brought him comfort. He needed her now more than ever. Cecilia's insight, her intuition, her judgment—Ronald relied on it.

He glanced over at his side mirror. *Looks like they're coming,* he thought, knowing Cecilia understood.

"Let them come. Let them all come."

Chapter 40

His Turf

The sun rose as they pulled into Idlewild, Michigan, also referred to by the name "Black Eden." It was a place where their family had always felt comfortable, even back during segregation in the United States. Being a blended family back then was hard. Acceptance was slim, but in Idlewild, the experience felt very different. It was where many of the entertainers and intellectuals of the past vacationed during times of segregation. Dr. Daniel Hale Williams, C. J. Walker, W. E. B. DuBois, along with the crème de la crème of Black entertainers, had visited, some even purchasing property there.

Gertrude's eyes popped open as if she had fallen asleep accidentally. "Did I sleep the entire drive?" She yawned, stretching her arms and back to shake off any residual restlessness.

"You obviously needed it," Ronald remarked, happy she got some rest.

"I guess so. Worry can do that to you. I have to admit, though, if the ride didn't do it, this scenery would have." She stared out her passenger window at the line of trees, outhouses, diners, bars, and cabins in their vicinity. Just behind the houses on her right, Gertrude could see the crystal blue water. It was the bluest lake she had ever seen. Parts of it shimmered like diamonds when kissed by the sun. "*Idlewild,*" she read the sign at the side of the road. "Wow!" She shook her head in admiration of it all. "This is where your parents' cabin is?"

"This is where *my* cabin is," Ronald corrected her, hoping it scored him a few more brownie points.

"I've read about this place. I heard the man who performed the first successful open-heart surgery owns property here on the lake," she gushed.

"I'll show you his house once we're situated."

Her eyes sprang open wider. "Would you? That would be wonderful."

"Anything to keep your mind from worrying about what's not here with us," Ronald responded.

Gertrude felt a little guilty for allowing herself to be so happy when her friends could be suffering. But would being miserable make her situation any better, she argued with herself in silence. As she looked over at Ronald, she realized everything she wanted from him he'd done it, whether or not she'd expressed it. How was he so inexperienced in the relationship department yet treated her just as a partner should? His father couldn't have been that bad of a man to have raised a man so compassionate, she reasoned. Maybe he was just spiritual, Gertrude further deluded herself. *I should relax and enjoy these couple of days away.* After struggling with her feelings for a while, she had finally made up her mind. Gertrude trusted Ronald, no matter his family's quirks.

Cecilia's plan to alert Gertrude to the contents of Ronald's bedroom closet to cause the end to the couple's tryst had failed miserably. The backseat had become a cold place for her to sit with her brother drooling over Gertrude every waking second.

"Look at him," Cecilia's apparition simmered in rage. *"He's forgotten all about me."* Cecilia dreaded the day she'd fade completely. *"It's all your fault,"* the teary-eyed entity grimaced at Gertrude.

Ronald heard it but neglected to respond, of course, with Gertrude sitting there beside him. He could see the evil glare plastered on his sister's face. If nothing else, he knew it meant trouble for them all. For Gertrude, their trip showed promise. She smiled, taking in the beautiful scenery around them. Ronald, on the other hand, couldn't escape the dread and loneliness Cecilia was feeling. The coldness of her heart permeated the car, turning up the hairs on Ronald's arms.

Gertrude glanced over, sensing his slight discomfort. "Are you cold? Let me get your jacket."

Ronald shook his head no. "It's fine. You don't have to do that."

She followed her first mind—removed her seat belt, then reached into the backseat to retrieve his coat.

Before Ronald knew it, a dog had run out into the street, causing him to swerve into oncoming traffic to avoid the canine's demise. Tires squealed as approaching vehicles parted to make way for the burgundy conversion van. Gertrude's body was tossed right, then left, slamming against the front seats. It was the same dog that had caused Ronald to force Tiffany over the bridge. The snarling animal had shown up out of nowhere, fangs dripping with saliva, even larger and more muscular than it was that day in the alley. As Cecelia's rage grew, so had her pet's.

Ronald struggled but managed to gain control of his vehicle, pulling over on the side of the road.

Passersby laid into their horns. They had even shouted obscenities from their car windows at him. Each of them insignificant, so Ronald paid them no mind. Gertrude remained his priority.

"Oh my God, Gertrude, are you okay? Honey, I'm so sorry. I was trying not to hit the dog," he professed, helping her back into her seat.

Gertrude winced, stretching her injured arm in hopes of relieving any discomfort.

"What the hell is wrong with dude?" Daryl criticized as they drove by Ronald to pull over at the gas station about a tenth of a mile ahead. "Why the hell is he swerving all over the place?"

"Maybe there's trouble in paradise," Joey speculated from the passenger seat of Daryl's loner vehicle.

"I'm okay," Gertrude answered Ronald, shaking off the scare. "How long until we reach the cabin?"

"Provided we don't have another incident, I'd say about five minutes."

"Let's try to get there without incident then." She smiled, telling him all was well between them.

Ronald shifted into drive, then cruised back out on to the road.

Pulling up to the cabin pushed a surge of excitement through Gertrude's veins. She hopped down out of the van, doing a 360-degree turn. "Look at this. Oh, Ronald, it's so gorgeous and peaceful," she declared with a smile that spanned from ear to ear.

For Ronald, it felt eerie. He glanced at Cecelia still seated behind him before he stepped down out of the van. His emotions were a mixed bag, remembering some of the memories the place held. He kicked at the dirt and loose foliage under his feet as he recalled a time he'd done the same as a boy.

Chapter 41

Not so, Home Sweet Home

Young Ronald kicked at the soil and loose foliage and dirt under his feet, so much so he'd dug a small hole out on their fifteen-acre property.

His father walked up behind him out of nowhere. "We don't dig up what was once buried, son," Mr. Doolally remarked with a warning note in his voice.

Young Ronald stared down at the dirt beneath his feet and knew then he was standing on top of someone's grave. "Yes, Daddy," he responded with a look of indifference.

"Is everything okay, Ronald?" Gertrude inquired, interrupting his trip down memory lane as she'd noticed the slight disconnect.

He looked over at her as if he had never even drifted off, giving her his full attention. "Everything's fine. Let's go inside."

Daryl and Joey watched from the woods nearby as they took cover behind the trees. "When should we do it?" Joey inquired, his impatience nearly having reached its boiling point. He was desperate to make the money Daryl's deal would provide. In fact, his college education depended on it.

"As soon as night falls, we'll make our move." Daryl popped a squat on a downed log nearby, preparing to relax for a while.

"Well, shit. If we're waiting, let's not just sit around. We could at least go back into town and get something to eat. I'm starving."

"If they see us in town, they'll know it's us and assume what we're here to do."

"I guess we better make sure they don't see us then," Joey countered.

"All right. I guess I am a little hungry. We can get food, but other than that, we're lying low. The last thing we need is our mugs plastered all over town after this is all said and done. We keep our heads down and no small talk. Got it?"

Joey rubbed his aching tummy. "Whatever you feel is necessary is fine with me. I just need some meat and potatoes."

Back in Hamtramck, Tom was busy kicking himself. He had underestimated Ronald. Having finally validated the notion, the old man concluded there was much more to Ronald than which lay there on the surface. *What if he had something to do with Peggy's disappearance?* Tom bet his life on it that Ronald had more than a few skeletons in his closet, all of which he planned to uncover. Something had to get Ronald off his back, he hoped. He needed to talk to him one-on-one, even if it meant showing up at his house. If nothing else, it would tell Ronald that Tom was willing to go to great lengths to ensure his secret remained just that . . . secret.

He turned on his wipers as droplets of water scattered down across the asphalt before him. Lightning flashed, then thunder roared, foretelling a hell of a storm coming. Still, it wouldn't stop him from going after Ronald.

The old man pounded his wrinkled fist at Ronald's door. "Come on, boy. Answer the damn door," he griped under clinched teeth.

After a few seconds, he repeated the action, only then, he'd given the security gate a pounding much harder and more repetitive than the last. Still, no one answered. "I won't go another day under this punk's thumb," he vowed. Tom had one more idea up his sleeve, and he knew just the person to assist him.

The doorbell at Aunt May's chimed, rushing her from the kitchen to the front door.

"Tom. I wasn't expecting to see you today." The old woman straightened the silk bonnet covering her hair. "Do you have some information about Peggy?" She unlocked the screen door, allowing him entry.

"I haven't heard anything about Peggy. I was wondering if we were still doing the stakeout for your niece." Tom took in the scene, realizing she was alone. "Is she here?" he whispered.

"Actually, she left me some half-ass excuse for a letter, saying she was going on vacation with her little boyfriend." Aunt May snatched up the note from the side table by the door, handing it over to him.

"Idlewild, Michigan," he mumbled, taking a mental note of the address scribbled on the paper. "I guess when they get back, we'll resume our regularly scheduled programming." Tom played it off as if he weren't about to go after them as soon as he walked out the door.

"I guess so. They made it difficult to follow them now. Quite frankly, I think they're on to us anyway," May replied.

"Well, I've got some other errands to attend to, so I'll get back with ya." Tom passed the note over to May, then backed out the door faster than he'd rushed inside. "Fare thee well." He tipped his plaid beige and black fedora.

Chapter 42

Murderous Intentions

Back in Idlewild, Gertrude kept herself busy dusting the furniture while she emptied the contents of their suitcases to fill the drawers in one of the bedrooms, the one she and Ronald had chosen to sleep in.

He peeked his head into the room. "Hey, there."

"Hey," she replied, seemingly relaxed in the atmosphere.

"I'm going to go check on the grounds. Make sure nothing is out of place. It's been awhile since I've been back for maintenance."

"I can tell," Gertrude agreed, running her finger across the dresser to collect caked-on dust. She held her finger up, showing it to him. "I think I'll be able to keep myself busy."

"Oh, you're going to clean? Maybe we can go fishing later, and I can catch us some dinner," Ronald eagerly suggested.

Gertrude rushed over to the window to look out at the lake, "No one has ever caught me dinner before," she admitted excitedly. "I don't think I've ever even been fishing with anyone besides my father when I was a little girl."

"Well, you're in luck. I'll get the boat ready while I'm out there. It's right out back."

The back door of the cabin faced the lake, where his fishing boat was tied to the dock. Ronald left to do his duty as Gertrude waved him farewell, not taking her eyes off the figure she spied in the distance. She couldn't really make out what or who it was, but whatever was there emitted a trail of smoke that drifted out into the atmosphere.

Ronald climbed a tree stand on the property, checking the rifle hidden inside. He cocked the weapon to ensure it was loaded. Not only was it loaded but also, there sat a case of bullets in the corner he had pulled out to survey as well. The last thing he wanted to check while he was up there was the line running from the deer stand to another positioned a foot lower. Ronald pulled at it checking to see if it was secure. He yanked it a few more times until he was sure. Everything looked to be in order. Knowing they'd attack eventually, he'd taken every precaution. His intuition told him he had until nightfall. Even so, he kept his eyes peeled, just in case Daryl and Joey would decide to attack in broad daylight.

Next, he had to check the stone. Ronald trekked along, pushing through jutting tree limbs until he made it to a small clearing in the land, which, as opposed to stepping into, he walked around. Once he made it to the giant boulder, he crouched down low, leaned his back up against it, then pushed as hard as he could until the tunnel was revealed. It allowed him to walk underground along the property through a series of four tunnels that were interconnected. The maze of tunnels had two other exits, one that led back to the cabin, the other to the edge of his neighbor's property.

At the property line, a metal pig trough nearby reeked of guts. Even worse, it attracted a hoard of flies. His father thought it the perfect spot for an exit you'd want to keep hidden. Ronald had to go down to make sure the corridors were clear, and the lanterns along the wall were in working order. Once he flipped the breaker to turn on the electricity that ran throughout the tunnels, each one illuminated. Damp cement walls surrounded him, taking him back to the first time he had been taken there to see what the tunnels were really used for.

Young Ronald was 12 when his father enlisted him to help him cart the duffle bags to the end of one of the tunnels. The exhausted boy pulled with all his might, not wanting to let his father down. Sweat poured down onto the sides of his face from under the helmet with the glaring bulb attached above its brim. Mr. Doolally didn't want Ronald to get lost down there, so he made sure he kept a light on his person at all times.

"Come on, son. We've only a few hundred yards left," he coached Ronald to continue despite his weariness.

For young Ronald, it felt as if the bag weighed more than he did. The adolescent boy breathed a sigh of relief once they made it to the edge of the tunnel. Mr. Doolally wrapped the straps of the first duffel bag around his shoulders, carrying it up out of the hole on his back. Ronald heard the thud from the loud sack hitting the ground before his father climbed back down the metal rodlike steps to retrieve the other. Mr. Doolally repeated the action with the remaining duffle bag so that Ronald could easily climb the makeshift ladder. When they both made it to the top, his father pulled a long pair of black rubber gloves from the back pocket of his jeans, using them to cover his hands and forearms. He leaned over, unzipping one of the bags. The malodor funk that escaped was worse than that of the pig trough nearby. After that moment, though, they became one and the same.

Young Ronald forced back the pancakes he'd devoured that morning as they threatened to escape his esophagus. He hunched over, then rested his hands on his knees in an attempt to regain his composure. Sweat, dizziness, and nausea threatened to be his demise . . . for the time being, anyway.

"Man up, Ronald. It has to be done," Mr. Doolally remarked with a hand rested on his son's shoulder.

His father reached into the bag, then pulled out the bloody, detached extremity. He knew the arm belonged to someone. He simply had no idea who. It didn't matter either way. Whoever it was no longer existed. Mr. Doolally tossed the arm and the rest of the body parts into the pig trough, eradicating all evidence beyond the blood-soaked plastic lining the duffle bags.

Disposing of Daryl and Joey the old-fashioned way would come naturally to Ronald, having lived through the process many times throughout his years.

Chapter 43

Lying in Wait

Back in town, Joey and Daryl shopped for disguises while waiting for their food to be prepared. A local gas station had a section of sunglasses, fishing hats, and shorts sets that proudly represented the Mitten State. They picked out what they thought would keep them from being recognized. Joey pocketed the majority of it. Not having the money to cover his purchases never seemed to present too much of an issue. Much of the time, he relied on a five-finger discount.

"Man, I'm not down with just sitting in the woods. Not only is it uncomfortable, but I heard somebody talking about the wolves up here. Maybe we should rent a boat instead," Joey babbled on.

"*We?* You got that much cash to put up? I mean, that might actually be a good idea *if* we had money to be wasting on a boat."

Joey wasn't giving up that easy. "I don't mind. Take it out of my cut," he offered.

The offer sounded great to Daryl since he was unwilling to foot the entire bill. "All right, cool. Now, we can blend in with the rest of the beach bums," the grimy hooligan agreed as he tried on the pair of silver shades, then checked his reflection in the mirror on the display case.

Back at the cabin, Gertrude searched every space, eventually finding herself in one of the other bedrooms.

The ruffled bed skirt and canopy above the twin-sized bed told her that it more than likely was where Ronald's twin slept when she was alive.

Cecelia stared, outraged by the intrusion. She bellowed at Gertrude to leave. *"Get out of here,"* she roared. *"You have no right to be here."*

But it was no use. Cecelia's scream echoed for no one to hear. That gift remained for her twin brother, alone.

Nevertheless, an eerie feeling washed over Gertrude when she sat on the edge of Cecelia's bed. It was so intense that she hopped up, leaving the room in an instant as the prickly feeling crept up along the nape of her neck. She was not welcomed there, and the energy surrounding her told her as much. Gertrude closed the door on her way out.

By then, she wondered what Ronald was up to. His company sure would be comforting in that strange, old cabin. Gertrude headed for the front door in a hurry to find him. As her hand clutched the knob, the door flew open in her direction, almost crashing into her forehead. Lucky for her, the edge of her shoe held it at bay. It was Ronald who had pushed it open. He had finally returned from prepping the property for their visitors.

"Oh my God." She threw her hands up over her pounding chest. Gertrude was shocked by him returning just as she went to look for him. "We must be in sync," she exclaimed. "I was coming to look for you."

"Look no further"—Ronald held out his arms—"I've arrived. Are you ready to do some fishing?" He closed, then locked the door behind him.

"Are you ready to catch us some dinner? I could go for some lake bass or even some perch if we're cooking outside."

"What do you know about grilling outside?"

"I know that all I need is some lemon pepper, garlic, butter, and some Lawry's, and I can make any meal a delicacy."

"Okay, well, let me catch the fish first. I've got a few poles already in the boat. You should get a jacket, though. It may get windy because of the storm just passing."

"I'll go grab one. I need to get my book too." Gertrude headed back to the bedroom.

"There's the cabin." Daryl pointed out the Doolally's log cabin to Joey as they rowed by. Each rowed a paddle opposite the other to get them close enough to see any activity around the cabin. That's when they noticed Ronald and Gertrude boarding the sixteen-foot Starcraft fishing boat. It had a lifted Wise seat, which sat at the head of the craft. The lower seat sat stationed at the back of the boat for the person steering the craft. "I think that's them, getting in that boat."

"Have a seat at the throne," Ronald directed Gertrude to the captain's chair.

"Oh no, my King. That chair is for you. I don't feel comfortable riding up that high in the air." Gertrude tugged down at her life jacket as it pushed up on her chin.

"So, I take it you know how to steer a boat?"

"We'll see. My crash course starts now, I guess." Gertrude took her seat at the rear.

Ronald then proceeded to give her the rundown on how to steer the boat.

"It works like a car in reverse. If you move the tiller to the left, the front of the boat will go right. If you move the tiller to the right, the front of your boat will go left. It's as simple as that."

She seemed to grasp the concept of what he was saying.

"I think I can handle that," Gertrude nodded, confident she could pull off the task at hand.

After Ronald got his pole and then took his place in the elevated chair, Gertrude took off into the open water like a pro.

He smiled proudly. "That's my girl." Ronald cast his line out into the water, and it almost felt like a real vacation. The temptation to forget about the two men in the boat who had followed them nearly won out. Fishing was always a time of true peace and enjoyment for Ronald. He'd have to find a way to make it so, considering the peculiar circumstances they were in. Gertrude, being none the wiser, depended on it. The fact that Daryl and Joey had not made a move yet confirmed to Ronald what he had surmised. The pair's plan required they wait until nightfall to strike, assured of the fact that they couldn't take him in the daylight.

Ronald and Gertrude fished for hours out on the peaceful lake. There were only, at most, five other boats out on the large, winding lake. With plenty of room to spread out, Gertrude felt like they were practically alone out there.

"Ronald?" Gertrude broke the silence that had blanketed them.

"Yes, Gertrude."

"Don't you get lonely, not having any family or friends around?"

Although Ronald did miss human interaction, he was never alone. Not even at that moment were they alone. Cecelia sat right at the center of the boat, glaring out at Daryl and Joey, who floated hundreds of yards away.

"I learned not to get lonely or bored at a very young age. Losing my twin sister, leaving me as the only surviving child, forced me to get used to being by myself. I've been an only child since first grade."

"I can't imagine how hard it must have been for you to lose your twin and your mother all within a few years. I'm sorry you had to go through that. I'm sorry your sister had to go through that. She didn't deserve to have her life cut short. When things like that happen, it pushes me to search for the silver lining."

"I'm curious. What would the silver lining be in my situation?" Ronald wondered how she could put a positive spin on his mother and sister's deaths.

"They're your guardian angels now. They protect you from harm. When there's no one else to turn to, you should talk to them. They'll give you a sign. My aunt May talks to her late husband all the time. She swears he's there when she speaks to him."

Ronald chuckled a little. "I always thought she was a little crazy."

"I'm serious, Ronald," Gertrude swatted playfully. "They're your guardian angels. Have you ever tried talking to them?" her voice turned serious.

Gertrude wondered just how much of his father's practices he had picked up. She didn't see it as misleading him, simply using what experience she had to learn more. It was how she justified it.

Ronald stopped reeling in the line to look Gertrude in the eye. "It doesn't frighten you, spirits and all that other supernatural stuff?"

"Nah . . . I read books. I've read about my heritage. My grandmother, much like her mother, practiced vodun. She was from Ghana."

"*I smell a liar. Her grandmother was from the gutter,*" Cecilia spouted. "*Go on, brother, tell her about the boat of bandits waiting to kill you two once you're back on land.*"

"What if I don't like what they are saying? Then what?" he replied to Gertrude's question, ignoring his sister completely.

"You know, I never thought about that." Her face wrinkled in contemplation of his inquiry.

"I'll tell you what. How about you let me worry about coping with my family's death? Which, might I add, was some time ago. And I mean that in the nicest way possible."

Gertrude dropped her eyes in shame. "I apologize. I shouldn't have overstepped."

Ronald shrugged it off. "It's not the end of the world."

"Coward." Cecelia barked at him before she vanished from view.

Up until that point in life, Ronald had lost every person dear to him. There was no way in hell he was going to let Daryl and Joey take Gertrude away from him. They had shown up at the wrong place and the right time as far as he was concerned. Much like his rifle in the tree stand, Ronald was cocked and ready. "I think instead of grilling, you should cook inside. I could go for some fried bass. I haven't had cornmeal-fried bass in years."

"You're in luck." Gertrude raised her chin, brandishing a wounded smile. Even though she felt sore about over-stepping her boundaries, she knew it was a faux pas he would soon forget after tasting the dinner she'd whip up for them.

"Let me guess. You'll make the best fried bass I've ever tasted."

Gertrude snickered. "That sounds about right."

"Well, I think about an hour more, and we'll have plenty of fish to fill us up for dinner."

"Can we go to the store in town and get some potatoes? I didn't see any at the cabin."

Just then, something tugged at his line. "Uh-oh." Ronald jerked up on his rod. "I got something," he proclaimed as he began reeling it in. "If this is as big as it feels, we might be able to stop now and head into town."

"Look at that fish he just caught," Joey gawked through a mini pair of binoculars he'd swiped from the souvenir station.

Daryl snatched the binoculars from his clutches. "We should show up for dinner. Get a sample of what Miss Lady's got before we trade her off." If Daryl's intentions weren't bad enough at first, their wait definitely made it much worse.

Another couple of hours passed as the translucent waters beneath them transitioned to opaque.

Ronald looked over at Gertrude engrossed in the book she'd brought along, *Twisted Entrapment,* by N'Tyse. She had barely taken her eyes off the pages to look out at the scenery. Still, he appreciated the fact that she had refrained from rushing him, as he assumed the typical woman would. Gertrude truly enjoyed time out on the boat with Ronald. But alas, they couldn't stay in that perfectly harmonious state. It was time to get back to reality, him from those waters and her out of the pages of the erotic fiction she had found herself swallowed up by.

"It's about time to head in," Ronald spoke up, stealing her attention away from the read.

"I'm ready if you are."

"Take us home, Captain," Ronald instructed, prompting Gertrude to grab the tiller, then head for the shore.

Ronald climbed out first, unloading their catch for the day, before tying the boat to the launch deck on his property. "Take my hand, baby." He extended his right hand to help lift her out of the boat and onto the dock.

She accepted the kind gesture as she stepped up onto the platform. "Thank you."

"The pleasure is all mine." Ronald picked up his line of six fish, then ushered her forward to head for the cabin. "Come on. We should get home."

She smiled, putting stock into the fact that he had referred to it as such. The words "we" and "home" in the same sentence sounded like music to her ears.

Chapter 44

Multiple Enemies

At the local market down the road, they were able to pick up the few things on Gertrude's list to make their fish fry complete. They grabbed a sack of potatoes, a bag of onions, a few bell peppers, along with the cornmeal. The box of pink wine on the shelf would have to do since Gertrude wasn't fond of the taste of beer. She and Ronald gathered up the rest of their items, then headed to the register.

"I wonder if they have a restroom here." She looked around in desperation, her bladder nearly ready to explode.

"Can you hold it until we get back? We're next in line."

"I'm sorry. I've been holding it since the lake. I should have gone before we came," Gertrude explained.

"You'll need this key, ma'am." The older woman behind the cash register interrupted, holding it out for one of them to accept.

Gertrude stepped up, snagging the key as she read the name tag on the woman's lapel. "Thank you so much, Bernadette," she expressed with gratitude.

"It's just outside on the side of the building."

It was at that moment that Ronald started to panic. Knowing the bad guys were out there watching them, waiting for a slip up, he worried about Gertrude being out of his sight and right out in the open. He walked her to the door, then watched as she bent the corner at the side of the building.

"Sir, are you going to pay for your items?" the cashier called out to Ronald to rush him back to the register.

He glanced at the cashier. Then on second thought, he turned back to look where he'd expected Gertrude to resurface. Of course, she wasn't there, but neither were any other cars, and more importantly, the van that had followed them to Idlewild.

Time dragged. The analog clock above the freezers ticked slow but loud. Kids jumping rope across the street in front of the motel moved in slow motion. Even the vehicles driving by seemed to take more time than needed to pass.

What's taking her so long?

"Sir, I need to clear my register. She's a big girl. I'm sure she'll be okay for a minute," the lonely, middle-aged woman complained, secretly jealous of the attention Ronald had shown Gertrude. Bernadette wished she had something more than a cat and bucket of butter pecan ice cream to go home to. She sucked at her brown, nicotine-tarnished teeth, gawking at him as he drew near.

"That'll be sixteen sixty-nine," she smirked, having found humor in the amount of change required for his order.

Ronald pulled a twenty from his pocket, slapped it down on the counter, then grabbed his bags. "Keep the change."

It was a nice gesture, him leaving extra cash, but something told Bernadette that Ronald wasn't giving it to be kind.

He rushed outside, headed for the restrooms. Gertrude plowed into him as he rounded the corner.

"Oh my God," a startled Gertrude shouted. Her body bounced off his, causing her to stagger backward, nearly losing her footing. Had it not been for Ronald, who grabbed her arm to stabilize her, she probably would have landed smack down on the pavement.

"I'm sorry. You took so long. I didn't know if something had happened."

"I'm okay, Ronald." She looked down, seeing he had purchased their items. "Are you ready to go?"

He looked around to be sure there was no danger in the immediate vicinity. "I'm ready."

Once they got back to the cabin, Gertrude put on a record, Barry White. Ronald stood in the doorway of the bedroom, having gotten dressed in his coveralls. He watched her dance across the kitchen, snatching up the three-pound sack of potatoes along with a knife to cut them. Her second glass of wine had loosened her up, putting her in a mood more jovial than he had ever seen before. It was nice to see someone truly happy, especially someone he held so dear. If only he didn't have to step out to commit murder, that night would have been perfect.

Gertrude turned, catching him amid admiration of her essence. "What are you staring at? See something you like?" she uttered with a twist in her hips. One side of her brows lifted over bedroom eyes.

"Very much so," Ronald admitted yet remained as cool as a cucumber. "But I should get to cleaning this fish. It's already dark out. It'll be hard to see where I'm gutting." He tossed and spun the blade round in his hand.

"You're pretty good with your hands. I have all the confidence in the world in you." She walked toward him at the pace of a lioness stalking prey.

Ronald grinned, surmising what she considered his hands were pretty good at. He certainly planned to test the theory that night.

"Give me about thirty minutes or so." He kissed Gertrude atop her forehead, then lifted her mouth to his with a finger under her chin. The space between her thighs moistened. Ronald tasted her full, soft lips with his tongue before theirs intertwined. She would have been content with the kiss never ending. So much so that when he leaned back, Gertrude remained frozen in a transient state, lost in his kiss.

"Would you like for me to grab some wood for a fire?" he smiled, witnessing her drift back to reality.

Oh, how romantic, she gushed silently. "A fire sounds perfect."

"I may need an ax then."

Chapter 45

The Element of Surprise

Daryl and Joey watched from the woods nearby. Between the two of them, they had one gun, which stayed in Daryl's possession. The mission was to kill Ronald and kidnap Gertrude. After selling Brenda and Gertrude to the buyer, they wouldn't have to worry about money for at least a couple of months. She and Brenda were to be sold to Daryl's new business contact from out of town. He liked the fact that he didn't have to do it often because it paid so well. Money had made Daryl the worst of the worst. Nothing was above it, and nothing stood in his way of it. He liked it quick and easy. Even so, it wasn't money that was the root of his evil.

Joey was still learning. Being out on his own and up from under the watchful eyes of his parents, he'd fallen prey to the wolves and since had become one of the pack. He didn't care what would happen to Brenda or Gertrude after getting rid of them. The sooner they got it over with, the better. As far as he was concerned, the job would only give him more clout out in the streets.

"Ole girl is probably up by now."

"It don't matter. She's tied up anyway," Daryl said.

"What if she has to use the bathr—?"

Daryl pressed his finger to his lips, halting Joey's rebuttal. "What the fuck is that?"

The music blasted from the outside speakers. "*My darling, I can't get enough of your love, baby.*" Barry White was loud enough for even the neighbors to hear.

That's when out of nowhere, the arrow pierced the tree Joey had taken cover behind. He screamed, taking off into the dark forest.

Inside, Gertrude sashayed across the kitchen, knowing the same tune playing for her, played for Ronald. If she only knew he was amid the act of murder, her two-step might not have been so graceful.

Outside, the ax Ronald planned to chop wood with ended up ingrained in the tree that provided cover for Daryl. "What the fuck?" Daryl screamed as he fired off into the woods in retaliation for the near-ax murder he had been subject to. "Joey! Come back. We've gotta stand our ground."

He tried swaying his cowardly friend, but it was too late. Joey had booked it off into the wilderness with nothing but the crescent moon lighting his path. Up ahead, the moon shined bright where he saw a clearing among the trees. He pushed through sharp twigs and hopped over downed logs to make it there . . . to make it to the point where his world turned upside down.

"Help me," Joey yelped, his body being yanked into the air like a rag doll. The rope had snatched at his ankles, pulling his feet up into the air before some netting cocooned him. Joey tried to scream again, but the combination of hanging upside down, along with inhaling the chloroform-soaked rope that pressed against his face, caused him to pass out within a minute.

One down, one to go. Ronald trekked through the woods, making his way to the tree stand for a better view, one where he had full vantage of his property. There would be nowhere Daryl could hide. Ronald's boot caught the first rung on the ladder against the tree trunk, then each after that in a flash.

Meanwhile, Daryl had found a toppled-over log to lie behind. It would be hard to see him wedged there between the tree and the dead foliage . . . he hoped. A bright strobe of light came closer, threatening to reveal Daryl's hiding place. He'd be out in the open. Target practice, he feared, sticking his face back down into the leaves.

That's when everything had gone black. Ronald's light was blown. Someone shooting from below had taken it out with one bullet. Daryl got up, hoping to take off far beyond where the light could illuminate, should it come searching for him again.

Ronald grabbed hold of his trembling arm. "Someone else is here, sister," he whispered. He could feel it in his bones. He scooped up his rifle from the corner of the tree house, ready to protect his property. The pressure to keep Gertrude safe and none the wiser had become more complicated than he thought.

Then, suddenly, *chop!* A blade sliced through the rope holding his first capture, sending Joey's body plummeting toward the earth beneath him. His skull cracked open upon crashing into the ground. He'd hemorrhaged and died without even waking from his chloroform-induced coma. And although he was no saint, a crimson halo formed atop the leaves under his head as he slowly bled out.

Hell-bent on finding them all, Ronald trekked through the darkness, though not lost. Ronald Doolally knew those woods well, from the trees, standing or downed, to the ground, grassy or soiled. But what he felt then under the soles of his shoe was damp earth. His boot kicked the corpse lying limp on the leaves, at which point a surge of reassurance coursed through his veins. Ronald harbored no doubt. He would kill them all. The question was, who had killed Joey?

On the other hand, Tom had Ronald in his sights through the set of infrared goggles strapped around his head. The old man was headed right for him. He wanted Ronald to see his face before his end. He made his way clear through the trees on Ronald's right. But just as he got close enough to call out to him in full view, he saw the butt of the gun crash down atop Ronald's head, sending his body crashing to the ground.

"I got you now, muthafucka." Daryl relished his capture. He'd flanked Ronald on the left, catching him unaware.

"How does it feel to get ambushed in your own yard?" Daryl aimed his weapon down at Ronald, at which point he heard the twig snap. "Who's there?" He held the gun up in defense, then quickly reminded himself of his comrade. He lowered the gun just a little so that either one of them, the newcomer or Ronald, could feel the bullet should he choose to pull the trigger. "Joey, come on out, man. I got him," Daryl professed, brandishing a sly grin.

Bit by bit, his face started to come into view as he took off his binoculars to speak. "I'm no threat to ya. Go on and do your business, then go on your way," Tom instructed.

Daryl's eyes squinted to see what he was already sure he had heard. That groggy-like robot tone in his voice . . . Those words. How could he ever forget? Daryl's heart pounded as the recollection bored a hole into his brain.

Young Daryl chased his football up the street into the neighbor's yard. When he scooped it up, that's when his eyes fell upon the man with smoke leaking from a hole in his neck. The man smiled at the adolescent boy, then pulled a candy bar from his pocket.

Young Daryl's eyes bucked. Chocolate bars were his favorite.

"Go on, take it. I'm no threat to ya."

Daryl wanted to trust the man. So much so that he did. Daryl headed up the porch, accepting the sweet treat with graciousness. "Thank you so much, mister."
He held the candy in his hands as if it were a bar of gold.

"There's more inside. Just grab a handful off the table,"
the man instructed as he casually puffed his cigarette.

A happy little boy went into Tom Swine's home.

Tom barely recognized the damaged man standing before him, but what he did find familiar was the look in Daryl's eyes. It was the same look they had all given him, every one of his victims at one point in time. Tom knew it well. With his weapon cocked and ready to fire, Tom didn't waste another second. He pulled the trigger on the off chance Daryl was one of the children he had come across and molested in his travels. However, to Daryl's advantage, Tom's goggles weren't over his eyes, making him less of a crack shot. Daryl attempted to take off into the darkness when Ronald grabbed hold of his foot, taking him to the ground. Once he was down, Ronald shoved the tip of the rifle against Daryl's chin, then fired, blowing off part of his skull and brains.

By the time Tom got his binoculars down and in place, Ronald had him dead in his sights. Even so, Tom was an old-timer, meaning he had more than a few tricks up his sleeve. He clicked on the flashlight strapped to his jacket, shining directly into Ronald's eyes.

"Shit." Ronald threw his hand up, shielding the light from blinding him.

The diversion gave the old man the time he needed to make his escape. "Maybe next time." Tom waved his white flag in retreat as he disappeared into the darkness.

Ronald knew where to find him, so he allowed him to slip away. He then focused on getting Daryl and Joey's bodies underground just in case Tom decided to call the cops. Plus, he still had to grab the wood from out back, then gut the fish. He would take care of the rest once Gertrude was fast asleep.

The moment Ronald crossed the threshold, Gertrude rushed into his arms. "Did you hear all that shooting?" she asked nervously.

"I did. Hopefully, somebody got a nice buck," Ronald answered, affirming her inquiry with a nonchalant nod of his head.

Two murders and not a spec of blood on him. Gertrude rubbed at his chest as he had finally returned home with their catch.

She nestled closer to him. "I've missed you."

Ronald dropped the chopped wood to the floor alongside him, pulling her in to allow the embrace. "Are you ready for me to light your fire?" he smiled, brandishing a sly grin.

Gertrude could tell he was merely setting the tone. "Indeed, I am, Mr. Doolally." She lifted to her tiptoes to kiss his strawberry-freckled lips, figuring she would usher things along.

That night, they made love on the bearskin rug in front of the fireplace as the gray wolves feasted on scattered, fragmented pieces of Daryl's skull.

Chapter 46

Freed from Afar

Early the next morning, the authorities were kicking down the door at Daryl's house. The anonymous call complained about gunshots fired inside the residence, which warranted a squad of police vehicles to the scene. Barnes and Alanis hung back while they allowed the tactical team to gain access. After kicking the door down, a mess of officers dressed in riot gear rushed inside the nearly empty abode.

Outside, Alanis griped that it was probably a false alarm and how their man-hours should be used for more constructive things. She argued they should have been working on the Columbus case.

Barnes looked up, searching his mind to find a rebuttal, which instantly came once he saw her walk out the front door of that house. It was Brenda. The lone survivor of Daryl's victims. The terrified woman quivered as if she were a cowering child, having been bound, gagged, kidnapped, then held against her will for hours. Barnes pointed, alerting Alanis to the emerging victim.

Brenda closed her eyes and thanked God once she saw the light of day. She held tight to the officer's hand, who helped to steady her as she stepped out onto the porch, tears pouring down her cheeks. She couldn't help but wonder if her cousin had suffered the same fate and not lived to tell the story. Brenda had overheard Daryl and Joey discussing the "sale" before dropping her off at the house. Ever since then, she had agonized about the torture and sexual abuse she would endure.

But luckily, Brenda was alive. She opened her lids, praising the Lord that she'd been spared, that she'd been given another chance to live a life worth living. Never again would she ever take anything for granted, her life, most importantly.

"Let's allow one of the paramedics to check her out before we take her to the station," Detective Barnes ordered as he approached with a blanket intended for wrapping over Brenda's shoulders.

Once they got her down to the station, Detective Barnes allowed Alanis to head up the questioning since Brenda was a woman who had recently been afflicted and preyed upon by men.

"Sweetheart, my name is Detective Alanis. I'm here to figure out who did this to you. Unless you already know who it was, that is. Do you have any idea who grabbed you?"

"I don't know where to start," Brenda admitted, shaking her head in despair.

"How about you start by telling us how you ended up at that house?"

A moment of silence passed, Brenda still silent, in tears.

Detective Alanis placed a hand atop hers, resting on the table between them. "It's okay. You're in a safe place now," she assured the frightened young woman.

Sure, there were things Brenda didn't want them to know. The fact remained she had to tell them something. She needed those men locked up. Brenda cleared her throat, then began her version of the story. "I was holding the phone to my ear with one hand, talking to one of my friends. And with the other hand, I was taking the trash to the front yard. There were two of them. One of them

was white. The other one looked just like you and me."
She looked up at Detective Barnes, her face oozing with
utter disappointment.

Barnes couldn't pretend her confession didn't bother
him. He could see how much it hurt her to be treated the
way she had by someone who shared the same skin color
she did, someone who had shared the same struggle.

Barnes mashed his lips together, having no answer for
her silent plea.

"The Black guy grabbed me first. I tried my best to fight
him off. I even hit him with my phone on the head a few
times. It had to have hurt him a little, at least. Anyway,
that's the last thing I remember before waking up tied
and gagged on the basement floor of that hellhole."

"Would you happen to know who these men are?"
Detective Alanis chimed in.

Brenda didn't want to tell them about her cousin
Tiffany for fear of them connecting her to the mall distur-
bance. She also didn't want them to know that Gertrude,
Ronald, and she had driven over to the house to confront
them. She had to tread a very thin line.

"I know one of them from school. His name is Joey. We
attend Wayne State University downtown."

Detective Alanis turned to her partner. "That's how
they must have picked her out. We need to cross-reference any missing women with Wayne State University
students. If these guys have been picking off girls from
the school, we're damn sure about to find out."

Chapter 47

The Cleanup

Between last night and that morning, Ronald had completed the task of getting rid of Joey and Daryl's bodies. The hogs would ensure not a spec of them remained. As far as their van went, Ronald made sure to park it where no one would ever find it. Even if they had, it was unrecognizable. That was one of the benefits of living in Northern Michigan. You could burn practically anything that wasn't a house, and no one would bat an eyelash.

All that morning, Gertrude worried about Brenda. Where was she, and what had happened to her? It's true; she was having the time of her life with Ronald. It was as if they were a married couple the way they had carried on for the last twenty-four hours. Even still, she wondered what fate her friend suffered.

Ronald could see something was amiss when he walked back inside from tying up some loose ends. She hadn't turned to him with a smile, showcasing those irresistible dimples. Gertrude had no cute little words or phrases to woo him. Her mind had wandered elsewhere, and Ronald could tell whatever was bothering her would not be a subject easily cast off. He was doubtful the dishes could have been so enjoyable that Gertrude couldn't bother to turn to greet him as he returned. He had to get to the bottom of the situation, and sooner rather than later. He needed to know Gertrude was with him, that she wanted what they had created as much as he did.

"Come here, sweetheart." He grabbed her by the hand, leading her from the sink filled with pots and pans to the worn plaid sofa in the living room.

Gertrude followed him in silence, then took a seat where Ronald had instructed.

"Why are you pouting? Tell me what's wrong. Did I do something?"

"Not at all. You're perfect, actually. It makes me feel kind of guilty, being here with you, having the time of my dreams while my friend and her sister are missing. I just can't help feeling like there is something more I should be doing other than running scared." Gertrude dropped her head, fearing she had disappointed Ronald.

"Well, Gertrude, if that's the way you feel, you should do something about it."

"What are you saying?" she looked up in hopes he truly understood.

Ronald cut right to the chase. "Would you like for me to take you home?"

"Can I stay with you?" Gertrude's brows wrinkled as if she assumed she was asking too much.

Ronald quickly set the record straight. "I wouldn't have it any other way."

Gertrude let out a huge sigh of relief, having no idea that on the inside, Ronald was doing the very same thing. He had business to attend to, and Tom was at the top of his list of priorities. Ronald needed to get back and hash things out between them. In other words, kill the old man and ditch any evidence that would prove he had even been murdered.

"How about we have breakfast? I'll tidy up the grounds around here, and then we'll head back to the city. I can have you home by three o'clock."

Gertrude gushed. "That sounds perfect. I'll whip up something for breakfast. Thank you so much for understanding, Ronald."

"You don't have to thank me, Gertrude. Compassion should be a simple courtesy."

Albeit it was wishful thinking on Ronald's part, to Gertrude, his words rang true. "You're wise beyond your years, Mr. Doolally."

You have no idea, Ronald thought as he leaned in to kiss her tenderly.

While Gertrude prepared to head home, Brenda couldn't wait to tell her and Ronald what had happened when their phone call ended abruptly. She knew Ronald would be interested to know what they'd done. Plus, she had to make sure the same thing didn't happen to Gertrude. Brenda pounded at the screen door, in addition to giving the doorbell a ringing or two. The second was what had sent Aunt May rushing to the door.

She unlocked, then flung open the door. "What has gotten into you, girl? Ringing and pounding on my door like the authorities. You nearly gave me a heart attack."

Aunt May's brief tirade caused Brenda to feel the weight of her mistake instantly. But just as she went to profess her apologies, Aunt May opened the screen door, having spied the bruise at the top of Brenda's skull along her hairline.

"Some little knot-head boy laid hands on you, I see."

"It's not what you think."

"Well, you come on inside here and let me know what it is I should think. Close and lock the door behind you. I don't live in a barn," the old woman demanded as she turned to head for her chair in front of the television.

"Now, usually, I don't do this. But since Gertrude isn't home during your time of need, I'll step in for a little while." Aunt May pulled the remote from her robe, muting Ricki Lake, then inched her way down into her seat. The old woman grunted as she worked out the kinks in her aching bones. "So, tell me," she said, finally getting comfortable, "who did that to your face?"

"My cousin got mixed up with a group of bad people. Of course, me, being the older cousin, I went to pick her up. Set things straight. Let's just say her so-called friends didn't appreciate it."

"Oh, my Lord, you poor thing. Go on in the kitchen and get some ice for your head. The Ziploc bags are in the cupboard. Clean clothes are in the hallway closet. You've got to get that knot down."

Brenda got up to do as she'd been told. Granted, she was no Gertrude, but Aunt May's age made her almost as good, if not better, to talk to. The girl clearly needed a shoulder to cry on—someone she could open up to about all that had transpired. Yet, Brenda remained apprehensive. She wasn't sure how much of the story Gertrude would want her Aunt May privy to. The last thing she wanted to do was cause trouble or get Gertrude kicked out of her aunt's house. Brenda had a feeling Aunt May wouldn't appreciate her niece getting involved in Tiffany's mess. *I really need my friend right now,* Brenda pouted as she searched the kitchen cupboard.

That day, the authorities had finally decided to follow up on the damage to the party store. Detectives Barnes and Alanis went to check it out since no one else had bothered to follow up on the call. Nadi, the party store owner, had befriended Barnes some years back, so when no one showed up to take a statement, he called in a favor.

"Nadi, my man," Detective Barnes greeted the man behind the counter as he entered the store behind his partner, "how's it going?"

"Better, now that you two are here," Nadi Salem replied with a goofy grin. Nadi was proud to say he had a good friend who worked on the police force. In his mind, it awarded him some sort of clout. It certainly boosted his ego, if nothing else.

"So, what's this I hear about vandals?"

Nadi unlocked the door, then pushed it open, giving them access behind the counter. "Come on back. I'll show you.

"You can't really get a good look at their faces on the tape, but I still wanted to make a report, just in case it happens again. I can't have these kids vandalizing and robbing my store. I'll never stay in business," he vented.

"I'm sorry this happened to you, Nadi. It's a shame youngsters these days have no respect for property, their elders, or themselves if you ask me."

Detective Barnes reviewed the video along with his partner, then took the report. Like the owner had explained, you couldn't get a clear view of the delinquents' faces on camera, but the mere fact that they'd viewed it, and he was able to take his statement, gave Nadi the peace of mind he needed.

His old pal promised to keep a lookout for any other cases that may come across his desk involving vandals. Mr. Salem held out hope that maybe someone would apprehend the hooligans the next time they decided to steal from hardworking citizens.

Chapter 48

Plotting His Demise

Meanwhile, Tom obsessed about what pain he wanted to inflict on Ronald and how he would go about committing the act. Seeing Daryl there had thrown him a real curveball. Since the surprise encounter, Tom had remembered the little boy who'd come inside for a chocolate bar that fateful day long ago. He reasoned, maybe it was best Daryl had been killed, especially since he'd run into him again after all those years. The look on Daryl's face told Tom he hadn't blocked out the traumatic memory, like most. As he pondered in hindsight, things were looking up. Daryl was dead, and Tom wasn't the one who'd pulled the trigger, which meant he was in the clear. The only person that knew of his despicable acts besides his victims was Ronald. Tom couldn't, for the life of him, figure out how he knew what had happened all those years ago.

Tom knew he had twice as much on Ronald than Ronald had on him. Hopefully, it would be enough to keep Ronald's mouth shut. All he needed to do was talk to him one-on-one. He remained optimistic that he could sway the angered brother.

Just as Ronald promised, he had gotten Gertrude home by three o'clock. She turned to her love as he made a right on to their street—her mind thanking him, while her body simultaneously craved him. Gertrude caught her bottom lip in her teeth. "I want you to know I had a wonderful time with you. The best I've ever had with anyone."

"I'm glad you enjoyed yourself. And just so you know, I feel the same way."

It wasn't the declaration of everlasting love she would have preferred, yet it was enough to keep her heart fluttering. In an instant, the look of lust plastered across her face turned to shock. "Is that Brenda's car in the driveway?" she inquired, squinting to see if her eyes had deceived her.

"It looks like it," Ronald confirmed her query. "That's a good sign, right?" he glanced her way, attempting to foretell what she was thinking.

"Let's hope everything is okay."

Once they got inside, Gertrude headed straight back toward the television room. "Aunt May," the concerned niece called out for a response.

Aunt May halted her niece's cries as she popped up in the doorway. "Poor thing fell asleep." The old woman tilted her head toward the couch, where Brenda lay fast asleep.

"You're back early. Is everything okay with you and Ronald? I was hoping we didn't have to pay rent next month," she joked.

Gertrude's eyes bucked. "Oh my God, Aunt May." Her freckled cheeks blushed over. She couldn't believe what her aunt had said. And with Ronald there behind her listening, Gertrude couldn't help but be embarrassed.

"Everything is fine, Aunt May. How are you?" Ronald peeked his head around the doorway, greeting the then-amused old woman.

She had no idea Ronald was there in the house with them. Aunt May chuckled as she slapped at her knee. The commotion woke a startled Brenda from her much-needed nap.

"What happened?" Brenda wiped the drool from her cheek, which had leaked from the edge of her mouth down onto the soft peach sofa cushion.

"Brenda, what happened to your head?" Gertrude blurted, frowning with concern as she noticed the bruised lump atop her friend's skull.

"It's a long story." Brenda shook her head in despair.

Gertrude walked over, sitting down right beside her. She wrapped an arm around Brenda, caressing hers. "I'm here now, friend. You can tell me all about it."

The fact that her friend was there made Brenda feel better, even considering what questions remained unanswered. She lay her head on Gertrude's shoulder, allowing herself to rest in the compassion her friend had shown.

Gertrude looked up at Ronald as if to say, thank you for letting me be here for this. Just from the look on her face, he understood. The understanding also came with a crushing realization. The realization that Gertrude's friends meant the world to her. *What will I do if she finds out what I've done? Will she forgive me, or will I have to say goodbye to the love we've created?* he feared. The same questions that had plagued him after he pushed Tiffany off that bridge plagued him then. Overwhelmed with worry, he felt the need to clear his head.

"I should let you two talk. There are a few things I need to take care of. I'll see you later." Ronald kissed Gertrude atop her forehead, waved farewell to Aunt May and Brenda, then went on his way.

There was no need to hear what Brenda would reveal. Ronald had already taken care of that. He had bigger fish to fry.

At the top of his list was none other than Tom Swine. He thought, why put off until later what could be done then. He trekked up the block, then around the corner on his way to visit the old man. On the way there, he thought about not only all he'd done but also all Tom was capable of. The old man wanted him dead; that was clear to Ronald. To make matters worse, he knew Ronald's secret about Daryl, Joey, and the cabin. There was no way in hell he was going to let him live.

He cut through the alley behind the houses, traveling it the rest of the way there. The fewer people that saw him, the better. Once Ronald got to Tom's backyard, he hopped the fence to get to the back door.

"Kick the door down, brother," Cecilia egged her twin brother on.

Ronald charged up the porch stairs. The heel of his boot crashed into the wooden structure, blasting it open and tearing the molding from the door frame, all with one swift kick. Natural light showed his way through the house. It looked exactly as he had seen it in his recollection, within the terrible memories Cecilia had shared with him. The brown shag carpeting felt soft under his feet as he crossed over into the dining room. He recognized the bobblehead dolls that decorated the bookshelf. To his disgust, right there on the table was a Ziploc bag full of Tootsie Rolls. He swallowed the lump of anger lodged in his throat.

From Cecelia's eyes, tears streamed down her pale, freckled cheeks. *"He isn't here,"* her apparition spoke.

He's close, Ronald surmised, continuing to take in his surroundings.

Chapter 49

Caught Unaware

Around the corner, Brenda poured her heart out to Gertrude about how she felt regarding everything that had happened. Brenda explained how she thought Tiffany was as good as dead. She admitted how she feared they'd probably sold her to the highest bidder. Brenda knew her cousin would never submit to a life of slavery. Tiffany would rather die. For Brenda, saying it aloud solidified the notion.

Her own life had fallen completely apart since her cousin's disappearance, and Brenda wasn't sure if she could handle the mental stress that weighed down on her. On top of all that, being snatched in her own driveway had her frightened to be alone. For the first time, Brenda didn't know how to deal with her situation. "What if they come back for me?" the teary-eyed woman inquired as if Gertrude had the answer to her prayers.

"I thought you said that the police raided the house. I'm sure they're searching for them. They won't let them get away with this."

"I can't depend on them to protect me. Detroit is a big place, and I'm sure the police have more important things to do," Brenda sulked.

"Why don't we go by your house and get some clothes? I'm sure Aunt May will let you stay here for a while. Come on. Please don't cry. Let's get your stuff. I promise I won't leave you," Gertrude said, hoping to stop her friend from weeping.

"Promise?" Brenda looked at Gertrude for reassurance.

"I got you, girl. Don't worry about it."

Brenda took Gertrude as a woman of her word, agreeing to what she had proposed. She prayed staying there would give her the emotional support she would need to make it through the entire ordeal.

Brenda pulled into her driveway, then sat there for a moment, afraid to go inside. "What if they're in there waiting for me?"

"You have a burglar alarm. Wouldn't it have gone off?" Gertrude quickly banished the theory.

"I guess you're right." Brenda shut off the car, not taking her eyes from the house. She looked for any movement she could spy through the windows, any bulge in the curtains she could spot. Thankfully, there was nothing. "Okay. I'm ready."

The women got out of the car to head inside. Lavender-scented potpourri pervaded Brenda's abode, placed strategically in decorative bowls around the house. As Gertrude expected, it was quiet except for the alarm that had sounded off, beckoning for her to enter the correct code. Although there wasn't a soul in the house beyond the two of them, Gertrude shivered due to the eerie feeling that washed over her just being in there. Even so, she had to be present for her friend in her time of need.

"Go get your clothes. I'll wait down here." Gertrude closed, then locked the side door behind them. "By the way, do you have any bottled waters?" she added, heading for the fridge to see for herself.

"Check the refrigerator. There should be plenty. Tiffany hasn't been by to clean me out." The epiphany caused her to smile at first. Then it almost instantly waned once she had considered why it was so. The pain of not having Tiffany there felt as if it would never subside. Not knowing her cousin's fate was destroying her piece by piece. The lump in her throat felt impossible to swallow. Yet, she had to go on. She knew Tiffany wouldn't want her just to give up.

Brenda tackled the stairs by twos to get to her bedroom, feeling the sooner she gathered her belongings, the sooner she could get back downstairs to Gertrude. More than anything, she preferred not being alone. The fact that Aunt May was willing to open her house up to a stranger spoke about the compassion she harbored for her fellow man. Brenda was Gertrude's friend and all, but to be honest, it wasn't as if they'd been friends for years. Aunt May put her trust in the fact that her niece had always been a great judge of character.

Gertrude opened the fridge, ready to quench her thirst. To her dismay, not one water remained. "Girl, you don't have a single water in here," she yelled so that Brenda could hear.

"Check the fridge in the garage."

"The garage? Oh, she has extra fridges. Doing it big, I see," Gertrude remarked as she walked out the side door to make it to the garage. She glanced left, then right. Not a soul in sight, except for the little boy riding his bike down the street, cards clicking in the spokes of his back tire. *If it's safe enough for him, I'm sure it's safe enough for me,* she thought, brushing off all nuances of fear as she moseyed on back.

Gertrude twisted the small brass knob, then crossed the threshold into the garage. A thin hanging chain near the center of the dark space brushed against her face as she navigated her way through. *Click.* She pulled the string, illuminating her surroundings. It was by no means a man's garage, but Brenda had almost everything she needed. Those she deemed essential were inside, including a power drill for hanging wall decor, a lawn mower, and a snowblower to ensure she could maintain her yard. Even a barbeque grill for nights Brenda preferred eating al fresco. Her father had always taught her never to depend on a man for the small things.

Gertrude darted over to the refrigerator, pulled it open, then reached in to retrieve water from the twenty-four-pack sitting front and center.

She snatched it up. "Got it." At which point, she turned to go back inside, colliding with the barrier in front of her.

"Gotcha," Tom replied before bending over to retrieve the water bottle that had fallen onto the cement slab under their feet. He handed it over to the speechless young lady.

"I believe this belongs to you."

Gertrude accepted it, not yet having caught on to his ill intentions. "Tom? What are you doing here?" she brandished a confused expression.

The old man pressed his finger to his lips, silencing her. "Quiet now. They'll hear you."

"What are you talking about? Who will hear me?"

"Anyone that can help," he answered, then grabbed her by the arm, spinning her around. He jammed his pistol into her side to convince her to behave.

Not at all convinced, Gertrude dropped the water bottle, then tried breaking away.

But Tom had a tight grip on her arm. "I wouldn't make any sudden moves if I were you, darling," he whispered into her ear, his hot breath warming the side of her neck. "Let's just get to my car."

"Why are you doing this?" she protested.

"We'll discuss that later. Just move your ass."

Moments later, Brenda rushed out the side door, noticing the garage door ajar. "Gertrude! Girl, I thought you said a water—not the case." Once she stepped into the garage, her face instantly drained of hope as she spied the water bottle there on the ground. "Oh my God." She covered her gaping mouth with her hands. "Gertrude!" she shrieked, stepping back out into the yard. Brenda did a 360-degree turn. Still, no Gertrude. She was gone, and Brenda had found herself once again all alone as the sun made its descent.

It was getting dark. She couldn't help but feel frightened. Brenda had to get out of there and fast. She locked up the house, then jumped into her vehicle, on her way to find the only person she thought could help.

Chapter 50

His Worst Fear

At the time, Ronald was busily canvassing the neighborhood with the hood of his jacket over his head. He had to sneak up on Tom if he were going to catch him. A car zoomed by, traveling the block just ahead of the persistent young man as he rounded a corner. The car looked familiar. In fact, much like Brenda's from what Ronald could tell from afar. His footsteps after that had become more deliberate. Something wasn't right. Ronald could sense it in his bones. As he rounded the next corner on Gable, he saw what his mind had already confirmed. It *was* Brenda, pacing the porch and pounding at his front door.

"Ronald!" She called out in a panic. Brenda tried her best to see into the windows of the residence. But, of course, Ronald barely allowed a view into his home from the outside.

"Brenda," he called out to her from up the street, garnishing her attention.

She jetted down the porch, tearing off toward him.

Ronald's heart pounded, his stomach twisted in knots, knowing whatever she was about to tell him involved the love of his life.

Brenda hunched over, hands resting on her knees, nearly out of breath by the time she coughed up the words. "Gertrude's gone," she cried.

"Gone where? What do you mean, 'gone'?"

"We went to my house to get some clothes. She wanted some bottled water, so I told her they were in the garage. When I went outside to the garage after getting my suitcase packed, she was gone. I don't know where she went. Do you think it might be the men that took me? Do you think they came back for us?"

Ronald knew that unless Daryl and Joey had come back from the dead, it couldn't possibly have been them. A fact he wouldn't dare reveal to Brenda. Quite frankly, he didn't have time to convince her that everything would be okay. Ronald had to find Gertrude—and fast. "I plan to find out," he assured her as he darted off. "You should go home, Brenda. It's getting dark."

Ronald rushed into the house, then slammed the door behind him. He had to find out where Tom could be holding her hostage. It was him Tom really wanted. Gertrude was merely bait. Ronald hoped the cameras on his property would spot something that could assist him in finding her. With the computer in his living room, he maintained a connection to his cabin in Idlewild. Ronald powered on the hard drive and monitor, then proceeded to pull up the cameras. After five minutes of searching, he found nothing out of the ordinary, just a few bucks roaming the grounds.

The phone chimed, grabbing his attention. Without hesitation, he snatched up the receiver to the big, black, outdated phone sitting on the desk beside the monitor, answering the call. "Hello."

"Ronald, we haven't seen each other in a while. We should meet up. Hash things out like gentlemen."

"Gentlemen kidnap women?" Ronald spouted angrily.

"I haven't harmed a hair on her curly head. Ask her yourself." Tom pulled the handkerchief from between Gertrude's lips, allowing her to speak while he held the phone to her ear.

"Ronald, I'm afraid, baby," she whimpered, sniffing loose mucus back into her running nostrils.

"Don't be scared, baby. I'm coming to get you. I promise. I'm so sorry I got you in thi—"

Tom pulled the phone away from her ear, abruptly ending their time to talk, "That's quite enough of that, lover boy. The directions where we are to meet will be on the windshield of your car. Drive safely. You know what? On second thought, don't." Tom hung up the receiver.

Ronald lowered his head as if he were about to pray. "If I've never asked for your help before, I'm asking for it, now. Come with me, Cecilia."

"Nothing would please me more, dear brother," his twin sister answered, revealing herself near the front door.

He had to get to Gertrude as fast as he could, and there was only one car that could take him there at that time. Ronald ripped the note from the windshield of the conversion van, then headed straight for his garage. Inside, he pulled the two iron pins securing the large metal door on each side so that he could lift it. He hopped into his father's cherry-red beauty, revving the engine to warm it up, before pulling out into the darkness in search of his woman.

On the way to his destination, he thought about the good times he'd had with Gertrude. Envisioning her dimpled smile and joyful laugh eventually led to Ronald admitting to himself how she made him feel so needed, yet at the same time, cared for.

"You really love her, dear brother."

"I've never experienced this kind of love before, Cecilia. I don't want to lose it. I don't want to lose her." He finally allowed the words to come off his heart.

"And what will you tell her about me? Do you plan just to ignore me forever when she's around? What if she

catches you talking to me? She'll think you're crazy. And your mission . . . You think she's not going to find out that you're a killer?" Cecilia griped.

"My mission? You mean *your* mission, Cecilia. I didn't ask for this. I don't enjoy killing people. It's because of you Tiffany is dead. Now, I have to live with the fact that I killed one of my girlfriend's closest friends. If you had just let me handle it, Tiffany would be alive."

"Oh, cry me a river. She knew what she was doing all those times she stole from those places. Yet, people like her get to live, and my life gets cut short. It's not fair," she spouted.

"So, you think stealing food or a few items is worth someone's loss of life? See, that's where your mission completely conflicts with mine. The punishment just doesn't fit the crime. Besides, when did we go from punishing sexual predators to petty thieves? Cecelia, don't you see that was someone's daughter, someone's cousin? Her only crime was taking items that probably didn't cost more than $100. And you killed her for it."

"No, dear brother. I think you are mistaken. You're the one who forced her over that bridge. You even looked into her pleading eyes as she plummeted to her death. No, dear brother, I'm sure of it. It was you that ended her miserable life."

Ronald glanced into his rearview mirror, catching the evil smirk his sister brandished. Even still, he didn't have the freedom to think thoughts he really wanted to. Cecilia wasn't the same. She sat before him, tainted. The evil she'd tried so desperately to vanquish, her will had fallen prey to.

"I won't do this anymore," he blurted, causing a feeling of release he'd waited for since he was a child. "I'm done, Cecilia. After this, no more killing."

"After this," she huffed. *"Why put off until later what you can do today? Right, dear brother? You want me gone? You can save your girlfriend all by yourself. See how well you do without me,"* the apparition threatened before disappearing into thin air.

Ronald knew it wasn't the last he'd seen of his sister. There was no way she would allow him to walk away that easily. She would be back with hell, brimstone, and fire behind her, he reckoned. Even so, at least for the time being, he could think freely. Getting Gertrude back was his main objective, and without Cecilia's intuition backing him, Ronald would have to strategize. Waltzing right in through the front wouldn't be an option if he wanted to gain the upper hand. He mashed his foot to the accelerator, zooming left around the vehicle in front of him, then took off down I-75.

His instructions on the map led him to a place he couldn't recall ever having been before. Ronald figured he could ride by first to get a good look at the layout. He was sure Tom would have taken some measures to be privy to when he would arrive. Therefore, it was a must he approached the situation with caution.

It wasn't until he exited the freeway on Jefferson Avenue that the buildings started to look familiar. The last time Ronald had been in that area, he was a little boy. Back then, whenever they'd have a family picnic, it was at Belle Isle. So much time had gone by that he'd practically forgotten about their special place. Seeing it all again, Ronald recalled the memory as if it were yesterday.

Chapter 51

Family Time

Young Ronald stared out of the car window in awe from the backseat. While passersby admired how beautiful his father's ride was, the little boy soaked up the scenery down Jefferson Avenue. Stunning brick architecture hiding the Detroit River behind it kept his awestruck stare. The trip to Belle Isle that day was in an effort to lift his mother's spirits. Mr. Doolally looked over at his wife from the driver's seat. Oh, how he loved her so. He would do anything for her, yet the one thing she needed he couldn't provide. Mrs. Doolally wanted their daughter back, alive and well. She gazed sorrowfully from the passenger window, remembering the times they had been to the island as a complete family—before their daughter's life had been ripped away from them.

"Look at the water, Mama," young Ronald shouted excitedly.

With Cecelia being gone, it was hard for her to take that trip, let alone put on a joyful facade. Only for the sake of her son had she tried to carry on with some type of normalcy. She didn't want Ronald to feel like he didn't matter. Mrs. Doolally loved her son, but losing her daughter destroyed the best parts of her. Much of the time, if not cold, she was distant.

That day, she had promised her husband she would be present in body and mind for their day outdoors.

"Yes, it's beautiful, son. Kind of makes me feel at peace," she answered, appeasing him for the time being.

"We're here!" Ronald cheered excitedly as his father turned on to MacArthur Bridge to access the island.

More than half of the 982 acres were covered by three lakes, a lagoon, and 230 acres of forest-inhabited wetlands. Since its development in the late nineteenth century, Belle Isle had become home to some of young Ronald's favorite places to visit. Among them was the beach, its giant yellow slide, Belle Isle Aquarium, the conservatory, the nature center, and the Great Lakes Museum. The island bustled with activity due to the addition of the Detroit Yacht Club, casino, and golf course.

As they crossed over the bridge, Mr. Doolally spied on his son through the rearview mirror. His bright beaming eyes and freckled cheeks blushed over as he sported a giddy grin.

"Would you like to go all the way around first?" Mr. Doolally asked, knowing it was a customary tradition for them, but could see the anticipation nearly bursting from Ronald's little body.

"Can we go to the giant slide first, then the aquarium? After that, we can go wherever Mom wants to go."

"How generous of you, son," Mr. Doolally admitted, yet in the same instance, snickered at the audacious comment. He looked over at his wife, expecting to see a glint of amusement, but there was nothing. Mrs. Doolally's mind was so far removed from the conversation that she had blocked out both of them. Her mind was transfixed on memories of Cecilia.

They cruised by the James Scott Memorial Fountain as others stopped to toss in a coin and make a wish.

"Wait!" Ronald shouted. A brilliant idea had dawned on him in a flash. Maybe it would work. Then his mother would feel better. "I need to stop at the fountain. It'll be really quick, Dad. Can you pull over?"

"I sure can, son." Mr. Doolally pulled over to the right, granting his son's request.

"I'll be right back, honey. I'm going to park right here." He unbuckled his seat belt.

"It's okay. I'm a big boy. I can go by myself," young Ronald insisted.

"I can respect that, son. But, unfortunately, I can't." He paused in correction. "I won't allow you to cross this busy street all by yourself."

Ronald lowered his head in disappointment, prompting his father to make a compromise.

"I'll tell you what. I'll get you across the road safely, and you can go up to the fountain all on your own. I won't stand over you. It's your business. Agreed?"

Young Ronald looked up with a smile, confirming it so. "Agreed."

Mr. Doolally was a man of his word. He accompanied Ronald across the street, then allowed him to approach the fountain on his own, as he promised.

"I forgot something." The little boy turned back to address his father. "Would you mind letting me borrow a quarter? I promise I'll pay it back in chores."

"One quarter gets me a yard void of apples on the ground," his father negotiated.

"Deal." Young Ronald shook his father's hand firmly, making it official before darting off toward the big wishing spot. Spouts of water streamed here and there, even crossing over one another. The fountain was a beautiful sight to take in. If any wishing spot would work, the little boy surmised it would be that one. Young Ronald's eyes beamed with wonder at the various streams of shooting water and white stone lion statues decorating the monument. With his speech already in mind, he tossed his quarter in, shut his eyes tight, and began to wish as hard as he could.

"God, please bring my sister back. My mommy isn't doing very well, and I don't want her to be unhappy anymore. I don't want my father to have to hold her another night in tears. I miss Cecelia. She was my only true friend. I don't want to be alone anymore. Please, God, send my sister back to us." He opened his lids when he finished, feeling as if maybe, just maybe, someone up there heard his silent plea.

Once they got back into the vehicle, Ronald reached over the seat, letting his hand rest on his despondent mother's shoulder. *"It's gonna be okay, Mom. Trust me,"* he declared before sitting back to strap himself in.

Mr. Doolally didn't say a word, but from the expression on his face, you could see that he was proud of his son for attempting to uplift his mother's spirits. *"So, the giant slide, right?"* his father inquired in efforts to boost his excitement even more.

His plan worked perfectly.

"Yayyy," young Ronald cheered, ready to take on the attraction.

When he spotted the giant yellow slide, he pointed it out, yelling, *"There it is, Dad! Look at it. It's magnificent."*

"It is, indeed, son," his father cheesed.

Mr. Doolally made sure to park near a shed close to the restrooms just in case his wife had to relieve herself. They all got out, Mrs. Doolally moving in silence. She stared out at the river, remembering how much her little girl loved the beach. Cecelia, often, would be as wrinkled as a prune by the time her mother could get her out of the water. Mrs. Doolally would wrap her daughter up in the towel, then scoop Cecelia up, keeping her snug in her embrace. Those were the good ole days, she fantasized.

"Are you ready, honey?" Mrs. Doolally's husband stole her attention.

"I'm going to use the restroom first. I'll meet you two over there."

"We can wait for you," Mr. Doolally insisted.

"I'll be okay, honey. The line will just get longer." She pointed out the line of cars waiting to park. "I'll meet you two at the giant slide."

"Come on, Dad. Let's go," young Ronald pulled at his father's arm rushing him along.

"Okay. Okay. Let's get you on that slide." Mr. Doolally blew a farewell kiss to his wife. "Until we meet again, my darling," he uttered as he had on many occasions in the past.

"Until we meet again," she replied softly.

Mr. Doolally and his boy darted across the median, then to the other side of the road where the line to the huge, hilly, yellow slide stretched around the gate encasing it.

"It's gonna take forever," young Ronald complained.

"Wait right here, son," his father directed him.

Ronald watched his as his father took his wallet out and handed something over to one of the kids near the front of the line. The next thing he knew, his father was motioning for him to approach.

Young Ronald reached his father. "Dad, how'd we get to the front of the line?" he whispered, nudging closer to him.

"Don't you worry about that, son. Your father has a way of getting what he wants," he bragged proudly, rustling his hand through his boy's soft, ginger curls.

His father purchased the tickets at the booth, retrieving their wheat sacks, then up the steep line of stairs they trekked. Young Ronald gawked up at the staircase they were to climb, feeling a bit defeated before they had even gotten a tenth of the way there. It was like looking up at a mountain's peak. Reaching the top always felt epic, no matter how many times they had achieved the feat. His adrenaline pumped every step he climbed.

Young Ronald started to think about how exhilarating it would feel sliding down. It's what gave him the boost he needed to conquer the summit of stairs. They had endured five minutes of stair-climbing before the pair finally reached the top. As the instructor demonstrated how they were to step into their sacks, Ronald turned to ogle at the river across the road. That's when he saw it. His mother stood seemingly in a daze at the edge of the pier.

"Dad"—he uttered ominously as he tapped at his father's arm—"isn't that Mama?" He pointed out into the distance.

"Oh my God. Stay over here, son," his father demanded before leaping down onto the slide, sack first.

Young Ronald watched along with spectators as his father made it across the road, then down the brick pier just in time to snatch her from falling into the depths of the river. Ronald didn't understand why his mother would want to leave him. He knew his mother was grief stricken, but he couldn't help pondering why wasn't he enough.

Chapter 52

Kill or Be Killed

Even then, that very question haunted him daily. A plethora of fond memories on the island had been tarnished by one bad incident. Ronald and his family had never visited Belle Isle again after that day. Nearly fourteen years later, he found himself crossing that bridge to get back to that island. He drove by the fountain, still spouting water, illuminated by colorful fluorescent lights. In the darkness, it looked magnificent.

The Detroit River was turbulent that evening. He could hear waves crashing against the cement wall at the water's edge. Ronald squinted to see, having shut off his headlamps as he came on the island. There weren't many parkgoers on a weekday at that time of the evening, which he hoped wouldn't make his vehicle stick out like a sore thumb.

Then there it was in the distance. He saw the flashing light at the peak of his favorite attraction. Ronald grabbed the pair of binoculars from the passenger seat next to him, using them to see exactly what it was. To his horror, it looked as if Gertrude had been covered in a wheat sack from head to toe. The old man had a firm hold on her arm as he waited for Ronald to arrive. Sticking with his plan to catch Tom by surprise, he made a right at the statue of Major General Alpheus Starkey Williams. If he could climb the back of the closed attraction, maybe he could sneak up behind them. Ronald thought it was worth a try. He pulled over near the aquarium, then got out, stuffing his father's .38-caliber pistol into his waistband, beginning his trek.

Meanwhile, Tom whispered into Gertrude's ear. She could feel his hot breath as it seeped through the tiny holes in the sack. "It's almost time. Your boyfriend should be arriving any minute, unless, of course, he left you to die like he did his little sister. How much do you really know about him anyway? I've got a feeling it's gonna get exciting tonight."

A shuddering Gertrude whimpered as she cringed at the feeling of the pistol barrel poking into her side.

Then Tom heard it loud and clear, the aluminum structure around him shifting. He turned just in time to see Ronald climbing over the ledge.

"That's not playing fair," Tom grunted before shoving Gertrude down the slide.

Unfortunately, she couldn't scream as her mouth remained gagged with a handkerchief.

"Gertrude," he yelped, his heart dropping to his stomach as he witnessed her go over.

The old man slid down afterward, taking the slippery hills with agility he hadn't previously shown.

Missing him by seconds, Ronald darted to the edge without a sack to ride down. He watched in terror as his love tumbled and flipped like a sack of potatoes. Ronald assumed her arms were bound together because she hadn't struggled to break free.

Tom reached the bottom. "Come on down!" he dared Ronald to take the plunge.

To which Ronald answered with confidence. Gertrude's heroic lover sat down, pushing himself off with his hands to get a bulletlike start on the aluminum slide, riding down with only his jeans covering his buttocks. The ride was hot, but he would never allow the expression on his face to tell it. Faux green carpeting at the bottom of the slide barely stopped him from crashing into the fence that surrounded the perimeter of the attraction.

"Come on now, boy! Get up. Get up and face the music," Tom menaced.

Ronald stood up, headed right for them. The gun Tom raised to Gertrude's sacked head caused him to stop dead in his tracks. Did he have enough balls to blow her head off right there? Ronald mulled it over as he stood no more than six feet away.

Tom knew that look. His mind had already begun flirting with the idea of going for it. "You should stay where you are if you want her to live. Now, let's cut to the chase. I don't like you. You don't like me. I know a lot about you. You seem to think you know about me. Nothing we have to reveal about ourselves would paint us in a favorable light. I've put measures in place to ensure that if a hair is harmed on this silver fox's head—if anything tragic should happen to me—not only will sugar tits know about you, but so will the entire world. I don't think either of us wants that to happen. So, do I kill her?" Tom teased, poking her in the head with the pistol as he waited for a reply.

Ronald couldn't risk another minute of Gertrude's life. He spoke up without hesitation. "Just leave us alone, and we won't say anything about this," he reluctantly agreed.

Tom studied his miscolored eyes for the truth.

"Let her go, Swine," Ronald demanded with more aggression, unwilling to wait.

The old man sucked at his teeth in disdain at his heroics. "Holster your weapon, lover boy," he continued with his ultimatum.

Ronald countered with one of his own. "Take your gun away from her head."

"Do you love her?" Tom inquired.

"I do," Ronald admitted. The revelation caused Gertrude's eyes to stream like a river under the bag.

She had never felt so frightened, yet so touched all at once. Gertrude prayed whatever crimes Ronald had committed, whatever foul act he had been a part of, was not so heinous she could no longer bear the sight of him.

Both lowered their weapons slowly but in unison, having agreed to each other's terms. *"He's bluffing,"* Ronald finally heard Cecelia's voice. She hadn't abandoned him after all.

Despite her presence, Ronald controlled his twitching arm as Tom backed out into the darkness, leaving Gertrude there on her knees.

"Don't let him go. Kill him. Kill him, now," Cecilia shrieked.

Ronald ignored his twin's outcry as he approached to uncover, then help Gertrude to her feet.

He pulled the sack from over her head. Black mascara ran down her face, painting her dimpled cheeks.

"Oh, baby, I'm so sorry this happened to you," Ronald apologized as he pulled down the bandanna between her lips before unbinding her arms.

Gertrude started in on him immediately, "What is he talking about, Ronald? Why would he say those things to you?" she cried, rubbing her bruised wrists.

Ronald let out a long sigh. It was apparent he had to tell her something. There was no way she would be willing to go on, not knowing why she had been taken.

"Tom saw me kill a man."

"You killed somebody?" Gertrude's eyes bucked. "Ronald, why? Who?"

"Do you remember the guys I had it out with the other day?"

"The men who Brenda claims kidnapped her?"

"They did. They also followed us to the cabin to get rid of us. I had no other choice but to get rid of them first. In actuality, it wasn't even me who killed Joey. I assume it was Tom who did it."

"I don't understand." She shook her head in denial of it all. "You killed a man while we were at the cabin? And why is Aunt May's friend doing all this?" She untied the sack covering her bottom extremities, then stepped out of it.

"Tom is a pedophile, and I know his secret. Unfortunately, he will do anything to keep it, including hurting the person most important to me."

"I'm the most important to you?" her voice softened as she gazed into his eyes, hoping to see the truth she had heard.

"You're the only one," Ronald confessed with teary eyes.

Gertrude wrapped him in her embrace. His admission having been exactly what she had been waiting to hear, Gertrude tucked her head into his chest. She wanted to feel secure, but even then, she couldn't deny that they were still in very grave danger. "Ronald, I'm petrified. What are we going to do?"

"We're not going to do anything. He's threatening to tell people everything, and I just can't risk it. I can't risk losing you."

"Losing her?" Cecilia seethed, appalled by what her brother had said.

"Let's get you home." Ronald lowered his head, wincing from the pain of the headache that seemed to hit him all at once. He squeezed his eyes shut. "Gertrude, you'll have to drive." He handed over the keys to her, feeling as if his head were about to explode.

"Come on, baby. Let's get out of here."

As the couple headed to the car, Ronald tried his best not to see what was breaking into his psyche. His breaths became panicked, his stare deliberate.

Cecilia refused to let him get away again.

"Ronald, your eyes. They're both gray." Gertrude couldn't believe what she was seeing. In fact, as she stared at him, she didn't recognize him at all.

Ronald backed away from her, darting off into the darkness.

Gertrude stood there, confused. "Ronald, where are you going?" she called out to him.

Ronald neglected to respond. He had left Gertrude there all alone to fend for herself. She rubbed her hands up and down her shivering arms, the Detroit River nearby sending a crisp breeze over the landscape. "What the hell is happening?" She frantically spied her surroundings in fear of Tom coming back for her.

I have to get to the car. She thought about pressing the button on the car alarm to show her the way.

Beep! Beep! The headlamps of the cherry-red Chevy Caprice illuminated, ushering the frightened woman forward in a hurry.

Once she made it to the car, she climbed inside the driver's seat, locking the doors immediately.

Ronald, on the other hand, was on the hunt. Cecelia had taken over, and the only thing that mattered at that moment was killing the man who had been responsible for past transgressions against the little girl. He hiked through the park, ignoring the couple making out atop a blanket in the grass. As he rounded the corner by the casino, he spotted Tom attempting to climb back into his car to scurry away. Ronald charged full speed ahead across the grass. By the time Tom noticed, he had come face-to-face with Ronald. The old man's body was being jammed between his door and the frame. Ronald let up a little, then slammed the door back into his wedged body.

Tom choked down the yelp he wanted to let out.

Over and over, he took the blows. But something had to give. His weapon was stuffed into his waistbelt behind him. He'd have to use one arm to push the door off and the other to grab his .45-caliber pistol. Tom decided it best he accepted the brutal blows as punishment for letting his guard down.

He quickly pulled his gun from his belt, holding it over the door to shoot, but on second thought, he remembered the park did have one or two couples there roaming about. He had seen them with his own eyes on the way back to his vehicle. Instead, he crashed the butt of the gun down against Ronald's skull. Once, twice. By the third time, Ronald was staring directly into his fear-stricken eyes. The old man couldn't believe he hadn't knocked him out. It scared him a little more than he liked. The emotion was seen plainly in his dilated pupils.

Ronald kept him pinned there in the door while he grabbed Tom's wrist, twisting it down toward him. For a moment there, the old man thought his arm would snap right in half, at which point, he dropped the weapon. Ronald flung him to the ground by his arm. Tom crawled backward on hands and feet across the grass.

"Now, hold on, now. Think this over. If you kill me, your secret's out. Then you're a dead man," he barked.

"I'm already dead," Ronald responded but in Cecilia's voice. Then he proceeded to kick the man in his head, knocking him flat on his back. He pressed the sole of his boot against Tom's stoma. Ronald wanted to hear the bones in his neck snap. Harder, he pressed down against the man's throat. Suddenly, headlamps in the distance caught his chrome-like eyes.

It was Gertrude. She had gone riding around the park looking for Ronald, having no idea he had checked out.

Tom coughed, attempting to heave oxygen into his blackened lungs.

Still, Ronald refused to pardon him. He grabbed Tom's foot, dragging him across the grass back to his car, then snatched up Tom's gun. "Step inside," Ronald threatened Tom with his own weapon.

The old man got up, then climbed into the driver's seat. Ronald sat right behind him in the back.

"Start the car. We're going for a little ride."

"Where do you want to go?" Tom asked, quaking in fear.

"To finish what you started." Ronald pointed toward his father's red Chevy crossing their path at the intersection.

"So, you don't love her?" Tom mumbled.

That's when the headache hit him again. Ronald pressed the gun to the side of his own temple, wanting to end it all, but the forces that had overtaken his mind and body would not allow it to be.

"What's wrong with you, man?"

"What's wrong with you, man?" Ronald counted as the pain he winced from subsided in an instant.

"I've never seen a grown man talk like a child before," Tom admitted.

"No talking, just touching, I reckon," Ronald seethed, firing off a round into one of Tom's hands that lay resting upon the steering wheel.

"You son of a bitch," he wailed, clutching his bleeding extremity.

"Start the car and drive," Ronald demanded.

Tom started the car, pushing himself past the aching in his hand which had radiated up his arm. Although he was in excruciating pain, Tom continued to speed up the street behind Gertrude.

The worry-stricken woman saw the headlights coming yet had no idea they were approaching at the speed at which they were. She'd since looked back down at the road in front of her by the time the station wagon slammed into the rear of her car.

"Oh my God," she shrieked, swerving across the asphalt as she tried to regain control of the vehicle. Gertrude gawked at the rearview mirror, noticing Tom's station wagon. "It's him," she murmured. "Ronald, where are you?" Gertrude cried as he plowed into the rear of her a second time.

The turn to get off that road was too far ahead, and she was already careening toward the curb, so Gertrude allowed the car to do its thing. The Chevy hopped the curb, crashing into garbage cans, park grills, and picnic benches. Still, it revved on.

Tom made a hard right, hopping the curb to go after her. If he was going to die by Ronald's hand, he didn't mind at all chasing Gertrude down to kill her first. The old man hit the gas, then rammed into her a third time, that time almost giving himself and Ronald whiplash. When Tom's body flew forward toward the steering wheel, he was able to grab the switchblade from inside his sock.

Even though he'd dropped Tom's gun, the jolt had been an advantage to Ronald as well. It launched him forward, then knocked him back so hard that Cecilia released her influence on him for a moment. He looked up, one eye gray, the other now brown, seeing his car ahead all bashed in with a frightened Gertrude behind the wheel. It all came clear to him at that moment what he had been a part of.

While he processed what was going on, Tom took the knife, plunging it through Ronald's wrist.

Ronald's reaction was immediate. He grabbed his pistol from the back of his waistbelt, unloading it into the driver's seat. Once the old man's body lunged forward against the steering wheel, the car veered left. Ronald put the gun to his own head, ready to blow his brains out. There was no way he could bear killing Gertrude. Just as he started to pull the trigger, the station wagon plowed into a massive boulder along the shore, catapulting the vehicle up through the air, then into the Detroit River. The car crashed into the water, headed straight for the bottom.

A man standing out on the pier saw the car as it took a nosedive into the water. He made a heroic leap into the brisk water to save whomever he could.

An hour later, the station wagon was fished from the river's bottom with a cable and winch. The authorities were on the scene, as well as an ambulance. Front and center was good old Detective Barnes.

Looming behind a tree nearby, shivering from the cold water, stood none other than his old pal Richard. His dedication had proved once more unwavering.

"Detective, I'm surprised to see you here and without Alanis?" another officer remarked as he noticed Barnes taking in the scene.

"Well, I'm here in a sort of unofficial capacity. The young man there"—he pointed at Ronald as he was being wheeled toward the ambulance—"that's the late Sheriff Doolally's son. I promised to look after him when his father died. I've been there ever since. I'd like to remain abreast of the happenings in this case."

"Sure thing, Detective Barnes. Anything for Sheriff Doolally. He was a great man," the officer undoubtedly agreed.

Gertrude stood in tears with a blanket wrapped over her shoulders as she waited to climb inside the emergency vehicle to sit at Ronald's side.

Chapter 53

Could It Be Happily Ever After?

After arriving at the hospital, Gertrude had to stay in the waiting room for hours, unaware of what was happening to the love of her life. "Please save him, Lord," she prayed, hands pressed together and nestled against the front of her face. It was the hardest Gertrude had ever prayed before.

With her head bowed, she heard his shoes first. "Yes, Doctor?" the worried girlfriend stood up, anxious to hear the news.

"Well, it turns out Ronald had a tumor pressing against his frontal lobe. It was affecting the sensory cortex. Had he been experiencing hallucinations? Complaining of headaches?"

"Oh my God. The headaches, yes. But hallucinations? Not that I know of, Doctor," Gertrude replied while further pondering his inquiry.

"He's fortunate to be alive. We were able to remove the tumor, but during repair, he experienced some hemorrhaging. Parts of the hippocampus were damaged. It controls his memory function. There will be some memories blocked or simply gone. I'm sorry. We are unable to determine which areas of his life will be affected.

He's been in recovery for the last two hours. If you would like to go and see him, he's in room 112."

"Thank you, Doctor. Thank you so much for all you've done for him," Gertrude professed as she rushed from the waiting room.

Ronald lay, eyes closed, head and wrist wrapped in bandages. His body felt like he had been hit by a truck. His head throbbed. The young man had no idea how he'd gotten to the hospital. The last thing he remembered was water flooding his lungs.

A soft knock at the door garnered his attention. Ronald finally opened his eyes to see who had come to visit him.

She pushed the door open. "Ronald, it's me."

"Gertrude," he smiled. "My beauty. I'm so happy you're here. I thought you would be gone."

"Oh my gosh," she covered her gaping mouth, eyes filled with wonder. "Your eyes—they're *both* brown." She closed in on him, reaching out to caress the side of his face.

"They are?" he asked. "Do you still love me?" He gazed into her pupils.

"I do love you, Ronald," Gertrude proclaimed with a smile. "Whether your eyes are brown, blue, green, or gray, I'll love you."

"What about hazel?"

"Hazel too." She flashed a waning smile. Gertrude wanted so badly to talk to him about what had happened. Yet she hadn't the audacity to burden him in such a weakened state.

But Ronald wanted to know. He was curious about how he had gotten there. Some parts he could remember; others he simply couldn't. One thing was for sure . . .

Cecelia's influence over him had come to an end. He couldn't feel, see, or hear his sister anymore.

"What happened? How did I get here?"

She turned to make sure no one else was in the room and the door was closed before speaking. "It was Tom, Aunt May's bingo buddy. He tried to kill us because you found out about what he had been doing to the neighborhood kids all these years. You stopped him, Ronald. You even stopped him from killing me."

Ronald looked out the window into the distance, wondering when his freedom would end. Either Cecelia would be back with her orders, or the police would be coming to take him.

"Don't worry. He was a terrible man—a terrible man that will never hurt anyone ever again. And your friend Detective Barnes arranged to get your statement without you having to come down to the office. He said not to worry and that your father sent him to help."

"Barnes?" he tried his best to remember, recalling one of his father's old partners.

The tall Black man always used to ruffle his hands through young Ronald's curls as he encouraged him to grow up to be a man of justice.

"No man is above the law, and no man is below it; nor do we ask any man's permission when we ask him to obey it. Theodore Roosevelt said that," he educated young Ronald.

Mr. Doolally chimed in, "Therefore, it is our duty to enforce it."

The memory slowly faded from thought. It was what he remembered most about Detective Barnes.

"Can I see that?" he asked Gertrude, eluding to the newspaper in her hand. He'd noticed the headline *"Backyard Nightmare"* on one of the articles folded back on the front page.

"Of course." She placed the paper atop the white hospital blanket covering his lower extremities.

"Although a mass of dismembered body parts was found outside the residence, inside, the bloody crime scene was void of anyone, including the man suspected of committing the crime, Arthur Columbus." He thought through what he'd read aloud.

If he had left Arthur's body there, who'd taken it? he wondered. *Maybe Barnes has been helping all along,* Ronald considered.

Just outside his room in the hallway, Richard sat on a bench reading that very same newspaper article. Doctors, nurses, and hospital staff passed by, neglecting to ask who he was there to see. The older gentleman certainly wasn't wearing a visitor's pass. Maybe it was because he looked trustworthy. How far he had evolved from the dirty beggar he once resonated with. Into what was the question. It was an answer to be determined by the perspective of the individuals he would encounter. Hopefully, for them, they were on the right side of the law.

One week later, Brenda walked down her driveway to the mailbox out front, coffee in hand. She opened the box, pulling out a postcard from Tennessee. It simply read, *"I'm okay, Queen. Don't worry about me. I miss you. I love you, and please know that I can make it on my own. Thank you for always being there."*

Tears streamed from Brenda's eyes as a feeling of immense joy had begun to heal her aching heart. "Thank you, God," she screamed toward the heavens, rushing back inside through the side door to call Gertrude.

Of course, Gertrude was busy nursing a bandaged boyfriend. Ronald hadn't seen or detected Cecelia since the accident. Seems his surgery had utterly blocked out her influence. Although his memories were coming back more every day, Cecilia remained a distant memory as far as his present state of being. The guilt Dr. Martyr talked about had finally subsided. Gertrude sat at his bedside, feeding him a bowl of homemade potato soup she had whipped up herself when the phone rang, interrupting Ronald's lunch.

She set the bowl atop the nightstand, then picked up the receiver next to it.

"Hello."

"She's alive! She's alive!" Brenda screamed into the phone on the other end.

Knowing her best friend's voice, Gertrude responded immediately, "Who's alive?" she asked.

"Tiffany! She's alive. She sent me a postcard," Brenda rejoiced. "I'm so happy she contacted me. All I wanted was to know that she's alive and well."

"Oh, thank God Tiffany's alive. She sent Brenda a postcard," Gertrude exclaimed as she relayed the message to Ronald.

A soft but sly grin surfaced upon his face upon hearing Brenda had received the postcard sent via Detective Barnes. Once Ronald realized his father's former apprentice had been helping him all along, together, they'd decided it best the girls assumed Tiffany was a fugitive from justice, alive and kicking. They would never know the truth about what happened to Tiffany that fateful night.

Ronald Doolally lay there feeling all was indeed well. . . .

The End